AUTHOR

BARRAS, L.

CLASS

F

TITLE

The chocolate cream society

The Chocolate Cream Society

A Novel

Leonard Barras

First Published 1997 by IRON Press
5, Marden Terrace, Cullercoats,
North Shields, Northumberland NE30 4PD, UK
Tel/Fax: (0191) 253 1901

Typeset by David Stephenson
in Palatino 9 point

Printed by Peterson Printers
South Shields

Cover design by Geoff Laws
Book design by Peter Mortimer

07215232

ISBN 0–906228–58–1

IRON Press books are represented by:
Password Books Ltd
23 New Mount Street
Manchester M4 4DE
Tel: (0161) 953 4009
Fax: (0161) 953 4001

Clarification

Between 1979 and 1991, IRON Press published four Leonard Barras books, two of short stories, one of poems, one of selected newspaper columns. This helped pass the time, and also ensured neither press nor author became rich and famous.

In 1994 Len rang me up to ask if we'd be interested in another collection of his short stories. I read them, chortled and gasped as is one's wont when reading the man, but decided IRON Press had already covered that area of the Barras universe. I went to see Len, deciding to tell him personally.

He was sat in an armchair, his complexion the colour of an unwashed handkerchief. Tubes seemed to be sticking out of his leg, and he was preparing to go into hospital for treatment of an ailment few people can spell.

'You're not looking at all well, Len,' I said, and added, 'By the way, we're not going to publish your stories.'

'Thanks,' he replied and fiddled with a tube. I went to see him in hospital and, as writers do, we conversed deeply on matters such as his ability, when sat up in bed, to see the three piece suite in his living room across the fields.

Len got better and I got to thinking about the Barras/IRON syndrome, and how I was missing something. I realised what it was and rang him up.

'Len,' I said, 'I think it's time you took on a new challenge, explored new territories. As editor of IRON Press I invite and challenge you to write a novel!'

After a pause, Len asked, 'Does that mean you guarantee to publish it?'

'No,' I replied.

'Hmm. And no advance, I suppose?'

'That's it, Len.'

'Thank you,' he said.

Ten months later the typescript of *The Chocolate Cream Society* arrived. Extended absurdity, surrealist satire, the Geordie culture subverted and celebrated simultaneously, and of course a talking ghost horse.

I decided IRON Press should publish it. Who else is writing novels as individual as this? Small presses have always avoided publishing novels, and no doubt I'll soon find out why. Meantime you have done your bit in buying it (you *have* bought it, haven't you?). Now read it. I can assure you the inimitable Mr Barras will not let you down. And of course, reading the book does help pass the time, even if, as Beckett puts it, it would have passed anyway.

The other short stories? They were eventually published elsewhere.

Peter Mortimer, Editor, IRON Press.

Justification

'Every piece of writing writes itself.' Did Ionesco write this? Or did it, by his own definition, write itself?

Thirty years ago, there surfaced a story called *Learning to Swim*. Shall we assume that it was written by somebody called Leonard Barras? Otherwise, Ionescoism will undo us. And may we consider it now, before coming to *The Chocolate Cream Society*'s justification for having been written (by whatever agency)?

People associate Barras with *Learning to Swim* and with very little else, except moral cowardice and sitting in the corner at damned silly parties, hating everybody in the room. If he ever writes a better comedy than *Twelfth Night*, there are those who will still come up to him and say 'Ah! The man who wrote *Learning to Swim*!' – after they have said, 'Ah! the man who was sulking in the corner, not drinking beer!' They will offer him beer.

He could point to several actors who have used *Learning to Swim* at auditions and thereafter had successful careers. This is not unduly significant, as all actors have successful careers, so they tell him. One actor landed a lucrative beer commercial. Barras might have objected to this, because he dislikes beer and abominates TV commercials, but it would have damaged his reputation as a moral coward.

If you bully him, he will admit that *Learning to Swim* is not the sum of his canon. He has written for stage, radio, press and television, unnoticeably. He has had five books published, attracting nobody's attention. He is boundlessly grateful for the near anonymity which has pursued him; if only he had avoided writing *Learning to Swim*, it might have been total.

He occasionally performs readings of his work, on the grounds that every craven nonentity has the right to make a nincompoop of himself. He recites ten verses, three essays and a short story. Afterwards, when the chairman has thanked him, through gritted teeth, somebody rises to ask, 'But what about *Learning to Swim*?' People on their way out, querying the purpose of life, come back to hear it. Afterwards, they pat him on the back and press beer on him.

Sometimes it occurs to Barras that *Learning to Swim* may well be the most successful piece of writing since Colley Cibber's *Love's Last Shift*. At least nobody dies in it. Why, he wonders, should it be so highly regarded? It says all that needs to be said about the human condition and says it in luminous prose, but apart from that – what?

As it happens, he bakes a very fine gooseberry sponge, but the world has not beaten a path to his door on that account. Nobody knows, therefore, how gratified he would be to have people come up to him and say, not 'Ah! *Learning to Swim!*' but 'Ah! Gooseberry sponge!' An actor who could pass an audition using one of Barras's gooseberry sponges would without doubt go on to drown every stage with tears and cleave the general ear. But there is probably an Ionescoesque cook somewhere who would say that the gooseberry sponge bakes itself.

So far, he has resisted writing a sequel to *Learning to Swim*. 'What could I do with all that beer?' he asks himself. Such a sequel might, of course, be completely ignored, but he would not risk writing it in that glorious expectation.

And so we arrive, by circuitous route, at the justification. *The Chocolate Cream Society* is a lament for a disappearing way of life. Not an idyllic way of life. Not even an especially rewarding one. Just a familiar one – and by that token precious. The citizens of Lastfort have built a cocoon about themselves to ward off the future they have sighted and for which they don't much care. They are honourable Luddites. They have the entirely human disinclination to part with either the baby or the bath water. Must the Pluvius thingie-fettling factory which they have long affectionately execrated be closed? Must their cherished unlovely town – built on the very spot where the Emperor Hadrian fell into the Tyne – fade and decay?

Well, Shaw once notably urged the miners: 'For heaven's sake, come up out of the earth!' Splendid advice, of course, if they could have come up on something like their own terms. Otherwise, into what sort of world would they have emerged? (We know now.)

The Chocolate Cream Society invites all decent regressives to weep for the days that we shall never see again. If the tears are tears of laughter, that will suffice. If, however, anybody invites the nincompoop behind it all to step forward, Ionesco will be invoked. Long live moral cowardice!

Leonard Barras
May 1997

Chapters

Chapter One

A Time-Served Thingie Fettler

Sir Rodney Eames gazed first at the clock and then at his secretary. "Dear me!" he said. "How the morning's flown! It's twenty-four-and-a-quarter minutes past ten already."

It was the signal for Elsie Pilbury to wince. She did so. "It's seven-and-a-half minutes to five, Sir Rodney," she said. "In the afternoon. You're reading the clock upside down."

"Again," Sir Rodney acknowledged.

Outside in the courtyard of the thingie fettling works, all was relatively quiet. The workers were poised to hurl themselves out into freedom the moment the five o'clock buzzer sounded. Miss Pilbury hovered. She too was hoping for early release, but there was a matter she wanted to raise with Sir Rodney as soon as she could nudge him into signing his three letters. Once there would have been three dozen.

Obligingly unnudged, Sir Rodney signed. But he was disposed to chat. "A bizarre old stick, you know," he said. "That's my reputation."

"Of course," Miss Pilbury agreed.

"Am I living up to it?"

"To the hilt," said Miss Pilbury. "Er – your finger…"

"What?"

"It's just that you did ask me to discourage you."

"But we both know my request lacked conviction," Sir Rodney said. He had a finger in a hole in his pullover, assiduously enlarging it. "I can't resist dynamics, you see. Are you familiar with Archimedes?"

"Gladys Button is."

"Who?"

"She has a loose cartilage."

"Can she resist dynamics?"

"Neither dynamics nor hydrostatics, she gives me to understand."

"Archimedes," said Sir Rodney, "claimed that if somebody would give him a firm spot on which to stand, he would move the earth."

"So Gladys said," said Miss Pilbury. "Her loose cartilage – it's in her knee. May I ask you something?"

But Sir Rodney was now considering Time. "Time goes on," he said. That was one thing he had noticed about Time. Who would have thought, for instance, that in Time's opulence his cherished little factory would be swallowed by a huge consortium?

Miss Pilbury uttered a sympathetic "Ah!"

"And as if a consortium were not enough," said Sir Rodney, "came another sombre day when we were nationalised. Belatedly. Ask me anything you like." He chuckled his self-deprecating little chuckle. Good heavens! Hadn't he always been a benevolent despot? "Did you know that my grandfather founded this factory in 1891?"

Miss Pilbury knew. "I've often wondered," she said, giving him the prompt he hoped for, "why it's called the Pluvius Works."

"He used to ride right into the factory courtyard on his horse."

Miss Pilbury said, "On his horse? Good heavens!" What a small world it had been in 1891!

"Do you know why it's called the Pluvius Works, by the way?"

"Why, no."

"Latin. The Emperor Hadrian fell into the River Tyne at this very spot when he was stepping back to admire the Roman Wall in pouring rain." It was the sort of gorgeous apocrypha much peddled at the Lastfort Nostalgia Centre. He chuckled again.

Miss Pilbury essayed a little more broaching. "What about the ladies' rest room?" she ventured.

Sir Rodney said the ladies' rest room was another edifice no doubt greatly admired, in pouring rain or not.

"Coupled with Gladys Button. That's what I wanted to ask you."

Sir Rodney had gone to the window overlooking the courtyard on the other side of which was the main factory building. He surveyed his beloved domain. There stood the trough from which his grandfather's horse had so often drunk, and over it the verse which the old gentleman had caused to be carved:

As the Roman Wall was built to last
So may our works withstand the blast.

It was in 1931 that Sir Rodney's father, Gervase, had thought seriously about changing the second line to read: "God help our works withstand the blast," because it was the time of the Depression and he was anxious to enlist the help of the Almighty. As it happened, the factory was forced to close for a while, but before too long God had introduced Hitler to ensure the need for thingies (especially the chuffled and thennioned variety) for the reviving defence programme.

"It's a long way off," Miss Pilbury continued. "The – if I may say so – ladies' rest room. Down two flights of stairs. And Gladys Button's 59, with a loose cartilage. I thought I'd mention it – discreetly."

"Any lady's age is safe with me," Sir Rodney assured her. He gazed out, a tear not far from his eye. First a consortium. Then nationalisation. And now, rumours abounded (when did they do other?) that further storms were brewing (as storms invariably did). His grandfather's horse was not merely turning in his grave, but rising from it. "I still stare out of this window at the horse's trough," he said. "An artefact which has resisted Time's buffets."

"Er – the ladies' rest room..." said Miss Pilbury, and gave up. Well, at least she had mentioned it. She had done her best, for the moment, for Gladys Button's leg. But would Gladys Button's leg go away?

Sir Rodney could see the ghost of his grandfather's horse even now, as clearly as he could espy Walter Lester, foreman of the thingie assembly squad, down in the courtyard, falling over a mild steel T-bar. But he had a sudden agonising recollection. "Lionel Judge!" he cried.

"What?" said Miss Pilbury.

"Judge! Judge! Judge!" said Sir Rodney, more over-wrought than you would expect in a third generation benevolent despot.

*

Walter Lester had been warned of the impediment by Jonty Harwood, his chargehand.

"Look out!" the grizzled Jonty had shouted, but it was too late.

The aggrieved Walter rubbed his leg. "Who left that mild steel T-bar there?" he asked.

"Mild steel T-bar!" said his scornful aide. "You'd trip over a bar of milk chocolate! Or its wrapper."

"I'm a plain man," said Walter, a known stickler.

They entered the large main fettling shed and proceeded to Walter's little cabin, tucked into the corner of the thingie assembly bay.

"What's worrying you, anyway?" Jonty demanded. "Your face is longer than a two-to-ten shift." They hadn't worked two-to-ten shifts since World War Two, but Jonty's images were immemorial.

Walter was undoubtedly careworn. "I didn't sleep last night," he confided.

"Have a bit kip now, then," Jonty barked. "You're a foreman – you're entitled to be dozy. It's expected of you."

"I had this dream," said Walter. "Shall I tell you about it?"

"Why else have you locked the door?"

It was a recurring nightmare. It was about the assembling of the jumbo thingie – for a jivelled pump equipment outsize protective shell – which was being completed for dispatch to Gledson's Pump, Scupper Hatch and Brass Bell Emporium, in cold blood. He dreamed that at the moment its assembly was completed it collapsed at his feet in a heap of metal dust. "Beth woke up screaming," he said.

"Your wife?"

"Who else?"

"That's none of my business."

"She got a fright."

"Next to you, who wouldn't?"

Walter took an agitated turn. "Less than six weeks and it'll be over."

"So your wife's leaving you?"

"Eh?"

"No wonder if there's somebody else."

"The jumbo thingie, you daft old coot! Five weeks come Wednesday, barring the end of the world, it's due to be dispatched to Gledson's. I worry, Jonty. Can I help it if I worry?"

"No, but you could stop in your cabin and keep your miserable mug away from the innocent public."

"Another thing," said Walter. "D'you know Beth's Auntie Dinah?"

"I've never heard of her. What's she done?"

"She's Beth's Auntie Dinah. That's enough."

"Anybody could be somebody's Auntie Dinah."

"You couldn't."

"I've never tried."

11

"She's coming to stay with us tomorrow."

"Have you got a spare room?"

"I never thought of that."

"You haven't all that much time to build one."

"She's a lovable old lady. I can't stand lovable old ladies. But Beth wants her to stay, so I can't exactly shoot her, can I?"

"Not you. Not exactly. You couldn't hit your own foot from three feet."

"I haven't got three feet."

"Nobody would know."

"That's all right, then. A glorious time for me, mind you, with any luck, God help me. Do I deserve to be foreman of the thingie assembly squad, I ask myself?" Pride in his office fought a perpetual battle with Walter's natural self-effacement. "It'll be the twenty-first jumbo thingie I've assembled." Not personally, of course. He was too modest to claim that. Under his diffident supervision the squad had assembled them. His squad! Jonty and Joe and Arthur and Tom and Clarence and the rest! If those were their names.

Jonty was exploding. "It'll be the twentieth! The twentieth! You lost count once you got into double figures."

Walter had the familiar feeling that Jonty was trying to teach him his job. He said as much.

"Bloody impossible!" Jonty shouted. "Even though I'm the finest fettler this side of hell!" And so he was, for the time being.

"It's twenty-one," Walter muttered, although he felt in his heart that he should know better than to argue with this irascible ancient, this obsessive contradictor, who ought to have retired eight years earlier, but had disputed his dispensability with the management, sedulously pointing out that the Pluvius Works would founder without him.

"It's twenty! I've seen a hundred-and-twenty! The oldest living chargehand in the Pluvius Works! Fifty-nine years come Dookie-Apple Day since I first walked into the factory, a little lad in raggy-arsed trousers."

"Back to front."

"Foremen! What's a foreman? Nothing but a tradesman with his brains bashed out!" Jonty laughed delightedly at this archaic sally.

Walter gave up. Perhaps that was the knocking-off buzzer he could hear, bringing relief from toil and torment.

It was. His tormentor was complaining that the buzzer was late as they went out into the fast-emptying courtyard. It was a diurnal gripe. "Timekeepers! Couldn't tell the time in a cuckoo clock factory! Come on, then! And mind that bar! I'll tell you something…"

"I'll tell you something," said Walter, with slight relish. "That stuff about a foreman's brains – they were telling that one a lot longer ago than fifty-nine years come Dooky-Apple Day."

He proceeded across the courtyard, savouring this small triumph, and tripped over a plain chocolate wrapper.

*

"I'd forgotten," said Sir Rodney.

"Indeed," Miss Pilbury confirmed. "Mr Judge is coming. You didn't mind my mentioning the ladies' rest room?"

"Headquarters people," said Sir Rodney, "might descend on us at any time." They had seconded Lionel Judge to the Pluvius Works to make it more efficient and if possible to get Sir Rodney to change his pullover. "The horse's ghost reproaches me, you know. Do you remember Hamlet?"

Miss Pilbury shook her head. "I'm only fifty-eight."

Oh, the horse's ghost neighed a frequent message to Sir Rodney. "You've let your grandfather down," was the burden of it. "You must fight them."

"How can they make us more efficient?" Miss Pilbury asked. "Against our will, I mean? We're English, aren't we?"

"Of course I didn't mind," said Sir Rodney, although he had forgotten what.

"Thank you."

"Stomach," Sir Rodney muttered. "I haven't got much stomach." Well, the horse thought not.

Was it surprising? The days of the eccentric individualist had departed. Specialised thingies with clargled cast iron sleeves were no longer required, for instance, for the shipbuilding industry, previously one of Sir Rodney's principal customers. Even in his father's day, there had ceased to be any building of arcane craft such as ferries for the Great Lakes, luxury yachts for maharajahs and small meticulously designed liners for Pacific cruises. Now, there was no shipbuilding at all on the Tyne, and not much elsewhere, requiring exotica such as clargle-sleeved thingies.

Sir Rodney still had his model ships. As a supplier to shipbuilding, he had acquired an avid interest in ships' models. In particular, there was his model of an eighteenth century tea clipper, which he hoped to launch on the Recreation Ground lake on the late summer Bank Holiday. He sidled to his drawing board and furtively studied the plans.

"My mentioning the ladies' rest room," Miss Pilbury asked, in search of clarification. "Is that what you didn't mind?"

Sir Rodney thought they had settled that. He regarded himself as a broad-minded despot as well as a benevolent one. "Mention the ladies' rest room to your heart's content," he said. He was also a latter-day Hamlet, he felt, urged on by an admonishing ghost.

There was a peremptory knock and Lionel Judge stepped in, already speaking as he did so, the embodiment of efficiency.

"Sir Rodney!"

The time was indeed out of joint, it seemed. Sir Rodney braced himself to receive some figures.

"I have some statistics," said Lionel Judge. He was a large neurotic young man, who scratched his knees and tugged at his ears. "They are in fact certain computer abstractions for the labour costs of the thingie assembly bay."

Miss Pilbury decided to excuse herself. "If that is all, Sir Rodney..?"

"What?" Sir Rodney was dreaming of the palmy days when they had supplied the QE2's thingies, complete with glurs and spaddled foddiffs, or vice versa.

"I have to rehearse, you see," said Miss Pilbury. "I'm reciting Omar Khayam at the club next Tuesday. And for an encore, given a vast amount of luck, Kipling."

"Throw in Mrs Hemans," said Sir Rodney. "For me."

"Goodnight, then." Miss Pilbury smiled and withdrew. Be it said that she was familiar with Hamlet, as she and Sir Rodney both well knew, although neither of course knew if the other knew.

Lionel Judge was spreading computer printouts in front of Sir Rodney. They did not tell a pretty story, he was saying. Decidedly ugly, in fact. "Not to be sneezed at," he was saying.

"Oh, Lord," said Sir Rodney.

His grandfather had ridden down to the factory through fields which rolled right up to the gates. The fields had long since disappeared under dispiriting three-storey tenements, which in their turn had given way to inglorious thirteen-storey blocks of flats. This was the twentieth century at work, like Lionel Judge's computer. But it didn't do to dwell on morbid history. After all, his grandfather had built the tenements.

Meanwhile, he had better not sneeze at Lionel Judge's statistics.

*

Oswald Gorman arrived home, not with jocund heart, because he knew that from the kitchen-diner would come the predictable barrage.

"That you, Oswald? Oswald! That you? Eh?"

"Nobody but," said Oswald.

Was this world a place in which hearts could be jocund? Part of the time, yes, but Oswald mostly felt, like Sir Rodney, that it was a pity Archimedes hadn't moved the earth.

"You're late," said Jonty.

"No, I'm not," Oswald said, quite gently.

"It's in the oven, then. You're late. It's in the oven."

"Thank you, Uncle Jonty," said Oswald. "What is it?" He laid down his newspaper and proceeded to wash his hands.

"I put it in the oven. Good job I finish work half-an-hour before you. Soup! Me, I've had mine."

It was true that Jonty arrived back at the flat they shared some time ahead of Oswald, but Oswald always regarded this is no sort of blessing. Jonty laboured under some compulsion to prepare their meal, and Oswald, eternally tolerant, was burdened with an equal obligation to accept this unwholesome arrangement. He lunched quite well in the staff dining room and had no need of an evening effusion, especially as his Uncle Jonty was a disgusting cook.

"Soup!" Jonty repeated.

"You're very kind," said Oswald from the cooker. "A pity you forgot to light this."

"It's only right we should, mind you," said Jonty.

"Oh, it is," said Oswald, "whatever it is – and why shouldn't you?"

"It's not boiled, if that's what you mean," said Jonty. "You don't boil soup! You boil bananas. I mean, us manual toilers are entitled to knock off before the penpushers."

"I don't boil bananas," said Oswald, mildly mordant, as always, in response to Jonty's threadbare prejudices. He poured soup.

"I mean, it's not the penpushers, sitting in their central heating, getting calluses on their arses, that'll bring down the costs of industry."

"I'm a contracts estimator," said Oswald, not for the first, or the fifty-first, time. It was a refinement of penpushing unrecognisable by Jonty.

"I'm not asking you to boil bananas. I'll boil the bananas. I didn't know you wanted boiled bananas."

"I'm quite happy with cold soup."

"Are you reading that paper? D'you want some ham next? What time is it?"

"I don't mind," said Oswald. "Where is it?"

"Eh?"

"It's twenty-to-six."

*

Is it perhaps time to reveal just what thingies are? If you were to call at the Lastfort Nostalgia Centre, we should be pleased to tell you their history. Meanwhile, shall we let it suffice to say that the thingie was reputedly invented by William Hedley, who perfected Trevithick's locomotive for an encore? In full, it is a Tensile Hydraulic Integrating Notchless Graduated Impermeable Equilibrator. Hedley has acquired additional posthumous fame in that he is the ancestor of an illustrious theatre director.

The uses of the thingie are manifold. It is one of the wonders of our glorious industrial past and like all of them will soon be obsolete.

You will be made welcome at the Nostalgia Centre, which is housed in the former Philosophical Society building. Philosophical societies? Are they already obsolete?

*

"I was thinking," said Jonty. "D'you know how long it's been?"

"I don't mind some ham."

"Fifty-one years," said Jonty. "It was there just now." He unveiled a plate of ham from under the tea cosy. "Fifty-one years I've worked in the assembly squad at that Pluvius Works! Is it twenty-to-six yet?"

"What's in that uncosied teapot? Or had I better not know?" It turned out to be very weak tea.

"Am I any better thought of? I was talking to Charlie Embleton."

"He's a spronker."

"I was going to say that."

"I know. In the zilted spindle shop."

"I was going to say that."

"I know. His name's Tommy Wrench."

"D'you know what he told me?"

"No, I'm not," said Oswald.

"You mean no, you don't."

"I mean no, I'm not. Reading the paper. I'm not going to read at the table."

"Why not?"

"I've left my glasses at the sink."

"He said the computer was going to do the thingie positive displacement final calculations."

"How does he know?"

"Bloody disgraceful!"

15

"How does he know?"

"Next thing, we'll all be derundant."

"It's better than being transposed."

As it happened, the rumour and its attendant rumpus had not gone unheeded by Oswald, and he intended to raise the matter at the next meeting of the Joint Unions' Fraternal Branch Action Group, of which he was minutes secretary. "It's not on the agenda for JUFBAG," he said. He was as susceptible as the next man to cryptic acronyms.

"Never mind the dishes if you want to get out," said Jonty. "And there's jelly."

"Blue and white collar brothers mingle at JUFBAG," Oswald reminded him. "Sometimes without fratricide."

"I'll wash the dishes if you want to go out."

"Computerisation's progress. I'm prepared to grant that. It's progress. But what price ideals?"

"Any daft beggar can wash dishes."

"Or boil bananas."

"Or peel taters. You don't need a degree to peel taters."

Oswald had the decent Luddite tendencies of any good trade unionist, but in his heart he acknowledged that if the computer calculated the thingie positive displacement figures common sense was served. In an ideal world, costing estimators would be released from the incubus of positive displacement calculations to expand their perceptions, sustained by the wealth which the new technology produced. In practice, men were released to the dole queue. Most sensible people knew how silly it was to have ideals. Oswald didn't consider himself very sensible.

"I'm the best dish-washer you'll meet in a day's march, even if you run," Jonty stated. "I mean, I promised your mother I'd look after you when she ran away with that Conservative, on the crossbar of his bicycle. 'I'll do my best for the young sod,' I said, choking back my tears. I wonder what time it is." He scooped up the teapot and hurled its contents into the sink. "Computers doing displacement calculations! What a liberty!"

"It's progress," said Oswald. "In an ideal world, realism rules. She didn't run away."

"Union meetings! What good did unions ever do? Bloody Trotties!"

"You've been a trade unionist for half a century."

"Marxists, every one of them!"

"She moved away," said Oswald. "With dignity." It was open to any mother to become a Conservative, he conceded. She had to accept the ostracism, of course. "Can you define a Marxist?"

"Eh?"

"That's what I thought."

"The unions are run by Trotties. Who lets them in, I'd like to know?"

"Did you vote in the last ballot?"

"I had diarrhoea."

"So had 87 per cent."

"Another thing – socialists!" Jonty made a disgusting noise.

He supported the Labour Party and had a virulent distaste for socialism. "Some of them Labour leaders have got two houses and drink wine. It was in the papers. Bloody traitors! I mean, I've been a trade unionist for fifty years. Not many can beat that. For why? Because I've got a trade. I mean, what am I?"

"The messiest potato-peeler I'll meet in a day's march."

"A time-served thingie fettler. When the likes of me came out of our apprenticeship in the thirties and went on the dole, we were fully qualified engineering craftsmen." Oh, in those golden days there had been turners, fitters, coppersmiths... Every man to his trade! What had you now? "Every bugger doing every bugger else's job."

"Nowadays," said Oswald, "demarcation is being eliminated." Which he favoured in principle, but would oppose in practice, being an honourable Luddite.

Jonty picked up the newspaper. "If you want to go out, I'll wash the dishes."

"What's this about jelly?"

There had been a time, Jonty believed, in those depressed thirties of his boyhood, when Britain's craftsmen were the best engineers in the world, in between being on the dole. "What's this, then?" He was flourishing the newspaper.

"Is there some jelly?" Oswald asked. "It's *The Guardian*. It's always there for you to thumb through, scattering its pages to the four winds."

"Here!" said Jonty. "D'you fancy some jelly? There's some jelly. It hasn't quite set, like."

He picked up a pan from the cooker top and from it poured jelly, totally unset, into a dish which he placed before Oswald.

"Thank you," said Oswald sorrowfully.

"People forget," Jonty pronounced, "that the greatness of British engineering was founded on demarcation. I'm off to get changed, then."

"What?"

"I'll leave you to wash the dishes," said Jonty. "I'm going to the club." He scattered *The Guardian's* pages. "I mean, you were late."

*

Auntie Dinah was greeted rapturously by Walter's wife Beth and their daughter Elaine. There were hugs and kisses and Auntie Dinah burst out sobbing.

"Well, well, it's lovely to see you," said Beth. "We've made a rice loaf, haven't we, Elaine?"

"So you got here!" said Elaine. "Sit down, Auntie Dinah, and take the weight off something."

Auntie Dinah dismissed the tears, but remained standing. "The bus was crowded. You'll remember Mrs Lockwood, Beth?"

An opening digression, Beth knew, and quite in character. "I thought she was dead?"

"You'd like a cup of tea, wouldn't you?" Elaine asked.

"I'm sure I don't know what you mean, Beth," said Auntie Dinah. Heavens above! She hadn't been in their house two minutes and here they were, confusing her.

"I'll put the kettle on," said Elaine. "Shall I take your coat?"

"I mean," said Beth, "she wasn't on the bus, was she?"

"I fancy a sausage roll."

"Oh, dear!" said Elaine.

"You thought who was dead?" asked Auntie Dinah.

"It doesn't matter," said Beth.

"That's no way to talk about death."

"We've got bacon pie," said Elaine. It wasn't a sausage roll, but they had it.

"I'll tell you this! She's been dead twenty years!" said Auntie Dinah.

"Mrs Lockwood?"

"I'm saying!"

"We've got lemon meringue pie and gooseberry tart," said Elaine.

"I'll never forget her stomach," said Auntie Dinah.

"We've baked some scones," said Elaine.

"How could she be on the bus?" asked Auntie Dinah. "Mrs Lockwood! She had practically no married life on account of her stomach."

"Shall I take your coat?" Beth enquired.

"I thought of her as the bus came down Stackpool Street." This was about as enlightened as Beth and Elaine were likely to be made about Mrs Lockwood, who was in any case now being dismissed from Auntie Dinah's horizon. "I thought about our Stanley last night."

Beth nodded. "You're fully entitled. He's your oldest, if you come to think of it." Auntie Dinah had ceaseless repinings for her far-flung sons.

"I was thinking about how he broke his glasses. What do they call that place?"

"Grimsby," Beth proffered. She and Elaine knew most of the chapters in Auntie Dinah's story of her life and sorry times. Grimsby figured in them, against its will.

"That place he went to, to make a lot of money."

"Grimsby," said Elaine.

"It's slipped my mind. He went in quite a lot for breaking his glasses, you know. Funny, the habits they pick up. He broke his glasses the day his dad died. On the night-shift. His dad didn't like it." She moaned. "And we'd had words, me and his dad."

It was about his sandwiches; Beth and Elaine knew. Beetroot sandwiches.

"'I can't spondle figgets on beetroot sandwiches!' he shouted. No nightshift canteens in them days."

"Shall I take your coat? I thought he findled spoggets, although I daresay it's much the same to a laywoman on a fast bicycle."

"No canteens at all! A woman had to provide what a man wanted."

"That's still true to a certain extent," said Elaine.

Beth sought a diversion of her own. "You'll have heard of young Oswald Gorman, Auntie Dinah?"

"When did he die?"

"He's alive and twenty-two and sexy in a bespectacled sort of way and Elaine's keen on him."

"That's a lie," said Elaine.

"Elaine's crazy about him."

"That's better," said Elaine.

"Does he break his glasses?"

"Not he! His habits are deadly unfunny, give or take the odd sally. But lovable."

"What d'you mean – I got here?" Auntie Dinah suddenly demanded. "Of course I got here! I keep your address in my hat, don't I? I was thinking about our Stanley last night."

"But why," Beth asked, "did you think of Mrs Lockwood in Stackpool Street?"

"What?"

"Mrs Lockwood."

"Mrs Lockwood never lived in Stackpool Street!" Auntie Dinah stated.

"That's what I'm saying," said Beth.

"Excuse me!" said Auntie Dinah. "That's what I'm saying!" Heavens above! She hadn't been in their house five-and-a-half minutes and here they were, telling her what she was saying! She took off her black mackintosh. "Are you not going to take my coat? And can a body not get a cup of tea in this house?"

*

It was on the following Wednesday evening that, despite an unfavourable wind, there was a meeting of the Joint Unions' Fraternal Branch Action Group, and there came a point when Elaine, if only to justify her presence, asked, "Do we have a quorum, chairman?" It was a pertinent question, because at that moment only she, Oswald and the chairman, Tot Needler, were present.

Tot's pensive reply was: "I've no idea. What's a quorum?"

To this, Oswald made the proud rejoinder: "It's the Latin 'of whom.'"

Tot retorted that he thought the minutes secretary was being a shade pedantic.

"Granted," said Elaine. "But he's gorgeous when he reads the minutes."

Tot said he knew what a quorum was, etymologically. But what constituted a quorum of the Unions' Joint Action Branch Fraternal Group? That was what he was pondering.

"Well, you're the chairman, Tot," Elaine cheerfully reminded him, "even though you've just bent the title a bit."

"Mind you," said Oswald, "he got through 'etymologically' with flying colours."

Tot assented. But he didn't profess to be a good chairman. He had never set out to be a good chairman. Merely to conduct their meetings with time-honoured lassitude. A Labour veteran, he had grown world-weary in the service of the unions. Without sacrificing any principles, except in practice, he had come to recognise the fallibility of human institutions, not least in the field of industrial relations, which he now knew were a sad comedy.

"Four," said Oswald.

"It was purely for altruistic reasons," Tot explained, "that I agreed to become chairman. And also because I'm a busybody."

"Four's a quorum," said the conscientious Oswald.

Tot said that for his part he would rather be in his quiet little room with Mozart.

Oswald said that Tot's devotion to duty was in those circumstances praiseworthy. Elaine asked if Mozart was better than sex.

"At my time of life, yes," Tot said, and added reflectively, "Or any time. Well, more accessible. But I believe in this great trade union movement of ours."

"I attend JUFBAG," said Elaine frankly, "because I'm an electronic typewriter operative and rather beautiful, some say, and noticeably nubile."

Tot said all this was palpable, Mozart notwithstanding.

"But the minutes secretary," said Elaine, "refuses to take cognizance of it."

19

Oswald asked that the representative of the monstrous regiment be called to order.

It was part of Tot's philosophy that lassitude was a prime virtue. It prevented a lot of aggression, he maintained.

"Was lassitude the reason why the Pluvius Works was nationalised five years after the rest of the thingie fettling industry?" Elaine asked.

Oswald knew the answer to that. "We got into the records of the wrong government department and were listed as an historic monument."

Tot confirmed that this was the accepted mythology, as laid down in the Nostalgia Centre. It was implausible enough to be true.

"After all," Oswald said, "the Pluvius Works is situated in Lastfort, which is so named because it is at the end of the Roman Wall and on the site of the most easterly stronghold."

"That may be very fine dramatic exposition, but it is not on the agenda," said the chairman, almost sternly.

"No," said Elaine, "but, as before, he was lovely when he said it."

Tot said they had in any case got through most of the agenda, including three apologies for absence. The other 753 members were absent without explanation. In other words, the traditions of their great trade union movement were being preserved.

"We're out of order," Elaine said.

"Not for the first time," Tot acknowledged. "Or the last, I hope. This is not the ideal world of Oswald's dreams. One of life's minor pleasures is being out of order. But in what way?"

"We're only three. You, Oswald and I."

"And Peter Quirk."

"He went out."

"Only to the gents'."

"Forty minutes ago," Elaine protested.

Tot said Time was relative. Sir Rodney would have agreed with him. And also about houseflies. "Houseflies are old at three weeks," he reminded Elaine.

"At what age do they retire?"

Oswald had been simmering unnoticed. "I have some 'Other Business,'" he stated.

"You said that in inverted commas," Tot said. "And I find that I'm sitting on the rule book. A symbolic posture, you'll agree." He retrieved the book and studied it. "It seems that three's a quorum."

"In that case, I move the closure," said Elaine.

Tot said he would like to think about that.

"My other business," Oswald persisted, "concerns the computer, which you in turn will agree is symbolically for progress."

"Will you walk me home, Oswald?" Elaine asked.

"I realise that we've got through a great deal of business, chairman," Oswald said, "including relativity, lassitude, etymology and Brother Peter Quirk's retention of urine, but I feel we ought to deliberate the computer's rôle."

"Point of order!" Elaine cried.

"It's hinted," said Oswald gamely, "that an additional visual display unit will be brought here from headquarters to monitor the positive displacement final

20

calculations. My question is: Where will it be sited?"

Tot considered this and said, "H'm."

"The meeting will have to be counted out," said Elaine. "We haven't got a quorum."

Tot counted heads. "We've got three."

"Two. I'm going to the ladies'."

Altruistic or not, Tot recognised a chance to get back to Mozart when he saw one and declared the meeting closed.

"Give Peter Quirk a knock as you go past," he suggested. "We don't want him to think he's wasting his time."

"All right," said Elaine. "And may I say this about the Joint Unions' Fraternal Branch Action Group? – it's worse than sex any day. See you outside, Oswald." She hurried out.

Tot and Oswald gathered up their papers. Oswald, incorruptible but ever tolerant, yielded the day. And after all, who wouldn't want to walk home with Elaine? Even Tot would have conceded that she could give *The Magic Flute* a run for its money.

"Just one thing, though," he said to Tot. "Unofficially, what about this piece in the *Lastfort Tinkle*?"

Tot put his tongue in his cheek. "Whatever it is," he said, "it'll be the machinations of the capitalist press."

Oswald read out the item. "Could the spectre of demarcation be raising its head again at the troubled Pluvius Works? Tall, 81-year-old, Beethoven-loving union leader Tot Needler refused to be drawn today on suggestions that there might be workers' reaction over the siting of a new visual display unit."

Tot nodded. "Very accurate, I'd say."

"What!" said the astounded Oswald.

"I'm of medium height, it's Mozart I love and I'm 62, but they spelt my name right," said Tot. "Goodnight, Oswald."

But you will not have failed to guess – not you! – that the spectre of demarcation would indeed be seen, although in a form not envisaged by either JUFBAG or the *Lastfort Tinkle*.

Or by Oswald as he walked homewards all but overcome by the presence of nubility.

*

And you will not forget, will you, to call in and see us at the Nostalgia Centre if you happen to find yourselves one day in Lastfort in a fantasy? We'll be pleased to show you the hoops. The hoops? More of those in a moment. Shall we proceed now – on another evening – to a choir practice?

*

"All right, lads," Elaine said. "You've rocked the cradle off its hinges. Very realistic."

Not only was she radiant and exquisite, for the sake of those romantics among you. She was also a wonderful typist. To boot, she was the acclaimed accompanist of the Pluvius Works Male Voice Choir. Yes, it was another evening, and in the factory canteen she was guiding the choir through *Rocked in the Cradle of the Deep*.

They had washed the muck of the factory from themselves and come back to the canteen. They had come from the thirteen-storey blocks of flats. They had come from the back-to-back houses with their cobbled backlanes along which the older among them had dashed barefoot as lads, their shirt tails hanging out, bowling their hoops. They had come from Rose Walk, the row of mid-Victorian cottages beside the Plodge Burn.

Rose Walk had been an idyllic retreat in the days when the Plodge Burn was still a meandering country stream pottering its way to the crystal Tyne. That was before Jasper Eames, Sir Rodney's grandfather, had built his factory and then constructed the town of Lastfort to house its workers and the town had had to find somewhere to discharge its filth. Well, the benefactor could hardly be expected both to provide the filth and dispose of it.

They had come past the bingo hall which had once been a theatre, past the former Philosophical Society premises which were now part used car showroom part Nostalgia Centre, and past the Working Men's Club which had some fifteen years earlier been lavishly refitted. Some had found the club impossible to pass, but they were a recidivist minority.

The bowling of hoops was one of those ancient childhood games now totally abandoned, except for its rehabilitation by us custodians of the Lastfort Nostalgia Centre (incorporating Poss Tub Museum).

"But where's the man with the baton, Elaine?" asked Ralph Wilkes.

"Where's the chief singer?" asked Dougal Claypole.

"Simple," said Elaine. "Dad and Jonty are working overtime." In another of their cantankerous partnerships, Walter and Jonty were respectively conductor and leading tenor of the choir.

"I bet they're lubricating their larynxes in the club," said George Carter.

"No, they're not, green eyes," said Elaine. "They're practising at our house these nights, believe me, after their half-shift. So you'll have to do your best for me, just me. *Bobby Shafto* next, right?"

Tot Needler spoke up from the ranks of the baritones. One of life's dedicated participants, he was inevitably a member of the choir. "Just for you, Elaine, we'll sing all night."

This was seconded by several approving voices in various keys.

"Or pretty near to closing time," Dougal Claypole amended.

"Oh, Dougal, Dougal, you're lovely," said Elaine. "Will you leave your wife for me?"

"I will, as soon as I'm married."

"Excuses, excuses! Come on, then, boys! Raise the canteen roof!"

She struck up. They sang *Bobby Shafto*. All in the same key.

*

The ghost of Sir Rodney's grandfather's horse had arrived at the trough. He drank and sniffed the air. So far, only Sir Rodney had ever seen him, because he was Sir Rodney's especial ghost; a ghost, be it said, as distinct from an illusion. Not that the element of illusion was absent. Illusion was what enveloped all of these Lastfortians. They all lived in the past, or in several and various pasts. Each lived in his or her own past, when times had been better; or worse, whichever they preferred. Even the young, who had no past of their own, lived in somebody's past. Well, that's the way we tell it at the Nostalgia Centre.

The horse, being a ghost, knew this. He gazed up at Sir Rodney's office window.

Chapter Two

——"Democracy Is A Ludicrous Contraption"——

Working late on his tea clipper, Sir Rodney had opened his window to catch the strains of *Bobby Shafto*. His paternal interest in his workers had descended from his grandfather and his father. He longed to hurry across to the canteen to wish all these choristers well, but was stultified by his inability to communicate with them. Damn the class system, for limiting gregariousness to the hoi-polloi! Society, stratified as it was, had undoubtedly proved to be terribly hard on the rich. Whenever he went into the tiggle-shaping shed or the kooming shop, or took it upon himself to go and view a jumbo thingie as it neared completion, he ached to call out benignly, "And how are you all getting on?" But he ended by mumbling, "Ah, yes..." to nobody in particular.

He stared down at the horse. The horse, who had promised to meet Shakespeare in a pub in paradise, shook his head and disappeared. Turning to pore over his ship's model plans while still listening enraptured, Sir Rodney met the purposeful gaze of the incoming Lionel Judge.

"Well, Sir Rodney!"

"My choir, Judge! What do you think of that? They're rehearsing for the next jumbo thingie dispatch reception, you know."

Lionel Judge said tepidly, "Very nice, I'm sure."

Sir Rodney did not think of his choir as very nice. "Celestial" would have been his assessment. Or "divine". Or "touching on immortality".

"These labour costs, Sir Rodney..."

Sir Rodney closed the window.

"They're eighty-three point-six per cent above budget," Judge accused.

What Sir Rodney now ached to call out would not have been benign, but he cravenly mumbled, "Ah, yes..." and hated himself.

"After all," Judge persisted, "why am I Efficiency and Methods Co-ordinator?"

Sir Rodney made an effort. "Eighty-three per cent?"

"Point-six."

"Eighty-three point-six? Yes. Per cent, eh?"

"I have here twenty-seven pages of errata." He flourished them at Sir Rodney. "They reveal outrageous culpability. And this is nothing to what I shall uncover as I co-ordinate efficiency to its utmost limits. I shall come to you daily with a dozen data-processed printouts."

"Good God!" said Sir Rodney, sinking into his chair.

"I might even – and I am capable of it – get you a P.C."

Sir Rodney was pretty sure Judge didn't mean a police constable. On the other hand, what would he do with a privy counsellor?

"I mean a personal computer."

"Good God, good God!" said Sir Rodney.

Judge scratched his knees. "The volume of sloth and negligence I shall detect will be stupendous. Take thingie assembly costs."

"I know," said Sir Rodney, showing willing again. "Eighty-three. Point-six."

"They can be axed."

"Can be what?"

"Bunting."

"Bunting?"

"Red, white and blue."

"Ah!" Here was a matter close to Sir Rodney's heart. Red, white and blue bunting was very dear to him.

"I've looked into this," said Judge.

"You've looked into red, white and blue bunting?" Sir Rodney was not following Judge, but was apprehensive.

"As a dispatching ceremony accessory. Exactly."

Sir Rodney nodded. Everybody knew about the red, white and blue bunting. It was draped around the platform at the send-off of every jumbo thingie. It was part of the heritage, like shuggy boats and bullickers.

Or the bouquet! It was at the send-off of Jumbo Thingie Number One in 1892 that Sir Rodney's grandfather had invited the prettiest girl in Lastfort to present a bouquet to the illustrious Russian lady who had performed the naming ceremony in French with the appropriately hackneyed words: "I name this jumbo thingie Pelican. Oo!" She said "Oo!" because Sir Rodney's grandfather, splendid old Victorian freebooter that he was, had pinched her bottom. He had then kissed the pretty girl.

The second part of this ritual had been carried on ever since. In 1892, the illustrious lady had been a Grand Duchess of all the Russias. This year she was to be, so rumour had it, the wife of a distinguished Secretary of State – if at all possible one of Her Majesty's ministers immersed, for the sake of maximum publicity, in fraud, espionage, sexual imbroglios and illicit arms dealing. A concession to the age, that, but the bouquet was to be presented just the same. It was a tradition that Sir Rodney cherished. Forlorn old bachelor that he was (no freebooter he), it afforded him a rare chance to kiss a pretty girl.

"A bauble," said Judge, oblivious of Sir Rodney's dreaming.

"What?"

"Red, white and blue bunting. A frippery."

Sir Rodney leapt up, aghast. A bauble and a frippery! The man would be calling it a gewgaw next.

"It's integral to our history!" he cried. "There's been red, white and blue bunting at every jumbo dispatch since my grandfather supplied a jumbo thingie for a yacht for the Tsar Nicholas or Alexander the Second or First." Fetching up at the window, he gazed out, shaken.

"It can be axed," said Judge, as implacably as an Efficiency and Methods Co-ordinator knew how.

"Good God!" repeated the appalled Sir Rodney. He was aware, of course, that headquarters' grip on his domain was tightening, but had it gone this far? "Oh, don't look at me like that, grandfather's horse!" he whispered, for the horse had indeed returned with reproachful mien. Shakespeare had not turned up. An unreliable chap, always off somewhere warbling his native woodnotes wild.

"What?" said Judge.

"Nothing." Well, at least his grandfather had seen the years of greatness. Years of the gifted amateur. No fetishistic efficiency. Flags of Empire flying. Jammed gatlings. The Raj in bloom...

"What are you doing, Sir Rodney?" Judge asked.

Sir Rodney was opening the window. From the canteen came the sound of the choir in full voice. They were singing *Land of Hope and Glory*. And here was the upstart Judge, proposing to abolish red, white and blue bunting! Good God! He would stop this! If he found the courage.

He had no idea what shuggy boats or bullickers were, but they were part of the heritage, weren't they?

*

The half-shift was over. Walter had brought Jonty home with him. They had showered and were now in the living room, spruced-up but far from relaxed.

"It needs a bit of thought," said Walter. He fetched up at the piano, studied it and began to take indecisive measurements with his hands.

Jonty eyed him sceptically. "Oh, aye. And what's your missus going to say about you shifting the piano?"

"Yes, well," said Walter, who preferred not to think of that. "Did I mention that Sir Rodney sent for me today?"

"That's right – change the subject."

"He told me I was doing a first-class job. Twenty-one jumbo dispatches! A splendid record, he said."

Truth to tell, Walter hated summonses to the sanctum. He always took the wrong turning and ended up red-faced in some remote uncharted department. On this occasion, when he had finally entered Miss Pilbury's office, tripping over her Indian carpet, she had said severely, "Sir Rodney does not like to be kept waiting, you know, Walter." Sir Rodney, as the world knew, was oblivious of time, but Miss Pilbury had the secretary's habit of voicing crushing reproaches in her employer's name.

And now he was being savaged by a ferile septuagenarian. "It's twenty dispatches, you daft ditherer!"

Walter said that changing the subject was the right of any normal incorruptible coward.

"And while you were up there standing to attention and licking the head bummer's boots, who d'you think was looking after the assembly bay?"

Walter concentrated on something else. "We'll shift this," he said, and began to pull the piano.

"Foremen!" said the scornful Jonty. With the aplomb of an engineering tradesman, he stood back to weigh the job up.

"Sho-o-o-ve!" said Walter, not realising that Jonty was still motionless. "From you! To me!" He heaved mightily. "We – can't – practise – in – here – with – all – the – double-decker – buses – rumbling – past – the – window..."

"If you heave yourself about much more," said his stationary chargehand, "you'll bring on your dandruff." His deliberations over, he began to push.

"So – we'll – shove – it – into – the – back – room," said Walter. "Argh!" Jonty had pushed a little too hard.

"What are you saying 'Argh!' for?" Jonty enquired.

"I often say 'Argh!'" said Walter, "when a piano's on my foot."

Jonty considered this. It was clear that Walter, jammed in the corner, had not sufficient leverage to free himself. Or rather, it would have been clear to Archimedes, Sir Rodney or Gladys Button, but Jonty had left his foot-rule in the assembly bay. He went out of the room and into the kitchen to deliberate further.

He was still absent when Elaine and Oswald entered the living room a moment later.

"Hello, dad," said Elaine. "Why are you pinned against the wall?"

"I'm waiting for the Fire Brigade," Walter explained, "to get the piano off my foot."

"That's all right, then," said Elaine. "I've brought Oswald for his supper, as luck would have it."

"I'll put the kettle on," Walter offered, "as soon as they've amputated my toe."

"No, no, silly! I mean, Oswald can help you. I've worked it out. He can lift the piano off your foot and I'll scramble eggs."

"Put in plenty of pepper, please," said Walter.

"There's just one thing, Elaine," Oswald said. "What's your mother going to say about this unsolicited piano-shifting?"

"Listen!" said Walter. "I can shift my own piano in my own house."

"Not very successfully, by the looks of it," Oswald suggested. "There we are." He had found a bit of space – something your average cost estimator could always do – and eased the piano from Walter's foot.

Walter said "Argh!" again, this time in relieved tones, and sat down.

Jonty returned and said he had worked it out. He rounded on the liberated Walter. "But you couldn't wait, could you?"

"Good heavens!" said Oswald. "So you're here!" He was not normally a young man to state the obvious, but we all make exceptions when sighting an unexpected great-uncle.

"Well! Am I not entitled to a scrambled egg?"

"No victimisation in this shop," said Elaine. "Just alliteration."

"No offence, Uncle Jonty."

"I needed that piano off my toe," Walter vouchsafed, "so that we could get in a bit of singing practice. Not for any selfish reasons."

"Did I take offence?" Jonty shouted. "I never take offence! Hey! I'll tell you something you haven't heard! In fact, I'll tell you anyway. I was talking to Charlie Embleton."

"That's Tommy Wrench," said Oswald.

"He's a spronker," said Jonty.

"In the zilted spindle shop," said Elaine.

Jonty glowered. "He said… I've forgotten what he said! No, I haven't. He said they're fetching in one of them what-d'you-call-its."

"Take it from me," said Oswald, "it's not official."

"It bloody is," said Jonty.

"It bloody isn't," said Oswald.

Walter asked Elaine what they were on about.

"The end of the world, dad," said Elaine. "Nothing important."

"A visual display unit," Oswald interpreted.

"Oh, yes," said Walter, unenlightened but alarmed.

"That worries you, dad?"

"Everything worries me," said Walter. "Without worry, what would I do?"

"It's not official," Oswald repeated. "I asked Tot."

"It's gospel, I tell you!" Jonty shouted. "And there'll be trouble!"

"It's only a rumour," said the patient Oswald.

"Trouble, did I say?" said Jonty. "There'll be a work-to-rule, that's what!"

"Rumour. Hearsay. Gossip."

"It was in the paper! 'Industrial action,' it said! You know who's behind it. Trotties! They're inciting the gubbible workers."

"That's gullible."

"I said gubbible!"

Elaine enquired if everybody accepted excessive pepper. Walter asked if they couldn't get on with some singing practice. Oswald pointed out that the piano was marooned.

"But my toe's a lot better," Walter said.

"What about the accompanist?" Jonty demanded. "I mean – she can't play the piano while she's scrambling eggs."

"I could if I were ambidextrous or Rubinstein," said Elaine. She disappeared into the kitchen.

Jonty now settled for unilateral obstreperousness and began to sing unaccompanied. "Bobby Shafto's gone to sea…" he carolled, in his undoubtedly fine tenor voice.

But he got no further than Bobby Shafto's silver buckles, because the front door was heard opening and closing and a clear soprano voice called, "Are you there, Walter?"

Walter's trepidation was patent. "Yes, Beth," he said.

Beth entered and contemplated the piano, stranded halfway between her coffee table and her india-rubber plant.

Walter launched into rapid exposition. "You see, Beth, it's too noisy to practise in here, what with all the double-decker buses and the young folks enjoying themselves vandalising the telephone box…"

"Walter!"

"Yes, Beth?"

"The piano – it's stuck in front of the telly!"

"I've explained."

"Have you? You haven't justified."

"The piano sort of finished up in that spot, you see, so we thought we'd leave it, just for the time being, you know, because Jonty has to practise and…" He failed to finish the sentence, not much to his surprise.

"What about Randolph Scott?" Beth asked.

Even less to his surprise, Beth had baffled Walter with a single question. Randolph Scott? He knew no Randolph Scott. Was he a shipmate of Bobby Shafto?

"He's in *Badman's Territory*," Beth said. "Nine o'clock. Movie Special."

Walter neither followed nor even tried. "The point is, Jonty's singing solo at the sending-off reception, isn't he? It's my twenty-first jumbo dispatch, isn't it?"

"I daresay," said Beth, "but I'm aiming to mosey to Dodge City."

"Could you not settle for a scrambled egg?"

"It's your twentieth dispatch!" shouted Jonty. "If it ever gets dispatched! Trouble! We're heading for trouble, I tell you! Trouble! Trouble!"

This elicited a despairing moan from Walter.

Oswald's carefully nurtured tolerance was beginning to crumble. "That's only a rumour, I'm telling you," he said.

"Is it?" Jonty shouted. "Is it? So what are you? – a boss's man?"

"I happen," said Oswald, "to be one of the newly-enlightened trade unionists."

Jonty made one of his disgusting noises.

"At least I'm consistent," Oswald responded warmly. "You change your mind more than you change your vest."

"I had a dream last night," Walter inserted wistfully, trying, not very hopefully, to create a diversion.

"And I should know," said Oswald, "because quite often it's *my* vest you change into." His warmth had become perfervid, because his patience had snapped. Well, no young man with an obnoxious uncle – let alone one yelling imprecations about Trotties, while a third party was trying doggedly to recount a nightmare – could maintain unsnappable patience, despite the alluring prospect of eggs scrambled by a beautiful woman. Even urbane old Sydney Smith, with pâté de foie gras in the offing, would surely have been tried.

And so, when Elaine returned, a minute later, it was to a confusion of voices. Oswald had increased his volume to get somewhere near Jonty's natural fortissimo. Walter was uselessly re-living his dream.

"Scrambled eggs for six," said Elaine, "if you'll fall in in the dining room."

"Scrambled eggs!" said Auntie Dinah, whom Elaine had recruited in the kitchen.

"Scrambled eggs!" cried Elaine.

"Scrambled eggs!" cried Auntie Dinah.

Nobody heeded.

What was needed was an authoritative voice. Nature usually provides one. It doesn't have to be loud.

"Quiet!" said Beth.

There was silence.

"Jonty..." said Walter.

"Eh?"

"Let's move the piano back," said Walter, "where it came from. We'll have some scrambled eggs. And then..."

"Eh?" said Jonty.

"Nine o'clock," said Walter. "Mount up. We hit the trail for Dodge City."

*

Sir Rodney was feeling mildly proud of himself. There was to be a meeting in his office at ten o'clock and he had remembered.

"Indeed yes," he said genially, in response to Miss Pilbury's reminder. Nor was he reading the clock upside down.

Not that he had accepted a briefing. He would attend the meeting in the English tradition of unpreparedness. In any case, perhaps the purpose of it all would emerge as they went along. If not, who would be any the worse off?

Miss Pilbury notified him that the Hun was at the gate. "Mr Judge is in the passage," she said, "telling Mr Needler about computer printouts."

Sir Rodney bade her let them in. "I am agog for computer printouts," he promised.

Elsie Pilbury ushered them in and retired.

Lionel Judge immediately said, "Shall we begin, Sir Rodney?" and tugged his ears in anticipation.

Sir Rodney wished them good morning and beamed vaguely at Tot. "Delighted to see you again, Mr – ah… So! I wanted to talk to you about computer printouts? Yes?"

"Strictly speaking, Sir Rodney," said Tot, "it was I who wanted to see you, inasmuch as I am chairman of the Joint Unions' Fraternal Branch Action Group." The word "inasmuch" was not in Tot's everyday vocabulary, but on official occasions he inserted a bit of trade union jargon. The world expected it.

"May I say, Mr Needler," said Lionel Judge, "speaking as a new broom, that I have looked forward to our meeting face-to-face across the table?"

"Yes, well," said Sir Rodney, "the purpose of this meeting is something I'm working on, believe me."

Judge was assuring Tot that he had himself laboured hard in Industrial Relations, from the management side.

"Making your fair contribution, no doubt," said Tot, "to many a satisfying rupture. How often have I too cavorted joyfully in the ritual dance!"

Sir Rodney ventured a guess. "The ladies' rest room," he said. "Is that it?"

"You were slightly nearer the first time," Tot modestly submitted.

"Was I really?"

No diffidence from Lionel Judge. "We are here," he said, "to discuss a putative visual display unit from the HQ link-up."

"Oh, that," said Sir Rodney.

"I thought, Sir Rodney," said Tot, "that you might allay the workers' fears about its siting."

Lionel Judge was sure he had the answer to that. "There is no occasion for trepidation, Mr Needler. None at all – er – Tot."

Tot greeted this equably. "So that's to be the tack?" He nodded, put his finger tips together and allowed himself a sapient pause.

Elsie Pilbury entered, put down a tray of coffee and biscuits and loitered. Lionel Judge said he rather liked the look of that morning's Financial Times Index. Tot, who had distrusted the *Financial Times* from early manhood, said nothing. Sir Rodney remarked sadly that there had been no commuters in his grandfather's day. Tot asked if he didn't mean computers and Sir Rodney said quite frankly he meant both.

"You will not forget, Sir Rodney," said Miss Pilbury, "that you have to visit the debunking shop?"

"Must I?"

"As a matter of urgency." She withdrew.

"You see, Sir Rodney," Tot pointed out, "I've heard on dubious authority that you're going to put it in an annexe to the wildgoose-bend loft."

Sir Rodney said that with the worst will in the world they could not put the ladies' rest room in the wildgoose-bend loft, let alone in an annexe. No women would rest in an annexe in his Pluvius Works.

"I'm speaking of a supplementary visual display unit."

Sir Rodney said there were none of those in his grandfather's day.

"We would reserve the right," Lionel Judge said, "to put new equipment – if any, if any! – in the site of our choice."

Tot said that as a trade union representative he recognised the first steps.

"The what?" said Judge.

"In the ritual dance."

"A paternal employer, my grandfather was," said Sir Rodney. "No unions, of course. His workers got a day off every Sunday. To go to chapel."

Tot said it was his bounden duty, jargon-wise, to warn Judge that there could be repercussions. Serious ones, it went without saying. The position and height of the wildgoose-bend loft afforded the wildgoose-benders a fine lunchtime view of the typists sunbathing on the Accounts Department roof. This was arguably frivolous, but wildgoose-benders were dour craftsmen who took their levity seriously.

"Ludicrous!" said Lionel Judge.

Tot was half-inclined to agree, he half-conceded. "But then, democracy is a ludicrous contraption. Lovable, but undeniably grotesque."

"But this is about nothing," said Judge.

"I hope so," said Tot. "The best disputes are."

Sir Rodney had wandered to the window.

"We are not even proposing," said Judge, "to bring in an additional visual display unit."

Tot was taken aback. "You don't mean that?" He allowed himself another pause. "Oh, dear! I see you do."

"We have an amplitude of V.D.U.s in appropriate forges, mills, furnaces and shops throughout the works. We have no wish to break a camel's back."

Sir Rodney had noticed that his grandfather's horse's ghost was at the trough again, reproaching him. He was tempted to ask his guests to come and look at it.

"Oh, Mr Judge, first blood to you!" Tot was saying. "Splendidly done – er – Lionel!" Well, the man had neatly removed a possible grievance. How would the rank-and-file take this?

At the window, Sir Rodney chuckled. How could he expect an efficiency co-ordinator or even an admittedly amiable trade union official to see the ghost of his grandfather's horse? What was that word? Ludicrous.

Tot was reviewing his position. "I think I can after all claim a victory. I can't say we've exactly forced the withdrawal of a visual display unit. But we might be able to claim that the arrival of one has been circumvented."

"But we never intended to have one!" Judge expostulated.

This was a point to deliberate and Tot duly weighed it. He then half-conceded that he was perhaps leaning towards unfair analysis. Meanwhile, Sir Rodney had returned to the conference table. He was sorry, they had his word on it, that the meeting was drawing to an unresolved conclusion; or a resolved one, whichever it was.

30

Tot suggested that on reflection they might be able to announce jointly that commonsense had prevailed. Judge said it seemed cosmetic and Tot congratulated him on his choice of jargon.

"Goodbye then, and thank you, gentlemen," said Sir Rodney. He uttered his self-deprecating chuckle. He had at least stamped a bit of his proclaimed eccentricity on yet another event.

Lionel Judge and Tot Needler departed and at once Elsie Pilbury re-entered with earnest intent. Nor was she alone.

*

There were many questions, be it said, that Tot Needler asked in his Mozart-free leisure moments, chatting with us in the Nostalgia Centre. Was it the aim of the masters of the thingie industry to concentrate production in a handful of large factories? Would all of the smaller concerns disappear like snow off the dike? Would the number of workers employed in thingie fettling be drastically reduced? It seemed likely, especially if the government were ever to find out where Lastfort was and that some old-fashioned industrial manufacturing was still going on there.

The concept of work as the country had known it since the beginnings of the Industrial Revolution was changing, he told us. But what about the generations to come? Would large numbers of them be occupied with something other than work? Or in some kind of activity which Tot and his contemporaries would not recognise as "work"? They couldn't all listen to Mozart.

Why not?

Incidentally, we might at this point have ventured a mention of the last horse-drawn tram's horse's nosebag which we have acquired for the Nostalgia Centre, but intelligence concerning Gladys Button's leg is perhaps more clamant.

*

"Sir Rodney," Miss Pilbury said, "I have brought my good friend Gladys Button. She is, as you will see, walking with the aid of a stick. You might like to look at her leg."

Sir Rodney said this offered a richness of choice. It was either Gladys Button's leg or go to the debunking shop.

"You don't have to go to the debunking shop."

"No?"

"No. That was a device." She had an array of devices for prising Sir Rodney out of undesired meetings.

Sir Rodney said he had half-thought it might be, and felt rather pleased with this stab at jargon. "Please have a seat, Miss – ah..." he bade his visitor.

"Mrs!" said Gladys Button, sitting. "I am the widow Button!"

Sir Rodney essayed a conversational gambit. "Would your late husband's ancestor have been the Timothy Button who built the first turbine-driven steam ship?" It wouldn't, as he knew, but any gambit will suffice for a shy man.

Gladys Button asked was he not thinking of Charles Algernon Parsons?

Sir Rodney said, "Of course, of course," abandoned gambits and looked longingly at his tea clipper.

Gladys Button felt he should no longer postpone looking at her leg, which she now extended. "It's my right leg, Sir Rodney."

Sir Rodney said yes, it looked like a right leg.

31

"My knee cartilage slipped out. It's easily done, you know."

Elsie Pilbury said this was true. "Take your eye off them for a moment, and out they pop."

Gladys Button asked if Sir Rodney knew that the human knee, ounce for ounce, carried more burden than any mechanism in the civilised world. "Shall I tell you what Archimedes said?" she asked.

"You've made your point, Gladys," Elsie Pilbury said, fearing that her friend might be overstating her case.

Sir Rodney said he was under the impression that Archimedes had intimated that if somebody gave him something to stand on, he could move the earth.

Gladys Button said it was as well nobody did. "What if he had been halfway through moving the earth," she demanded, "and his knee cartilage had slipped out?"

Elsie Pilbury asked if Archimedes had not been in the habit of sitting in a bath, displacing his own weight in water. Gladys Button retorted that a genius would always find something to sit in. In any case, all innovations began as fatuities, and so did all fatuities.

"He was the father of hydrostatics, so they say," said Sir Rodney.

"Exactly. Where would you and I have been if he hadn't invented the spiral pump for raising water?" She rose. "Would you care to see my other leg? It's not entirely infirm, but bears inspection, I like to think."

"You've made your point, Gladys," said Elsie Pilbury, rather more anxiously.

"Well, well," said Sir Rodney. "I'm sorry your husband was not descended from Charles Algernon Parsons. But I suppose not everybody can be."

Gladys Button said no woman's husband chose his ancestors. "But at least I've made my point, Sir Rodney." She flourished her stick and went out.

"I wonder what the devil Timothy Button invented," Sir Rodney said.

Perhaps he should have gone to the debunking shop. But the eternal paternalist in him had been stirred by Gladys Button's leg.

*

"It's just that nobody else would take it on," Oswald said.

"You've started a conversation in the middle, Oswald," Elaine replied.

They lived not far apart, so it was natural that they should frequently walk home from work together; not a fixed arrangement, but one they had slipped into, although not entirely easily on Oswald's part, because his native reserve rendered him a hesitant purveyor of small talk.

"Minutes secretary of JUFBAG," he explained. "I couldn't say 'No.' I'm not one to be negative."

"Except to me," Elaine thought sadly.

There was a pause, while Oswald cast about for his next non-negation. "So would you," he said at last, "if you lived with Uncle Jonty."

"Be a disjointed conversationalist, you mean?"

"That's it."

"In any case," Elaine said, "only half of any conversation is spoken. The other half's in the head."

"How did you know I was going to say that?"

"It's my mission to read your script."

"Well, anyway," Oswald said, "that's how it's carried on."

"Trade unionism?" Elaine asked, reading some more.

"That's right." Like much of the world's necessary labour, trade unionism was performed, Oswald believed, by pedestrian enthusiasts or reluctant misfits. And who benefited from this worthy work? The apathetic majority, which included a few caustic contrarietists, as exemplified by his Uncle Jonty.

"I like walking home with you, Oswald," Elaine said. "I even enjoy the pauses."

There was a pause, then Oswald said fiercely, "Thingie fettling!"

"What?" said Elaine, surprised.

"There must be a better life somewhere."

"There is, there is!" said Elaine. "And you're only twenty-two."

"Ah!" said Oswald glumly. "But how would he manage without me?"

Elaine, reading his script, reflected that she did not care to consider Oswald's unspeakable Uncle Jonty. "Do you fancy another scrambled egg some time?" she asked.

"Yes, please. He'd be hopeless by himself, and I rather promised my mother when she joined the Conservative Party and made her bed in Jarrow – two hazardous decisions – that I'd keep an eye on her belligerent old uncle."

"So he's really your great-uncle?"

"Yes. Have you ever had one?"

"I'm a girl. Mine's a great-aunt." She added "H'm," a little sceptically. She was wondering if his piety disguised an aversion to marriage. Or something.

They had reached her gate.

"See you," said Oswald. "I'm quite articulate, really."

"See you," said Elaine. She went up her garden path.

Oswald continued on his way. He had only a slight aversion to marriage, and none at all to something. But he had many other matters on his mind. There was his motor bike, JUFBAG, Lastfort Harriers... There was Newcastle United's home match every other Saturday... There was also the fact that he was – well, not exactly shy, but just a bit self-absorbed, taking himself seriously and conducting in his head great debates about the state of the world. He also took Elaine seriously, which wasn't the case with about eleven other girls he could name, but wouldn't. And it wasn't just her scrambled eggs. But he expected she knew that, if she'd been reading his script.

Oh, he was splendidly articulate in his head.

*

"Alas, that Spring should vanish with the Rose!" said Elsie Pilbury. "That Youth's sweet-scented Manuscript should close!"

She concluded her Omar Khayam recital on a sigh of relief, because she was an extremely nervous performer, and disappeared from the club stage to almost no applause.

Tot Needler grasped the microphone. "Thank you, Elsie Pilbury," he said. "That is the end of the mandatory amateur versifying for tonight."

"Hear, hear!" said a voice from the back.

"Elsie wanted to do some Kipling," Tot continued, "but of course we couldn't allow her to kipple in front of a family audience."

"Gerroff!" said the voice.

Ever the indefatigable improviser, Tot adopted facile Master of Ceremonies patter as easily as trade union jargon. He promised that the next poetry reader would be hung in the passage. "Last drinks, ladies and gentlemen," he then said. "Sup up." He was club M.C., part-time ambulance man, dominoes secretary, charities appeals organiser, choir committee member and sick visitor. He was the universal volunteer.

The Lastfort Social Club looked from the outside just like any other dismal building in a street of dismal buildings. It had once been equally drab inside, but the £400,000 spent on it by the brewery had given it a magnificent interior. Enormous chandeliers glinted, sumptuous plastic mock-panelling covered the walls, the stage was beautifully fitted and there were carpets so deeply piled that short-arsed members, so it was said, were frequently lost in them.

Oswald, arriving for a last-minute pint, following a training session with Lastfort Harriers, drifted to the corner table where Elaine sat with her mother and father and his Uncle Jonty. He was in time to hear Beth remark, "Walter, you're weeping into your Federation Special again."

Walter, seldom free from mournful speculation, was gazing absently into his glass. Too much was expected of him. Head foreman of the thingie assembly squad and conductor of the factory choir: one man should not be asked to shoulder all that. Not simultaneously. Not on one crucial day. On the eighteenth of September, at three o'clock, he had to get that jumbo thingie safely dispatched, amid all the attendant ceremony. Oh, God, if something went wrong! He sipped his pink paraffin. Or was it extra strong ale? A man in deep depression wouldn't heed the difference.

And at seven o'clock in the evening of that same day, he had to be at the Julius Caesar Hotel with his assembled choir, ready for the reception. Sir Rodney would make his ritual speech about the Pluvius Works family tradition and how that tradition had been handed down from grandfather to father to son. That included, of course, grandmothers, mothers and daughters; he was not one to forget the ladies. The tears would form in his eyes and he would reach his predestined peroration:

"Pluvius people stand together, firmly bound:
Like well-made jumbo thingies, stout and sound."

He would then call on Walter to conduct the choir in singing *Bobby Shafto*.

Tears came to Walter's own eyes. The choir! But the choir was depleted!

"It's depleted, Beth," he said. "Since they cremated Sidney Grout, and Tom Blackett became teetotal again."

"Death and virtue," said Beth cheerfully. "An unholy trinity, but for bad arithmetic."

"I'll tell you what!" Jonty shouted, "We all know what they say about thingie fettling workers."

"What's that got to do with death and virtue?" Elaine asked.

"He doesn't know," Beth said, "but he'll tell you."

"Not yet," said Oswald. "He has to forget first."

"If it comes to that," Walter said, "take the red, white and blue bunting. It's no gewgaw, you know. Sir Rodney told me."

"And yet you're still unhappy?" said Elaine.

Walter said it was every person's right to be inconsolable. And if a man couldn't be miserable on his night out, whither democracy?

Jonty thumped the table. "I'll tell you what!" They waited, not very expectantly. "I've forgotten! I've bloody forgotten!"

"He'll remember," said Oswald. "He'll bloody remember."

"Eighty-three point-six," said Walter.

Beth gazed at him wonderingly.

Jonty remembered. "You know what they say about thingie fettling workers: you'd never get a donkey in the fettlers' union." He laughed uproariously.

Into the pained silence, Walter said dismally, "The assembly costs are up eighty-three point-six. Imagine what it's doing to Sir Rodney."

"And his pullover," said Elaine.

"Would you laugh," said Jonty, "if I fell off my seat?"

"Mind you," said Oswald, "there's a quite simple method of cutting the labour costs to nil. Pay off all the workers. That's what they've done in shipbuilding. That way, they've got no ships – at no cost."

Walter pulled at his Federation Special and said Oswald had no right to try to cheer him up. Oswald said this was true; every man was entitled to his despair. Walter said either he or some other dejected sufferer had just said that and added, "They'll scrap it, you know."

"Scrap what?" Beth asked. "I don't understand you, Walter."

"No, well, that's part of the marriage packet, isn't it? I'm talking about red, white and blue bunting." He then enquired why Beth's Auntie Dinah hadn't accompanied them to the club.

"It's quite simple," said Beth. "You locked her in the cupboard under the stairs."

"I thought that was tomorrow."

"You couldn't wait. You were always an impetuous fool. D'you remember our honeymoon?"

"No," said Walter. "What happened?"

*

At the Pluvius Works, a car drove up the dimly lit street and stopped at the main entrance. The nightshift gateman greeted the figure which loomed up at his little gatehouse. "It's you, sir," he said. "Can I help you?"

"Just popping across the yard for something," said Sir Rodney. He turned into the darkened courtyard and headed for the office block.

*

Tot had clambered back on stage to make his closing sally. "Ladies and gentlemen, here's Charlie Embleton, sometimes known as Tommy Wrench, or vice versa – although why a man would want to be known as vice versa you might well ask but probably not."

"Gerroff!" shouted the voice.

Charlie Embleton, inept zilted spindle spronker by day, alias Tommy Wrench, very loud folk singer by night, stepped on stage. "Now then, folks, like," he said, "what I'd like to sing, like, is something you all know, like, so if you want to join in, like, please yourselves, like. If not, like, you can fall into your beer for all I care, like." He sang the final song of the evening. Nobody was quite sure what it was, but as it was a folk song. they wouldn't, would they? At any rate, it was very loud.

It was not loud enough, however, to drown a contentious voice which was raised at Walter's table. Jonty was belatedly challenging Walter, or anybody else who might be remotely challengeable. "Will they hell!" he shouted.

"What?" said Walter.

"Will they hell scrap the red, white and blue bunting!"

Beth was still lost. "Is that a bird, sometimes known as a crossbill?"

"Bloody management!" said Jonty.

"Shush, shush, Uncle Jonty," said Oswald. Any inveighing against management was trade union official prerogative, he felt.

Tommy Wrench sang on.

"It goes on the platform at the dispatching ceremony," Walter explained.

"What does?" said Beth.

"The red, white and blue bunting," said Elaine.

"I'll have every man in the factory out!" Jonty shouted.

"You'll what?" Oswald demanded.

"Why do they want a bird known as a crossbill on the platform?" Beth asked.

"I'll bring the place to a standstill if they try to scrap it!"

"You're not a union officer!" Oswald shouted back.

"What the hell's that got to do with it?"

Tommy Wrench sang on.

Suddenly, above the loud quarrel and the very loud folk song, sirens were heard.

"Fire engines!" somebody cried.

There was a rush to the door. Three fire engines were hurtling past.

*

In the darkness, at the Pluvius Works, flames were issuing from the first floor of the main office building. A figure was framed at a window.

Chapter Three

——————— *Horses Feel No Guilt* ———————

Tot arrived in Sir Rodney's outer office next morning to be greeted by a divulgent Elsie Pilbury. "Well, anyway, they got him out, Mr Needler," she said. "They got him out."

"I heard it on local radio," Tot said.

There had been extravagant versions of the story on Radio Clarts that morning. Later, the accounts became more sober. "Last night, fire appliances rushed to the Pluvius Thingie Fettling Works. It seems that the blaze was accidental. The Fire Brigade was originally called because the company chairman, Sir Rodney Eames, had locked himself in the ladies' rest room. The gateman heard his cries and telephoned for help."

"The Fire Brigade got him out," said Miss Pilbury.

"From the..?"

"Quite!" said Miss Pilbury. Sir Rodney had mysteriously fused the lights, it appeared, and could not find his way out. In the darkness, the gateman could not find his way in.

"I gather the fire chief had to light his lads in with matches," said Tot. "But what was Sir Rodney doing in there?"

"He was seeing if there was a case for condemning the ladies' rest room."

"There is now. First recorded example of a fire chief starting a fire."

"Mind you," said Miss Pilbury, "the fire chief did have a torch, but Sir Rodney dashed it out of his hand, thinking he was a burglar disguised as a postman."

"Postmen don't wear firemen's helmets."

"They might if their disguise is especially cunning, Sir Rodney reasoned."

"True," said Tot. "Good morning, Sir Rodney."

Sir Rodney was framed in the doorway of his office, in dirty old trousers. "Good morning. How are you, Mr – er..."

"Needler," Elsie Pilbury supplied.

"I'm chairman of JUFBAG," Tot supplemented.

"Splendid! And what's that? Please forgive my trousers."

"The Joint Unions' Fraternal Branch Action Group, Sir Rodney. You wanted to see me."

Happy though he was to see Tot, whom he acknowledged as a decent chap, Sir Rodney sighed. There had been no fraternal action in his grandfather's day. "A postman set fire to my trousers last night, you know." He chuckled. It had given him the excuse to come to the office in his dear old gardening togs. "Be it said, my housekeeper tells me I have fifteen suits. I wonder where they are. Strange creature."

"Is it to do with the non-acquisition of a visual display unit?"

"Hardly likely; she's already non-provided with one of those damned things,

37

fortunate woman. What was I saying?"

"You have fifteen suits."

"Why should I want to see you about that? Or take my grandfather."

"Did you want to discuss the visual display unit?"

"At the moment, I want to talk about my grandfather; it's one of the rights I assert from time to time."

"Hear, hear!" Tot supported such assertions.

"A paternal employer, my grandfather. His fitters worked a 72-hour week for a gold sovereign. Splendid fellows!" He often thought of those hard-working craftsmen of bygone years. Strange how so many of them dropped down dead in their forties. They didn't eat the right grub, probably, poor innocent chaps.

"Sir Rodney, speaking of the visual display unit..."

Sir Rodney said it was odd how people kept speaking of that.

Miss Pilbury decided it was time to intervene. "You were going to confirm, Sir Rodney, the finality of the board's decision, were you not?"

"You put that jolly succinctly, Miss Pilbury, but I'll tell him, you know."

Tot had accepted the much-promulgated V.D.U. non-acquisition. But he had his more militant members to consider. They liked to have substantial grounds for useful suspicion.

Sir Rodney was torn between staring out at the trough, sidling up to his tea clipper model and fingering the hole in his pullover, but he owed some attention, he knew, to this polite and worthy representative of his workforce. "Now! – what did I want to say?"

"I've said it, Sir Rodney," said Miss Pilbury.

And Tot was still pondering that he had to achieve a fine balance between (a) acknowledging to his militants that the employers were, as usual, up to something sinister and (b) assuring them that there was nothing sinister for anybody to be up to anyway.

"Yes, well, the Board have only this morning made up their minds," said Sir Rodney.

That was it, Tot decided. He would have to find a formula to convince his militants that if the employers had been up to something sinister (which they hadn't), it was militancy that had stopped them in their tracks. And there would be no demarcation dispute about visual display units. What then? In the unhealthy labour climate of the last decade, Tot reflected, there hadn't been a single demarcation dispute. His militants would be asking if the millennium was postponed.

"And now," said Sir Rodney, "I must tell you what the Board concluded."

"I've told Mr Needler," said Miss Pilbury.

"Rot!" said Sir Rodney jovially. Really, did nobody ever listen to him? He chuckled delightedly. "Mr Needler! Miss Pilbury! We're going to build a new ladies' rest room!"

Paternalism was not dead.

*

"Jonty!"

Jonty responded to Walter's agitated call and stepped into the foreman's cabin. "Well, then," he asked, helpful as ever, "and what can I put right for you this time?"

"Eh?"

"You're the foreman, aren't you? You'll have come up with another bundle of bollockses. Have you unpopped the wrong poppets? Or jammed your big toe in a limber hole?"

"It's the missus," said Walter bleakly.

"You're on your own on that one."

"Her Auntie Dinah's arrived from Hexham."

Jonty failed to see what the problem was. There was no harm in aunties, in moderation. He had even had one himself once. She had died. They all died. Life was a leveller. Old aunties worked out of the system, given time.

"Have I not got enough troubles?" Walter moaned. "Did I tell you I had a dream last night?" It was the same one. He was shaking even now as he recalled it.

"Sit down, man!" said Jonty. "You're trembling like a haddock."

It was all very well for Jonty; there was no Auntie Dinah in his life. Walter loved the human race, but Beth's Auntie Dinah was an exasperating old besom, the poor soul. "By the way, Jonty, somebody's uncrossed the crossover shove-ups."

Jonty knew. He had re-crossed them. Where would bloody management be if it wasn't for the likes of him putting right all their bloomers in his quiet way without a word of complaint?

"Nationalisation!" he shouted.

"What are you on about?"

"Bureaucrats! Next thing, we'll have fitters in clawhammer coats!"

"It's eighteen years since we were nationalised," said Walter wearily. "And you voted for it. Haddocks don't tremble."

"There's too many looking for a cushy number. Bloody left-wingers!"

"You voted Labour."

"Of course I voted Labour! Every working man should vote Labour! It's this bloody socialism that gets my back up!"

As always, Walter realised that his own troubles were being submerged. "*You'd* be trembling like a haddock," he said, "if you had a wife and her Auntie Dinah had come from Hexham and haddocks trembled."

"Whose fault's that, then? Nobody asks the likes of you to get married and buy your houses and your fitted carpets and your front-loading deep freezers. You take all that on, and you've got to get a job as a foreman to keep it up! And what happens? It kills you before you're fifty!"

Walter sat down. "Thank you, Jonty," he said. "I don't know how I'll manage if you retire. Or if you get strangled, lynched or garrotted in the natural course of events."

*

"Not that I ever got a sausage roll," Auntie Dinah said.

"So?" said Beth.

"Still, I've enjoyed staying with you."

"It's only two days since you got here."

"I don't want to outstay my welcome. But I would have liked a sausage roll."

Elaine intervened to enquire if this was a private misunderstanding, or could anybody join in? "Besides, you can't leave yet," she said. "You haven't seen Lastfort's latest attraction."

"I was thinking about our Dan," Auntie Dinah said.

"That's understandable; you've had a heavy dinner."

"If it comes to that, I was thinking about our Stanley. And just to round things off, I was thinking about our..." The tears arrived. "I was thinking about the one I lost."

"Well, anyway," Elaine said, "you can't leave Lastfort before you've made a tour of the Nostalgia Centre."

"Up to now, I haven't even had a sausage roll."

"One thing at a time. You've been locked in the cupboard under the stairs. Not everybody that comes here gets locked in the cupboard under the stairs."

This was an event too recent for Auntie Dinah to dwell on. "I was thinking about young Casablanca," she said.

Ah! Another undisclosed early chapter! Much fresher in the memory, that. "Who was young Casablanca?" Elaine asked.

"I don't think I'll tell you."

"That's pretty mean, when I've taken a whole afternoon off work."

"You stood on a burning deck with him?" said Beth. "You and Humphrey Bogart?"

Auntie Dinah said she wished they would shut up while she was explaining. "It was 1938," she said. "We were on a camping holiday, a group of us madcap young things. A camping holiday. Under canvas. With tents."

"They thought of everything in 1938."

"I can picture him now," said Auntie Dinah. "He had a bike and a moustache. Most of the lads had bikes and moustaches, if they'd saved up for them, in 1937."

"1938."

"You're listening, then? I'd been for a swim. I had bought a purple bathing costume for the king's abdication. Mind you, I'd have bought it anyway. I'd have gone bathing even if he'd stayed on the throne. And it wasn't purple. It was black, but I dyed it purple, except that it ran. Not that I could tell the difference, being colour blind, because my father was kicked by a mule before I was born. Well, there I was in my tent. I'd just taken off my bathing costume when he came in."

"A young man with a bike and a moustache?"

"Well, it wasn't the king, was it? He left the bike outside. He apologised and stroked his moustache. He said he should have knocked. He was wanting a penny for the gas, he said. He made that up."

"Never!" said Elaine.

"It was a good job my hair was down. Well, I told everybody it was." She heaved a huge sigh. "He was good-looking in a bandy-legged sort of way." She heaved another. "Casablanca I called him. It wasn't his real name."

"My word!" said Elaine. And to think they thought they had heard her entire repertoire.

"He had a three-speed gear on his bike. I sometimes think of his three-speed gear when the wind's in my chimney."

"Why when the wind's in your chimney?"

"If you've got to think of something when the wind's in your chimney, it might as well be a three-speed gear."

"I wonder where it is now," said Elaine.

"In the Nostalgia Centre, probably," said Beth. "Alongside the curling tongs."

"And the donkey boilers?"

"And the stays. I wonder what happened to stays and donkey boilers."

"The R.S.P.C.A. put a stop to them," said Elaine.

Auntie Dinah felt the conversation was slipping away from her. "What do they call that place again?" she demanded.

"Grimsby," said Beth.

"No, no!"

"Where your Stanley went?"

"Our Dan!"

"Inverness," said Elaine.

"Inverness!" said Auntie Dinah. "He went there to shoot the rabbits. He was always one for adventure."

"It was the Rocky Mountains," said Beth, "and he went to shoot the rapids."

"But the R.S.P.C.A. put a stop to it," said Elaine.

Auntie Dinah rose from the sofa and her knitting. "I think I'll have a bath," she stated.

"On top of a heavy dinner?"

"I've outstayed my welcome? Is that it?"

"Nothing like that," said Elaine. "It's just that I've left my stays on the towel rail."

Auntie Dinah proceeded majestically out of the room. "Which of you is going to wash my back?" she called from the stairs.

"D'you think she meant Casanova?" Elaine asked.

"Certainly not!" said Beth.

*

"Sir Rodney?" said Lionel Judge. "Judge here. Judge. Lionel Judge, speaking from Computer HQ." He had decided to telephone Sir Rodney, because he was finding their personal confrontations ever more frustrating. "Please note, Sir Rodney, that computerised output re assembly labour costs continues to escalate. What?"

His change of tactics wasn't working. Sir Rodney was mumbling something about jargon. Jargon? What jargon?

"We must look," he said, "to overheads contiguous to the jumbo dispatching ceremony. Sir Rodney, please do not go off tangentially... Tangentially! Your what? Your grandfather? Please! The bill for the bunting – we must institute some back-tracking on historical contract data... No. I'm sure your grandfather had his methods. But as Costing and Systems Co-ordinator, I've been seconded by HQ to promulgate the printout info which the computer memory bank is currently stockpiling..."

He took a deep breath. He really must get this point through to Sir Rodney. "There are rumours... Rumours! About unrest vis-a-vis certain personnel re pending decisions concerning bunting – i.e., red, white and blue bunting for the dispatching ceremony. You should scotch them... Scotch!" It was no use. "Yes, I know your grandfather was philanthropic. However, these are hard-nosed times... Sir Rodney... Sir Rodney!"

In his office, Sir Rodney had drifted to his tea clipper model. On his desk, his telephone jabbered away, unattended.

*

In his little room in his daughter's house, Tot Needler reclined. To him came his daughter, bearing a newspaper.

41

"Did you see this, dad?" she asked.

"What's that, Avril?"

Avril read from the *Lastfort Tinkle*: "As another jumbo dispatch looms up at the Pluvius Works, certain questions are being asked."

And even if they weren't, Tot knew, it was as good a way as any to start a canard.

"In the face of mounting costs, will traditional ceremony be removed? Will there be no more red, white and blue bunting? Are workers seething at these possibilities?"

No, but was the *Lastfort Tinkle* drooling at them?

"This should be seen against the background that when the current jumbo thingie is completed, no further work is in the pipeline for jumbo thingies and very little for tiddler thingies. What does the future hold for the Pluvius factory?"

"Chocolate creams," Tot suggested.

Avril said, "Naturally. That'll be something Shaw once said?"

It would, not surprisingly, as Shaw had said something about everything. "I'll look it up in my Shaviana files," Tot said. "Later."

"After Mozart," Avril said indulgently.

"After Mozart. It comes back to this Time Warp theory of mine. You've heard of my Time Warp theory?"

"No."

Bless her! It was a loving daughter who pretended she hadn't heard something her rambling father had told her a hundred times.

"Mind you," said Avril, "I haven't heard about chocolate creams."

"Wouldn't you rather hear the Time Warp theory?"

"Yes."

Bless her again. "Here goes. We're in a time warp. You see, the rest of humanity's in the nineties, but we're living in the fifties, with disbelief in abeyance. Some of us."

"Or even earlier?"

"Some of us." It was all, Tot believed, thanks to Sir Rodney's inability to forsake the epoch of his grandfather; an attitude of mind that was beguilingly transmissible.

"Can it last, though?"

"Not a hope." Sir Rodney was an old man, in an old world. It was an inefficient, incompetent world, on the way to being lost forever. The beguilement lay in the fact that they were losing it.

"But perhaps, dad, another generation, given good or bad will, can bring it back."

"Hardly. You see, for another generation the nineties might be the lost, inefficient, beguiling world. Heigh-ho."

"Heigh-ho?"

"As Victorian novelists used to say when the moment came to change the subject." He changed the subject. "Where's that husband of yours now, then?"

"Last heard of halfway across the South Atlantic," said Avril. "He's thinking of leaving the Merchant Navy, you know, and looking for a shore job."

"Oh?"

"Yes, the romantic fool! He thinks he's just as likely to find the Mary Celeste on dry land."

"Or a lost beguiling world?"

"That's it," said Avril. "Well... I'll have to get the bairns off to bed. We'll leave chocolate creams in abeyance."

"Why not?" said Tot. In any case, to expand on chocolate creams he would have to find Shaw's *The Apple Cart*.

An agreeable chore, but needing a fair bit of time, given the anarchy of his piled-up library.

*

As it happens, here in the Nostalgia Centre we have no donkey boiler. There is room for one in the alcove, but Mrs Thirlaway is there and we don't like to shift her.

*

"Yoo-hoo!" said Elaine. "Entertained any good rumours lately?"

"Come in, Elaine," said Miss Pilbury.

"Thought I'd look by, Elsie, to collect a new ribbon cassette and any disgusting gossip that's going around."

"It's a good job I know you."

"Hard luck for you. It's ignorance that sustains the human race. I got that from a clever young man."

"How *is* Oswald?"

"Still running from my arms."

"That's one way to catch you. One of my grandfather's old saws, that." She inserted paper into her typewriter.

"I never knew you had a grandfather."

"Sir Rodney's not the only one. Entertain this, by the way: It's not true that the red, white and blue bunting's going to be scrapped."

"It was on local radio," said Elaine. She had heard Mel Queasy of Radio Clarts announce it in his breakfast round-up, slip it into his lunchtime request programme and interrupt his evening *Pick-a-Disc* to insert it again. "That's three times; it must be true."

"Not so," said Miss Pilbury, "whatever Dr. Goebbels might have told you. Mind you, I am typing this instruction – that previous bunting costs have to be researched."

"A job for Oswald, that," said Elaine, "if he can shut up the unspeakable uncle: the only man who'll get the last word with the last trump."

"His bark's worse than his bite."

"It needs to be, or we'd all have hydrophobia," said Elaine. "Will you be entertaining at the club tomorrow night?"

Miss Pilbury nodded. "I'm reciting Omar Khayam every week until Christmas."

"That's the stuff. See you there."

"Turn down an empty glass," said Miss Pilbury.

*

The ghost of Sir Rodney's grandfather's horse had arrived at the drinking trough. He had come to haunt Sir Rodney, but Sir Rodney was in the debunking shop, for no reason, which for Sir Rodney was the best reason of all. The horse studied the drinking trough verse and reflected on its provenance. The verse was there because Sir Rodney's grandfather's mother had left her son her rhyming dictionary on her deathbed, or under it. What was it that young Oswald had said, the horse asked himself, about the cussedness of human nature? Or perhaps young Oswald hadn't said it yet. If not, he would say it shortly. Or perhaps it was that chap Tot Needler. The horse was a little confused; in heaven, the time was out of joint.

The fact was, he felt he too could do with a rhyming dictionary. Of all the verses old Jasper Eames had composed, there was none to a horse. Was this fair to a faithful beast? Didn't that omission indicate something about human nature's cussedness? The horse had decided he would write a verse to himself. Time dragged a bit in Eternity, if you were a horse. It was all right for former human beings; they had their guilt to fill their days. Horses feel no guilt. That was one of the curses of having no soul.

He had started to write a verse, but the first line ended with an awkward word. Yes, he must acquire a rhyming dictionary. As far as he knew, there was no rhyme to "equus".

*

On the following evening at the club Miss Pilbury declaimed:
"The wind of Life keeps oozing drop by drop;
The leaves of Life keep falling one by one."

wine? (don't recognise quote as Omar)

Sir Rodney's grandfather's love of verses had not stopped at placing them at various points in the factory. The Lastfort Working Men's Club had originally been the Eames Institute, founded and built by old Jasper Eames for the respectable recreation of his employees and their families. There were several stipulations in his will designed to inculcate and preserve a high moral tone in the workers. One of them was that there should be occasional readings of elevating poetry on the premises of the Institute. It was written in due course into the club constitution. Miss Pilbury was the latest in the line of estimable verse-purveyors. For her, it was more than a duty; it was an honour and a pleasure, which was even worse. And it did her nervous system no good at all.

"Thank you, Elsie Pilbury," said Tot Needler. "What about a big hand, folks?" He applauded, unaccompanied.

"I haven't finished," Elsie said.

Just so. And she was supported from the floor.

"The woman hasn't finished!" Gladys Button called. "What is this? Sexism?"

Tot said he didn't see how such a charge could be levelled against the club with regard to female performers. After all, there were strippers every Saturday. This was true; it was a contingency which Sir Rodney's grandfather's proscriptions could not have foreseen.

"Those strippers are female!" shouted Gladys Button. "There are no male strippers! We haven't seen a single willie on that stage!" She added that but for her loose cartilage, she would step up and give the chairman a black eye.

Tot said he hoped that would not be necessary. "Of course it won't be necessary," Elsie Pilbury inserted. "You don't have to do this for me, Gladys," she told her friend. "I'm quite capable of giving him a black eye unaided."

"You most certainly are, Elsie," Tot said. "Carry on versifying."

"Thank you," Miss Pilbury said, and continued: "Here with a Loaf of Bread beneath the Bough…"

Gladys Button interrupted again. "Elsie!"

"What is it, Gladys?"

"That's a great deal of balderdash, isn't it?"

44

"Since you ask me, yes," said Elsie. "Why don't I come down there and have a gin with you?"

She did so.

As Tot had thought many times (and so, to be fair, had Shaw), no man was a match for a woman, except with hobnailed boots. Very slightly chastened, he made his final announcement. "On Saturday, at lunchtime, gentlemen, we've got Dawn O'Day, exotic undresser, with pease pudding and saveloys."

He left the stage.

*

At the Lester family table, Jonty was saying, "Is it my turn to get the drinks in?"

"It is," said Walter sombrely, "which is why I've got them."

"I'm jammed in, you see."

"I know," said Walter, "and you worked hard at it."

Beth addressed Oswald. "By gum, you're quiet, my lad."

Oswald said he was the kind that simmered silently – most of the time – and continued preoccupied.

"Like Vesuvius," said Beth. It occurred to her that Auntie Dinah and Oswald were possibly unacquainted. "Oh dear, I'm forgetting my manners. Auntie Dinah, I don't know if you remember Oswald Gorman?"

Auntie Dinah studied Oswald. "Are you better, son?"

"Better?"

"They were putting it about that you were dead."

"Club members don't die nowadays," Beth assured her. "There's a new miracle cure. It comes exotically undressed. We haven't got those male strippers yet, that Gladys Button's on about, but it won't be long. Civilisation needs it."

"Where's Elaine, anyway, young fellow?" Auntie Dinah asked.

Oswald explained equably that he wasn't Elaine's keeper.

Auntie Dinah said, "Aha!" She was sure she had heard a rumour to the contrary.

Elaine was absent because it was her badminton night. Among the young men who would be playing were Ian Webster, Bob Ashley, David Norfield, Albert Anderson, Tom Yates and Mike Stanford, all of whom were handsomer, more sociable and more amenable than Oswald and none of whom she was in love with, although any one of them would have settled for less. At a pinch, they would even have eschewed Saturday lunchtime pease pudding and saveloys.

Jammed in or not, Jonty had decided to expand. He brought up a running theme. "So!" he said portentously. "They're going to do away with the red, white and blue bunting."

Oswald had a constant resolve to ignore his Uncle Jonty, and he constantly broke it. "They're not," he said tersely.

"Unions!" said Jonty. "Fancy letting the management scrap the bunting!"

"They're not," said Oswald.

"Of course not," said Beth, "and I speak from celestial ignorance."

"That's right," said Walter.

"Fiddling themselves jobs in headquarters!" said Jonty. "Should be looking after their members!"

Oswald was becoming less than temperate. "Who?"

"Who? Who, he says! Union officials, that's who! While the bunting's being scrapped!"

"It's not!" cried Oswald, Beth and Walter.

"And I'm a union official," Oswald reminded him warmly.

"I don't care if you're King Kong!"

"I want it on record," said Oswald, lapsing instinctively into jargon, as all do when the union hat is put on, "that I'm technical staff representative – and I happen to be jealous of the rights of my members."

"Bloody penpushers!" said Jonty.

"Listen!" said Oswald.

"Shush, love," said Beth, smilingly discouraging.

Oswald, smilingly discouraged, shushed.

"Is it my turn to get the drinks in?" Jonty demanded.

"Probably," said Walter. "That's why King Kong'll be getting them."

"I'm jammed in, you see," said Jonty.

*

Elsie Pilbury sipped her gin.

"It's your right knee, Gladys, isn't it?" she asked.

"You know it is, Elsie." Gladys sipped hers.

"Yes."

They both sipped.

"Right or left," said Gladys, "I could still hand out a black eye."

Elsie said she had always been given to understand that the knee had an inner cartilage.

"It's nature's bounty," her friend stated. "An inner and an outer."

"A fair balance, that seems."

"Not exactly. One's stronger than the other. I'm not sure which."

"Ah! So vigilance is the essence?"

"Quite! Have you ever asked yourself, Elsie: Could Leonardo da Vinci have invented the first bicycle if his cartilage had slipped out?"

"Why not, Gladys? You for your part could hand out a black eye."

"I was boasting, Elsie. Another fact about Leonardo: he irrigated the plains of Lombardy."

"That's enough for any woman."

"He wasn't a woman."

"That wasn't his fault."

"He was a restless genius."

"Ah!" said Elsie.

She went for two more gins.

*

"Beth!" said Auntie Dinah.

"Hello?"

"I was thinking about our Stanley last night. What do they call that place?"

"Grimsby."

"He won't come back."

"You never know. He could get homesick for beetroot."

46

Auntie Dinah shook her head. "He took his best cap. I keep thinking about the ninth of May, 1941."

"The Second World War was raging."

"Our Stanley was born."

"That as well."

"Old Dr Wrigley came on his bicycle with his black bag and his gas mask on. Just as well, really."

"There was an air raid?"

"No, but he was ugly. 'It's a boy, missus,' he said, handing our Stanley over. I wasn't expecting a boy, but he'd come to the wrong house in the blackout."

"Heaven knows what else was in his black bag," Beth said. "I see you've brought your knitting."

"Only because I've got no minty bullets. I love minty bullets."

Oswald gathered up empty glasses and murmured, "Well, it's my turn to get them in by proxy…"

"Still, a woman can't suck a minty bullet," Auntie Dinah said, "when she's drinking small brandies."

"As far as I can see," said Oswald, "you're not drinking small brandies."

She fixed him with a solemn gaze. "A lass can live in hope," she said, "when there's a good-looking young man buying."

Oswald said that kind of talk would get her a double and went to fetch another round.

Auntie Dinah watched him disappear. "From him, I'd settle for a quick single and a slow cuddle," she said. "D'you know, he reminds me of somebody…" She resumed her knitting.

Walter roused himself. "By gum," he said, "those are fearful-looking needles."

The needles were imposing relics of Auntie Dinah's earlier days. "Steel!" she said. "None of your modern plastic rubbish. Sharp as a tallyman, these are! Many a time I took them to the pictures. You never knew when a young man might feel your knees in the back row." She smiled. "And not only the back row."

"You lived in hope," said Beth.

Jonty glowered around the room. He was encouraging a grievance to boil up.

Oswald proceeded glumly to the bar. He understood, of course, why his Uncle Jonty was inveterately cantankerous. An old man needed an interest in life, and what better than misanthropy? All very gratifying, and despite a tendency to wash Oswald's socks, Jonty showed every sign of hating the human race, apparently forgetting that he was himself a fringe member. Well, every man was entitled to his obnoxiousness, but he ought to practise it in private. Oswald for his part was forbearing. He believed fervently in tolerance and was prepared if necessary to knock down anybody who didn't. He carried a laden tray back towards the table, fighting to keep calm. "Oswald! Be stoical!" he told himself. Halfway across the room, he met Charlie Embleton in his Tommy Wrench persona.

"What cheer, Oswald," said Charlie. "Did I ever tell you the story about the escalator, like? That's barmy, like, because I've just made it up, like. Hold on and I'll try it out on you, like, before I put it in my act, like."

It was a pretty good test of stoicism.

*

Elsie Pilbury and Gladys Button had downed another gin each.

"You see, Elsie," Gladys said, "Leonardo could have irrigated the plains of Lombardy even if his cartilage had slipped out. That's what a restless genius can do if he applies his mighty mind and can find the water."

"Ah, but could he still have invented the first bicycle?"

Gladys said that would have had to be left for Michelangelo. "And would Michelangelo then have had time to design the fortifications of Florence?"

"Let Florence fortify herself!" said Elsie Pilbury. "Had she never heard of Emmeline Pankhurst?"

"I don't think you know what I'm talking about, Elsie," said Gladys Button.

"Neither do I, Gladys," said Elsie. One way and another, it seemed to her that the human knee cartilage had a lot to answer for. "Do you mind if I quote Omar Khayam?"

Gladys Button said she would speak frankly. "Elsie," she said, "I'm sick of hearing you quote Omar Khayam. Why don't you and I sing?"

"Sing what?" Elsie sipped her gin.

"A song, for a start."

"You're quite sure you wouldn't rather I quoted Rudyard Kipling for a change? Mrs Hemans?"

Gladys Button said she would rather have inflammation of the inner ear on top of her other afflictions and she knew her best friend wouldn't want to wish that on her best friend. She sipped her gin.

Elsie Pilbury had already started.

"The boy stood on the burning deck –
Whence all but he had fled."

She stopped. "You may be right," she said. "What shall we sing?"

Gladys Button said she was giving it some thought.

*

"Our Dan," Auntie Dinah was saying, "was born on the eleventh of August, 1942. He went to Canada to dive for rubies. I remember it nicely. He grew up and he went out of the back door. 'I'm going to dive for rubies,' he said. My second, he was."

"You can't dive for rubies in Canada," Oswald said, plying her with brandy.

"He knows that now," said Beth.

"You're a good lad," Auntie Dinah told Oswald. "If it had been you in that tent fifty-five years ago…"

"What's all this?" Oswald asked.

"Never mind," said Beth, "but I can tell you she would have put her hair up."

Oblivious of these exchanges, Jonty now transferred his glare back to his immediate companions. "And what about the Union Jack?" he demanded.

"What about what?" said Walter, aroused from the contemplation of tragedy into which he had relapsed.

"They're going to put the Union Jack in the incinerator!" Jonty shouted. "Who are, you ask! Well, go on, ask! The management are! Burning it! The Union bloody Jack!"

"Hold on!" said his goaded nephew.

"Oswald…" Beth murmured, with an eye to his volatile forbearance.

48

"And what about the ceremonial platform? Ask me about the ceremonial platform!"

"You're talking rubbish," said Oswald.

"They're chopping it up!"

"Rubbish!"

"They're chopping it up for firewood!"

"Rubbish! Rubbish!! Rubbish!!!" cried the goaded nephew.

He had lost the struggle. Again. No young man who spoke with three exclamation marks could call himself a stoic.

*

"Give a bit of order, please!"

It was a voice from the stage. It was the voice of Gladys Button, echoed by that of her best friend, Elsie Pilbury. Having had a third gin each, they had decided on their song. It was *Hey, Big Spender*!

They weren't very sure of the words. They hadn't much idea of the tune. But Omar Khayam would have applauded the philosophy.

Chapter Four

—————Dropping An Ominous Question—————

Jonty resumed his tirade. What a monument of egocentricity the man was! It was magnificent. And why not? It had been seven decades in the making. "They're putting an end to everything that's decent! Diabolical! I mean – scrapping the red, white and blue bunting!"

Oswald muttered, "Oh, God!" But he fought hard and contained himself. Perhaps Burke was wrong and forbearance would be forever a virtue. Besides, somebody might manage to change the subject.

Would it be Walter? "Cheers!" he said, raising his glass.

"Aye, aye, cheers!" said Jonty, and carried on heedlessly. "No more champagne for the handing-over ceremony, you know. They're going to send jumbo thingies off with dandelion and burdock."

Would it be Beth? Yes, you could put more money on a sterling attempt by Beth. She gazed frozenly at Jonty and turned to Auntie Dinah. "You'll remember Elsie Pilbury?" she said.

"What did she die of?" Auntie Dinah asked.

"Nothing yet. She's just been singing, for want of a worse word, and now she's sitting down with Gladys Button and her fourth gin."

"Elsie Pilbury, did you say? I thought she dropped down dead in her poss tub."

"That would be her mother," said Beth. "Elsie recites poetry."

"You think that's better? Not that you'd expect dropping dead in the poss tub to run in the family."

But Jonty was erupting again. "Rumours!" he shouted. "Who starts them?"

Auntie Dinah, who had not so far acknowledged this malignity with which she was sharing a table, now fixed a searing gaze on it. "Are you talking to me?" She turned to Beth. "Is he talking to me?"

How could the impervious Unspeakable Uncle detect a snub? "That's the trouble with the modern world," he pronounced. "The daft beggars believe any old rumours."

Miss Pilbury walked past, relatively steadily.

"That's Elsie Pilbury, Auntie Dinah," said Beth.

"She does look poorly. Blood pressure, I'd say. Both high and low, if I know anything."

"I'll tell you this!" said Jonty. But he had forgotten. Why were people blathering about poss tubs? "What was I saying?" he asked Walter.

"You were asking if my glass was empty," Walter suggested.

"It's not!"

"I know, but they're calling last drinks."

"I'm jammed in, haven't I said?" As Walter and Oswald stood up and ostentatiously made way for him, he grudgingly rose. "You're drinking halves, aren't you?"

"Pints!"

Jonty made off for the bar counter, curses on his lips, and Auntie Dinah, who had been studying Oswald for much of the evening, now addressed him. "You're not unlike that young chap I was talking about."

"What?"

"*He* had blue eyes and a moustache."

Beth offered an interpretation. "Auntie Dinah knew somebody like you in her disgraceful youth, Oswald."

"You don't have a moustache, do you?" Auntie Dinah asked.

"I've never had the courage," Oswald said. "For you, however," he added gallantly, "if this were the arena, I'd kill the bull."

"He ravished her in a tent," said Beth. "Or vice versa."

"I can picture him now," said Auntie Dinah wistfully. "'Pass the towel,' he said. 'Your back's damp.' Only it wasn't my back he was looking at."

"And you didn't pass the towel," said Beth.

"'Get out!' I shouted. And out he went, the rotten coward!" She mournfully sipped her brandy. "I had to seize my First Aid Manual."

"For your damp back?" Beth asked.

"No, no! There was this scream of pain, you see. He'd fallen backwards over a guy rope and sat on a red hot primus stove. I threw on my beret and dashed out. What an awful sight!"

"Oh, dear," said Oswald. "I bet his trousers were badly charred."

"He wasn't wearing his trousers! Were you born yesterday?"

Oswald sighed. "The day before."

"This was in the non-permissive thirties," Beth said. "No wonder you called him Casanova, Auntie Dinah."

"Casablanca!"

"Sorry!"

Tears were trembling, not much bidden, in Auntie Dinah's eyes. "Oh, Beth, Beth! What a handsome lad he was! Where is he today, I sometimes ask myself? Well, I know one thing." She sobbed. "Wherever he is, he's got an X-shaped burn mark on his bum, left cheek."

"Ah!" said Beth. "But the time came when you lost your heart to another."

"Did I? Oh, aye. If you miss one bus, you can always catch the next. Well, you have to. You can't stand all your life at a bus stop."

"And so you married a beetroot sandwich addict."

"That I did. When you come to think of it, life's a rotten bus service."

Jonty returned, notably empty-handed. "Listen!" he said. "I'll tell you what I was going to tell you." He paused. "Damn it! I've forgotten again. But listen! I'll tell you something else."

They were pretty sure he would.

"What about the drinks?" Beth asked.

"I'll tell you about the chap I've been talking to."

"I think you mean talking at."

"Charlie Embleton, that's who!" said Jonty.

"That's Tommy Wrench," said Walter. "What about the drinks?"

51

"Charlie Embleton – him that's a spronker in the zilted spindle shop. D'you know what he's been telling me? They're not going to do it."

"What about the drinks?" Oswald asked.

"The red, white and blue bunting! Charlie Embleton says they're not going to scrap it. You see – it's just a parcel of rumours!"

"What about the drinks?" asked Beth, Walter and Oswald.

"Eh?"

"You've been to the bar for the drinks!" said Walter.

"I haven't, you know," said Jonty. "I've been to the bog for a Jimmy Riddle."

*

It was Lionel Judge's punctilious sense of duty that brought him to the meeting in Sir Rodney's office.

"All I ask, gentlemen," he said, mustering patience in a very small quantity, "is that we get on with the business in hand."

Tot Needler thought this was eminently reasonable. "I concur, Lionel. What is the business?"

Sir Rodney had been about to ask the same question, and was also prepared to concur. He too was reasonable. They both looked enquiringly at Judge. To be fair to him, it was only because his sense of duty overwhelmed all his other senses that he failed to recognise a conspiracy of apathy.

"Regular consultative meetings, Sir Rodney," he said irritably, "are agreed procedure, the two sides of industry being represented."

"Which is unfair to your side," Tot pointed out, "as I outnumber you by one to two." It was a fairly hackneyed barb; he was inserting the mandatory opening jocularity. Besides, he knew it was all perfunctory in the light of the nugatory trade union legislation of recent years.

Judge said they had to consider developments in the seemingly long years since nationalisation. They were still a publicly-owned concern, despite the current political climate.

Sir Rodney replied, "No." It should have been "Yes", but he couldn't always guess right, could he?

Judge acknowledged that nationalisation was still a dirty if now archaic word, but felt that Sir Rodney ought to brace himself. They might well be half-poised for another partial recession. The position was delicate, to say the least, and he was prepared to say more than that, if they wished, or no more, if they didn't, whichever applied.

Sir Rodney said rather testily that he was a scion of a family that needed no such injunction. Brace himself indeed! His grandfather had rowed for Cambridge in 1884 when they had lost gallantly.

In any case, Tot interposed, the Pluvius factory's nationalisation had been five years behind that of the rest of thingie engineering, rendering even that token gesture to socialism half-hearted.

"The delay was occasioned," said Judge, "because the works is adjacent to the site of an ancient monument – viz., the last fort of the Roman Wall."

"If only the weather had kept fine," said Tot, "it would have been called the Solarius Works."

"And the Department of the Environment," said Judge, "entered a caveat via a Green Paper, by pre-concert. This much you surely know, gentlemen."

Some more interesting apocrypha, Tot thought. And just the right amount of gobbledygook.

"Our position is fraught," said Judge. "We became publicly owned – significantly – five years behind the rest."

"Rendering even that token gesture to socialism half-hearted," said Tot.

"We are repeating ourselves," said Judge.

"For the joint benefit," said Tot, "of Sir Rodney and myself, both of us being famously forgetful."

Sir Rodney gazed out at his grandfather's horse's ghost and said, inserting his contribution to self-repetition, that his grandfather wouldn't have liked it; he had been a benevolent despot.

"We are all aware," said Tot, "of the prevailing political winds."

"Our principal current concern," said Judge doggedly, "must be the progress of the latest jumbo thingie, which will be dispatched in four weeks. Four weeks. God," he said glumly, "and industrial relations willing."

"There was a charabanc trip once a year," said Sir Rodney, "for the destitute widows."

"God is not a thingie engineer, Lionel, as far as I'm aware," said Tot, "or even a trade unionist. A socialist, yes."

"There was a boot fund for starving infants," said Sir Rodney. "Deserving ones, you understand."

Judge tugged at his ears and drummed the table. "May we get on with the business?" he implored.

"Oh, yes," said Tot. He had decided to honour the spirit of the meeting by making a few more token trade union noises. "After this latest jumbo, what?"

"What?" said Judge.

"There are no more jumbos on the order book. Are there?"

"No…"

"So?"

Judge felt obliged to hedge. "In such circumstances, one has to rationalise."

"In other words," said Tot, "you connive at the disappearance of the country's industrial base?"

"A benevolent despot, was my grandfather," said Sir Rodney. "He knew what was best for his men."

"But we shall resist compulsory redundancy," said Tot.

Judge said frustratedly that the discussion was proving inconclusive.

"The fear of dismissal," said Sir Rodney. "Best possible incentive. That's what the chaps liked. Decent traditional principles." He sidled to his model tea clipper.

"And if you tell us, Lionel," said Tot, "that there is no work, we shall withdraw our labour. Traditional union practice." He began to gather up his papers. "The eternal element, Lionel."

"What?"

"Humanity's waywardness."

Lionel Judge tugged at his ears, scratched his knees and uttered a moan of despair.

Thus Sir Rodney and Tot, in tacit unholy alliance, jerrymandered every meeting, both acting in the name of tradition, heritage, old-fashioned values and their own particular vested interests.

*

By much the same token, Elaine's designs for Oswald were time-honoured. Was her vision of conventional romance with him an acknowledgement of male domination? Well, after all, she lived in the male chauvinist North-East. Conceding this, she sensed in her heart that, having won him, she could dominate when it mattered. Hadn't her mother learnt that trick? It was the reverse side of the "walking the other way" technique.

"Bye-bye, then, Oswald," she said. They were walking home from work.

"We haven't reached your gate yet," Oswald pointed out.

"No, but you're having one of your longer-than-usual pauses." There was time, however, to voice a theory. "I know what soured your view of marriage."

Oswald didn't know that he had a view of marriage. And could a saint of atheism be sour?

"When your mother ran away with that Conservative, taking the gas cooker: that did it."

Oswald was prepared to admit that it had confirmed him in his non-belief, no more. "By the way, when you put it like that…"

"Mm?"

"That 'running away' version is Uncle Jonty's. It's coloured and garbled."

"All the best stories are."

"And the devil has all the best stories."

"Why did it confirm you in your atheism?"

"The man was a God-fearing Tory."

"Aren't they all?"

"Besides, if we can't thwart Tot's old favourite, the cussedness of human nature, we go along with it. Otherwise, we go mad."

"You might go mad anyway, just going along with human nature. Did your father have no inkling that your mother was leaning to Conservatism?"

"Well, yes, he was pretty sure she kept Disraeli up in the loft. And of course she got Adam Smith out of the Library. And Adam Smith sat uneasily with William Blake."

"Your father had William Blake?"

"Under the bed."

"Are you telling me your mother became the first person in living memory to read Adam Smith?"

"I can't swear to that, but with one partner in the loft and the other under the bed, strains are put on a marriage."

Elaine said it seemed quite normal to her.

Oswald said yes, perhaps they both failed to make allowances. "He took to wearing ragged trousers, to go with his philanthropy. She didn't even notice, so he ran away from her – a move that misfired, because *she* had simultaneously run away from *him*."

Elaine said that was the tragedy of socialism. "It means well, but it misfires."

"Capitalism doesn't mean well, but it misfires anyway. That's *its* tragedy."

"You may think," said Elaine. "that you've got the last word, but I'm still wondering how they got a gas cooker on a bicycle. Bye-bye this time. See you in the club tonight."

She ran up her garden path.

Oswald went on his way, telling himself that he loved Elaine; possibly more than he loved Newcastle United, the union branch and moral philosophy.

His love of moral philosophy was undeniable. He had some firm ideas about right and wrong, the firmest being that he didn't know which was which. He advocated tolerance, which was why he always felt you should allow a man at least one moral luxury – in his Uncle Jonty's case, contradictious bigotry. In fact, he had to stop his Uncle Jonty doing him good turns, such as ironing his shirts and washing his socks. There were two good reasons for this: he could not have another man ironing his shirts and he had no wish to be the worst-groomed man in Northumberland.

If this advocacy of tolerance prospered, it was just possible that in forty years he would be the Tot Needler of that age, benign and ineffectual. It was a thought that had not occurred to him. Did he hope to be far away from thingies by then, jumbo and tiddler alike, and living a wholly different life? If so, Tot could have told him (via Shaw, of course) that reasonable men never change anything.

*

They saw each other in the club. Elaine waved and Oswald joined Walter's table, where Jonty had got the first round in, qualifying, Beth claimed, for the Guinness Book of Records, or a kick under the table if he hadn't.

"I got them in!" he was shouting. "Pints! And shandies for the women!" The women hadn't drunk shandies in fifteen years, but Beth was now murmuring about gift horses. "Pints I got!"

"No need to make a three-act farce of it," Oswald said.

"I mean, some folks are spreading it around that I don't stand my whack."

"Rumours," said Elaine.

"Who starts them?" said Beth.

"Cheers!" said Walter miserably. He had caught himself several times during the day being almost optimistic about the forthcoming jumbo dispatch, but was now resolutely resuming gloom.

"Organised, that's me," said Jonty. "Oldest living chargehand in the Pluvius Works. Take the red, white and blue bunting…"

Walter moaned.

"They're not going to scrap it. That's the trouble with you lot – believe any old rubbish."

"I don't know how they'll manage when you retire," said Beth, unconsciously echoing Walter. "You are going to retire?"

"Soon?" said Elaine.

"Tomorrow, why not?" said Beth.

"Mind you," said the insensible pantaloon, "they're researching costs for the bunting. Did you know that? Oh, aye. There's been one of them what-d'you-call-its from that bloke with the itchy knees."

"Judge, they call him," said Walter.

"Who?"

"Lionel Judge."

"I forget his name," said Jonty. "Clever man. Went to college."

"A memo," Oswald said.

"Eh?"

"The what-d'you-call-it."

"Judge! They call him Judge," said Jonty. "Not that you need a degree to wash socks. I say, you don't need to be a professor to wash socks, Oswald."

"Unless it's a pre-programmed automatic," said Oswald.

"Eh?"

"What's washing socks got to do with the bunting?" Elaine asked.

"A memo! He sent a memo!" said Jonty. "I wash Oswald's socks, don't I?"

"You don't wash Oswald's socks."

"In his mind he seeks to wash my socks," said Oswald, "although Kant would have said that washing socks was forever inaccessible to his mind."

"I'm just saying," said Jonty, "there are blokes in Oxford and Cambridge that couldn't iron shirts. Not that I iron Oswald's shirts. Let him iron his own bloody shirts." He took a pull at his Federation ale and made a grand pronouncement. "Researching costs, is it? I'll take care of that. Oh, aye. I'll take care of the bill for the bunting."

There was a silence into which Oswald would presently drop an ominous question.

*

At another table, Gladys Button was showing her leg to Elsie Pilbury.

"I've got a little bit of swelling in the bursa, Elsie," she said.

"Oh?"

"Also a touch of knee arthritis and just a hint of synovial infection."

Elsie said that in that case there would be no singing that night. A coloratura on one leg was a wounded amazon.

"No singing tonight," Gladys confirmed. "Mind you…"

"Yes?"

"If pressed, I could manage some farmyard impersonations, or card tricks, or necromancy, semi-recumbent."

"How long have you been in touch with the dead?"

"Starting tonight."

Elsie said that was all right then.

*

Oswald dropped his ominous question.

"You'll do what?" he said, leaning menacingly towards his Uncle Jonty.

"I mean, I'm chargehand of the thingie assembly squad," Jonty said. "I'll take care of the bill for the bunting. I'll draw the rolls of red, white and blue linsey-woolsey from the General Stock Store…"

"Just a minute!" said Oswald.

"I'll jot down the rate per foot on my matchbox…"

"You forget," said Oswald, "that I'm an estimator."

Jonty went on without regard. "I reckon it'll take a couple of assembly labourers and that purple-haired job-training lad about a day-and-a-half to knock it up. There'll

56

be half-a-pound of clout nails…"

"I'm the technical staff shop steward," said Oswald. "Remember?"

Jonty pulled up at last. "Eh?"

"In the ethics of demarcation, which are, quoting you," said Oswald hotly, "the foundation of British industry, it's my department's job to estimate the bill for the bunting. Inter alia," he added, not forgetting the jargon, even under stress.

"What are you on about?" asked Jonty. He appealed to the company. "What's he on about?"

"Whether it's the chairman's boot polish," said the angry young shop steward, "or the disposal of forty tons of mild steel, estimating is for estimators."

Philosophers are the first to forget their own philosophy, unlike bigots, who remain true to their bigotry. Is there a lapse in logic there? Please make allowances. Kant is inaccessible to us at the Nostalgia Centre. "If anybody tries anything different," the advocate of tolerance stated, "I'll bring out the entire office staff, technical and commercial. After a ballot," the eternal democrat added.

At this, Walter uttered a piteous moan, Beth said, "Oh, dear," and Elaine, touching Oswald's arm, said despairingly, "Oswald, Oswald…"

Jonty, never winded for long, had recovered his breath. "Hold on, hold on, clever clogs," he said. "I've been fettling thingies since pussy was a kitten." So he had. And he had jotted many a figure on the back of a matchbox and lost the matchbox. This presumed bunting cost research was something new, but its possible ramifications eluded Jonty. What he knew was quite simple. He repeated his recital. "What I'm saying is, I'll jot down some figures…"

"Shut up, you silly old bugger!" Oswald shouted.

All eyes in the club were on them. At a nearby table, a man was writing eagerly in a little notebook. He didn't know how to spell "linsey-woolsey". Or what it was. But he would get the silly old bugger's name right. And also clever clogs's.

*

"Gladys!" Elsie Pilbury said.

"Hello?"

"Do you sense a crisis?"

"Yes."

"Well, now's the moment to call some spirits from the vasty deep."

Never a better moment. But Gladys's bursa wasn't up to it.

*

So it came that the *Lastfort Tinkle* that Friday pushed off the front page possible leads about perennial pollution in the Plodge and the Nostalgia Centre's newly acquired gobstopper display and replaced them with a startling scoop on a threatened demarcation dispute in the Pluvius Works.

"This is unique," the story ended, "in that no previous demarcation issue has pitted blue collar workers against office staff. 'Who Does What' disputes have traditionally concerned such alleged infringements as slotting by debunkers or chipping by picklers. The members of St. Mark's outdoor draughts club were given a talk by Mr. Samuel Beech-Davington on the head-shrinkers and stomach-compressors of 19th Century Borneo." This incongruous juxtaposing owed its insertion to the torpor of a sub-editor who was eaten with disillusionment because he had never got nearer to

57

Murdoch's Wapping than Stockton-on-Tees.

Lionel Judge waved the Tinkle at Sir Rodney and Tot Needler and asked with trembling voice if they had read the earth-shaking news. Sir Rodney's face lit up and he said, "Ah!"

"What?" said Judge.

"I opened it, you know."

"You opened it?"

"The Nostalgia Centre's gobstopper display." The story had been relegated to Page Three, but Sir Rodney had caught it.

Tot nodded. "I was there, Sir Rodney. If I may say so, it's all that a gobstopper display should be. But did you also take the opportunity to look at the warming pan and chamber pot collection?"

Judge waved the *Lastfort Tinkle* and said that this portended dispute was much more serious than debunking by chippers.

Perhaps. Or even than pickling by slotters. But in the factory, predictable stances were being taken up. The assembly squad complained of the everlasting arrogance of the pen-pushers. The commercial staff muttered about the perpetual chips on the shoulders of the debunkers, slotters and picklers. Even the chippers. It was Tot who pointed out mildly that there had been bunting at every jumbo dispatch since Ethelred the Unready.

He repeated this now to Lionel Judge.

"Ha!" said Judge, waving the *Tinkle* some more. "So why should there be trouble over this matter?"

Sir Rodney asked Tot if he had noticed the curling tongs and the flannel bloomers. Or, if it came to that, the copper kettles and aniseed balls.

"Please!" said Judge.

"Ah, Sir Rodney!" said Tot. "But what about the gas mantles? The netty door snibs? The starched dickies and Gregory powder aperients?"

"Please!" said Judge.

Tot felt constrained to point out to Judge that in essence there had merely been a few warm words exchanged in the club, nothing more. The chief reporter of the Tinkle, who was not a member, had fortuitously been signed in by his brother-in-law, a twaddler, and had overheard. Twaddlers were, of course, a notoriously foolish lot, as any ellipser or priming cutter-off would tell you. Nothing would come of it. Perhaps.

"The bottles of caraway oil!" Sir Rodney said. "Potter's Purple Paregoric Pills!"

Judge continued his desperate brandishing of the *Tinkle*.

And of course Tot knew in his heart that most of the human race, not least its garblers and cutters-off, would rather have the grievance than the remedy. He could not forbear, nevertheless, from enthusing with Sir Rodney about the gobstopper display. And the Nostalgia Centre's other delights. The bustles! The stays! The clay pipes! The bodices! "But most of all I was overcome by the exhibition of claggy paper for sticking on Co-op checks!"

Lionel Judge tried to tell Sir Rodney that it was only in the interests of rationalisation that he had sought in the first place the generation of statistics concerning bunting costs. No specific decision had been taken about the current jumbo thingie. And such information might well cut incipient redundancy by as much as nought point two per cent. To think that instead there should be the menace of industrial action!

"But this is not the worst of it!" he cried. "The HQ computer! It has got over-excited because some barbarian let hot air into its air-conditioned stable! It has been coughing all night!"

In a paroxysm of anguish, he beat his brow with the folded *Lastfort Tinkle*.

"Goodbye," Tot said.

"Goodbye?" said Judge.

"I must go home for a shave," said Tot. "I'm appearing on Radio Clarts tonight." He excused himself and left.

Judge turned to Sir Rodney, but Sir Rodney was dreaming of claggy paper. "Claggy"? What was this "claggy"? No matter! It was worth a dream.

*

May we now take you back and slightly diagonally? Elaine had coaxed Oswald out of the club and bidden him take her home.

"It wasn't worth it," he said, still shaking, as the resolutely patient do, when resolve falters and patience dissolves.

"You couldn't help it," Elaine assured him. He could, but it wasn't the time to say it.

"I still feel as if I'd been through a mincer."

"Put it behind you. It's the Unspeakable Uncle who's not worth it. Bye-bye."

"Bye-bye. Relations are going to be strained under the family roof, if family is what we can call it."

And strained they were, although only Oswald was noticeably uncomfortable. After about eighteen hours, Jonty had half-forgotten what had caused the rumpus. After two days, he had forgotten there had been a rumpus. He was vaguely aware that he had somehow annoyed Oswald and offered to wash his socks.

"No, thank you," Oswald said.

Next day, Jonty had forgotten even that his barmy nephew was upset. "There's custard," he said, when Oswald arrived home from work. "It's a bit lumpy, like."

"Dear God…" said Oswald.

Jonty sat dribbling his custard and began to remember that the daft young beggar was unaccountably vexed. After a while, he rose, said, "To hell!" and went out, muttering, "Just because I haven't ironed his bloody shirt!"

He hardly knew why, but he was pretty sure he was the injured party.

*

In fact, it was two shaves later before Tot appeared on Radio Clarts, but he had felt he must escape from the meeting in Sir Rodney's office. It was either that or start to feel sorry for Lionel Judge,

"Tonight's guest on *Pick-a-Disc*," said Mel Queasy, "is Tot Needler, chairman of the Pluvius Works Joint Union Fraternal Branch Action Group." He had got the title completely right, a rare accident on Radio Clarts. "Good evening, Mr. Needler."

"Good evening," said Tot.

"Will you tell us something, Mr. Needler, of your motivation as a fettling inspector?"

"Examiner," said Tot.

"Er..?"

"I'm an examiner."

"It's not the same?"

"No."

"I see," said Mel Queasy. "However, you are a dedicated trade unionist?"

"I prefer to be thought of as a dedicated socialist."

"It's not the same?"

"No."

"Oh."

"Trade unionism is not socialism," said Tot. "Trade unionism, as Shaw said in 1910, not that many were listening at the time, or any time, is the capitalism of the proletariat. I'm a trade unionist by necessity and a socialist by conviction."

Mel Queasy played his strong card. "I'd like to ask, Tot, what you have to say about the sensational 'Who Does What?' dispute which is currently threatening the Pluvius Works."

Tot's natural reaction was to adopt the stance of the necessary trade unionist. "Ah, well," he said. "Is it, though?"

"Isn't it?"

"Some are hinting as much."

"I'm thinking of the ugly scenes," said Mel Queasy, "in the Lastfort Social club. Raised voices. Threats of inter-union industrial action. Internecine, I'd like to say, but I'm not sure how to pronounce it." He wasn't far off.

"The media, you see," said Tot, calculatedly tantalising. "Manipulation of the news. Seize on a rumour, elevate it to the proportions of a fact and report it with lip-smacking sanctimoniousness."

"You think that is what has happened?"

"Well," said Tot, "I'm giving the regulation reply to your rehearsed standard questions. It's the old ritual dance, isn't it?"

Mel Queasy resorted to another ritual he was rather better versed with. "Tot, would you like to select a record?"

"Thank you," said Tot. "Mozart."

"Of course."

"*Abendempfindung.*"

"Why not? That's better than 'internecine', I'm sure."

The strains of *Alexander's Ragtime Band* issued forth and stopped abruptly after twenty seconds.

"Thank you," said Tot.

"That's not Mozart, is it?" said Mel Queasy.

"No," said Tot.

And it wasn't the same.

*

Injured party or not, Jonty was in good voice as he rehearsed *Bobby Shafto*, his fine tenor tones filling the Lesters' living room and overflowing to the bus shelter.

"That's it, Jonty," said Walter. "Perfect! Well, pretty good."

"I don't understand," said Elaine from the piano, "how he can sing fairly like an

60

angel when his soul's as black as the inside of old Nick's hat."

"What a protracted simile!" Oswald said. No, he didn't. He might have done, but he wasn't there. He was at home, tending his indisposed motor bike.

"Life's a funny old thing," said Beth, entering with Auntie Dinah, "which doesn't answer your question, Elaine, mostly because I didn't catch it."

The piano was back in its accustomed place, and there was uneasy agreement that Walter and Jonty could rehearse as long as the saddles were empty in the old corral.

"Poor Oswald, I was thinking," Elaine explained.

A party who felt injured made the stock response. "Bloody office workers!" he said.

"Now, now," said Walter anxiously. Any threat to peace put his thingie dispatch in jeopardy, not to mention the dispatching reception. "Let's just think of the choir."

"That's right," said Elaine. "Concentrate on the food of love and play on."

Jonty had remembered that quite without cause he had been called a silly old bugger. "Just because they work in the office," he barked, "they've got more edge than a broken brown ale bottle."

"Excuse me," said Auntie Dinah, moving him aside. She was looking for her knitting.

"I'm not making his tea tomorrow, I'll tell you that," said Jonty. "If he wants a fried egg and Tizer, he needn't look at me."

"I left my knitting round about here somewhere," said Auntie Dinah. "Is it on the piano, Elaine?"

"No. Just *Bobby Shafto*, *On Mother Kelly's Doorstep*, with *Sweet Rosie O'Grady*."

Walter picked up *Bobby Shafto* and urged it on Jonty. "One more time, eh? Then you can have a can of beer on the house."

Jonty ignored *Bobby Shafto*. What was *Bobby Shafto* compared to a wallow in self-pity? He had now recalled the injustice. "Adding up the bill for the bunting! I'll tell you what! – I started to serve my time when I was thirteen-and-a-half."

"What's that got to do with it?" Beth said routinely.

"How should I know?" asked Jonty, equally so.

"Sing, Jonty," Walter pleaded.

"One-and-a-tanner a week, I got," said Jonty.

"And what's that got to do with it?"

"Sing!"

"And I had to pay my board out of that. I got a new body shirt every third Guy Fawkes Day."

"The old one went on the bonfire," said Elaine.

"He took it off first," said Beth.

"Pity!" they both said.

"Verse and refrain, Jonty?" said Walter.

"I wonder where my knitting is," said Auntie Dinah.

Walter opened a can of beer and filled a glass.

"It's got nowt to do with owt!" said Jonty. "I'm just saying! Bill for the bunting! What's to stop me adding it up? I bet I'm the only copper-plated writer left between Jarrow and Jerusalem." He seized the sheets of music and glared at Walter. "One more time, then! What are we waiting for?"

He began to sing and Elaine hastily picked up the accompaniment, but they were barely six bars into Bobby Shafto when he stopped and embarked instead on a maudlin monologue. "The old times are gone. Kids were brought up properly in those days. No cheeky young 'uns." Walter tried to hand him his beer and he looked the other way. "I got a hiding once a week. It made me the man I am. And what about entertainment? Eh?"

"Sit down and sup up," Walter suggested.

"It was entertainment if the coalman's horse galloped up the backlane and chewed the washing off your granny's clothes line."

"The old times are gone," said Auntie Dinah.

"The old times? They're gone, missus!"

"That's what I said!"

"Excuse me! That's what I said!"

"You cannot turn the clock back."

"I'll tell you this, missus!" He had lapsed into appalling melancholy. "You cannot turn the clock back. You cannot roll the years away. You cannot tear the calendar up." He sniffed. "There's something else you cannot do, but I've bloody forgot it." He rounded on Walter. "Where the hell's my beer, then?"

Walter pressed the glass into his hand. He took a long gulp, circled the room in an orgy of martyrdom, deposited his glass angrily on a window-sill, flung himself down on a distant armchair and instantly leapt up again with a yell of anguish.

"So that's where my knitting is," said Auntie Dinah.

"Neither in Jarrow nor Jerusalem," said Elaine.

"Ha! The lethal needles!" said Beth.

Jonty was squealing extravagantly. "I'm bloody punctured!" he shouted.

"You're right," said Elaine.

"Eh?"

"Bloody's the word. It's seeping through the seat of your trousers."

"What! She's stabbed me! I'm wounded! My God! I'm dying!"

"Off with them!" said Beth briskly.

"Eh?" said Jonty.

"No time for modesty," said Elaine. "D'you want to bleed to death on an alien carpet? Trousers down!"

"No, no!"

"I'm a first-aid woman," said Beth.

"So you are!" said Elaine. "You're just the one to tend a perforated bum."

"Leave my arse alone!"

But Beth had seized him and pushed him face down on the floor. He struggled vehemently and yelled protests, but they yanked off his trousers.

"Now let's have a look," said Beth. "Cloth, Elaine! Oh, dear!"

"What is it?" Jonty bawled.

"Well, well," said Elaine, handing a cloth.

"Is it fatal?" Auntie Dinah inquired.

"I wouldn't say that," said Beth, mopping up.

"Superficial lacerations," said Elaine.

"Give me my pants!" said Jonty.

Auntie Dinah came across and stared interestedly at the afflicted area.

"But I'll tell you this, Auntie Dinah," said Beth.

"What's that, Beth?"

Beth pointed. "We've found your Casablanca."

"Ee!" said Auntie Dinah.

She put on her knitting glasses to look more closely at the X-shaped burn mark on Jonty's left buttock.

"That's entertainment!" said Elaine.

"Too true," said Walter. "And never mind the coalman's horse."

Chapter Five

—————————— *Lost Amid The Battle Cries* ——————————

It was not that Elaine was running out of sympathy for Oswald, but she was beginning to get very slightly short of patience; enough to want to thump his head rather brutally as they walked home together from the office – no more than that.

"Don't let it worry you," she said.

"What?"

"You know what."

"Elaine, Elaine, I'm always quiet! You know that this communion between you and me is one of tacitly harmonious minds."

"Reflectively quiet, yes – but this is distractedly quiet."

"I'm not worried."

"Communion tells me that your mind's discordant, unless I've gone tone-deaf."

There were certainly tell-tale signs. He shook his head agitatedly as they proceeded homewards. He was abstracted, as well as distracted. His tongue popped in and out. He tapped his brow.

"What about Abercrombie's Ague, then?" Elaine asked.

"What?"

"I looked up your symptoms in the family first-aid manual. If you're not worried, that's what you've got."

"Elaine, I'm not bothered about the bill for the red, white and blue bunting."

"You see! You've mentioned it! And what is there to worry about? Nothing's developed! There's just talk – of what might be." Perhaps she should be more soothing, she decided. People might notice if she thumped him in public; they might think she loved him. "Please don't get upset."

But the ever-conscientious union representative inside Oswald was churning away. "There is an issue here," he said. "Who adds up the bill for the bunting?"

But nothing had happened, Elaine protested. "All right – you've had a stand-up row with the Unspeakable Uncle. You called him idiotic. He called you daft. You're both right. Or wrong. See how dispassionate I'm being? You're barely talking to him. And he's stopped burning fish fingers for your tea. Apart from that, what's changed? The Pluvius Works is still limping along, next to comatose."

"Yes, well, Uncle Jonty's rather difficult to live with."

"That's just his bum. A sore bum takes some living with."

"It's not just his bum. He's rather pleased with his bum. After all, it's a long time since his bum was in the public domain. But putting aside his bum, he's difficult to live with."

"You said that."

"I didn't hear myself the first time."

"He's not difficult to live with. He's totally impossible to live with. But as for issues, ignore them and they'll go away. That's how civilisation survives."

"It's how barbarism survives."

"That as well."

A philosophy guaranteed to appal the punctilious Oswald. "Anyway, it isn't just between him and me," he said. "It's a major matter of principle. Nobody," he stated fiercely, "is going to add up that bill but my members."

"That's your trouble," Elaine sighed. "You're incorruptible."

"The First World War was just talk of what might be until Gavril Princip thought of assassinating an archduke. That's all it takes."

"Nobody's going to assassinate you, I promise."

"They're doing worse than that."

"Worse?"

"They're eroding differentials! That's what we've got to guard against!" Oswald was prepared to put up with a lot, but he would be first to the barricades when differentials were eroded.

"See you tomorrow," Elaine said. "I'll thump your head."

"See you tomorrow," Oswald said, not hearing her.

He went home. Because of his quarrel with his Uncle Jonty, he now had to make his own tea and for that he was profoundly grateful. He was happy with an apple and a slice of brown bread. Jonty, staring at this abstemious fare, cleared up his own mess of half-warmed tinned soup or blackened toast and believed that Oswald was justifiably suffering for being a cheeky young beggar.

As it happened, Oswald was quite likely to have a quiet meal out later in the evening or indeed, if he wanted to stay in and wrestle with *The Guardian*'s editorial solecisms, to prepare for himself some mildly esoteric dish; he rather fancied his skills in the kitchen. His errant mother had left her cookery book behind; no recreant is entirely infamous.

The fact that he did not put on his chef's hat more often was entirely because, forever diffident, he hesitated to assert himself. In any case, it was only at weekends and weekday teatimes that of necessity his and Jonty's timetables mingled significantly.

So, that evening Jonty went snorting to the club. Oswald settled down to read of the advancing nemesis of political mis-allegiances. Later, he would concoct a modest bouillabaisse.

*

Tot Needler's arrival in Sir Rodney's outer office had puzzled Miss Pilbury. "You say Sir Rodney didn't send for you?"

"I can't remember," said Tot.

"Because either way he's forgotten."

"He and I have a perfect management stroke union relationship. He's an absent-minded old fathead and I'm a forgetful old nincompoop." Oh, there was none of the abrasive stuff that had been traditionally reputed to bedevil British industry, nationalised, privatised, or somewhere in between. Well, not much; just enough to keep the ritual dance going.

"He's in his office, rehearsing his speech."

"Good. Which speech?"

"Well, he's not sure, but I suspect it's the one he intends to deliver to the new intake of apprentices." This was entirely reasonable from Sir Rodney's point of view, since, like every other manufacturer, the Pluvius Works no longer had intakes of apprentices. "What have you come to discuss – or not – if you're not supposed to be here?" Miss Pilbury then asked.

Tot was hardly likely to be pinned down as easily as that. He screwed up his eyes and said, "Ah."

"The current dispute, perhaps?"

Tot shook an innocent head. "You've got me there."

"I mean this Who Does What," said Miss Pilbury. "Who adds up the bill for the bunting?"

That was not really off the ground, Tot assured her. Interested – not to say prejudiced – parties were working on it, no doubt. "Odd how people act in terms of the myth."

"Is it? Do they?"

"In this case," said Tot, "the myth of trade union intransigence."

"You mean the myth comes before the reality?"

"Oh, yes, that's how it works. First the myth. Then people feel they have to live up to it. And so the myths are moulded into fact and get taught in schools as history."

Elsie Pilbury said she had made some coffee, and that was no myth. "Is the current myth," she asked, "that we're threatened with an inter-union quarrel?"

Good heavens! Was she asking him to confirm that there was even the possibility of a dispute? He screwed up his eyes again.

"Be a devil," Miss Pilbury urged him, "and hypothesise."

Tot chuckled delightedly. Now she was testing his polemics. What a treat! Hypothesise he would, mind you, at any time. Jaw, jaw was better than war war. Good heavens again! He could even agree with Churchill. "Times have changed," he said. Now that was one thing he would commit himself to – a platitude.

"Yes," he went on, "I'll admit that the white-collar workers are quite likely to be militant these days. A strange irony, that – now that militarism is frowned on in the once proudly militant Labour Party. There was a time when the office workers were just a branch of management. A pretty low-down sort of branch."

"Lackeys?" said Miss Pilbury, tongue in cheek.

"Lickspittles," said Tot, no less so.

"Flunkeys?"

"Mind you," said Tot, "if you want a real old-fashioned dirty word, what about nationalisation?"

"Now you've gone back twenty sentences. Or eighty years."

Tot said that was good trade union practice – when in doubt, refer back. "I think I can claim," he stated, "that the combined wool-gathering of Sir Rodney and me contributed notably to the delay in this factory's nationalisation."

"Don't you believe in nationalisation?"

"Even if I do," said Tot, "beliefs can't be expected to conquer character, can they? – especially one as lethargic as mine. As it happens, I believe in public ownership, not the same thing at all. But the socialist movement was long ago diverted into a movement to form a Labour Party."

"Not the same thing at all?"

"Not the same thing at all."

He felt seized by a certain ennui. It had been with leaden spirit that he had eased himself earlier that morning into the shell of the jumbo thingie.

"Not a bad day, Tot," said the glutter, or possibly glunter, who was working above him.

"Humph," said Tot.

Ten minutes later, the glunter dropped some hot solder down the back of Tot's neck.

There was many a solder scar on his back. He had broken finger nails and battered knuckles. They were the marks of his trade. He was a craft worker. How many more such tradesmen would the future see? He didn't know. Following so-called rationalisation, thingie trade journeymen had become what they called interchangeable.

They were expected, it seemed, to be one thing one day and something else the next. Well, he reckoned that if a lad learned his job by example from an older hand and acquired enough skill to call himself a genuine tradesman, that ought to satisfy his employer. By that same token, he could acquire a bit of pride. Not too much. But let nobody dent it. Good heavens once more! He seemed to have a lot in common with a certain irascible old bigot.

"No, not the same thing at all," he said. "Mind you, I'm still a believer."

"In the Labour Party?"

"And in a coffee break."

Elsie Pilbury poured him coffee.

*

In his office, Sir Rodney addressed his hatstand.

"I impress on you, as I impress on every intake of apprentices, that you must get your foddips right. Do that and it follows that the mattells, gleaks and glurs will present no problems. For the spronkers and tritchers, of course, the essence is that they must pick up the clolling, which oddly enough is done not by clollers but by stenters or even more surprisingly by shimbucklers. For myself, I like nothing better than to watch the thennions being hoisted into place from the peccable bed. But the aristocracy of the thingie fettling industry are rightly the assembly team with their complete mastery of pambing, jadging, nomping, jivelling and spoodling. That leaves only the contriving of the heffies. What is there to be said about the heffies? Not a great deal. As my dear grandfather used to say…"

*

"So you see, Elsie," said Tot, "the Pluvius Works is the last representative of primitive independence. The days of thingie fettling are numbered. No more do sons follow fathers. Sons are unemployed. As for me, not for much longer will you hear my motto of: 'Do good by lethargy…'"

Not that Tot in his lethargy scorned the activists; the world needed both their like and his. If something had to be shifted, sometimes you needed a hammer; sometimes a bit of oiling did the trick.

The communicating door opened and Sir Rodney looked out. "Ah, Mr. Needler," he said.

Sir Rodney had remembered his name. This would never do. "Good morning, Sir Rodney."

"Did I want to see you?" Sir Rodney benignly asked.

This was better. "I really don't know."

"What about?"

"I've no idea."

"Splendid!" said Sir Rodney, happily thumbing his pullover. "Come in and have a look at my tea clipper."

*

It was another badminton night for Elaine, so she was not at home to accompany Jonty's rehearsal. Not that his heart was in it. He had got no further than singing that barmy bit about *Bobby Shafto* coming back from sea and marrying some lass or other when he interrupted himself to say, "Huh! Cheeky young beggar!"

"Sing, Jonty!" Walter urged. "Forget Oswald!" He knew – they all knew – that it was very gratifying to have a grievance, but a fine voice was a gift to be treasured while its short life lasted. An injustice could be whistled up at any old time.

Jonty was not to be urged. "I could add it up on my matchbox! I could add it up in my head! I could add it up standing on my head! Bloody penpushers!"

"Why are you forever argey-bargeying?" Auntie Dinah inquired from her knitting.

"You might die, Jonty," Walter said, "and then where would you be?"

"I mean, I wouldn't use a big sheet of foolscap, the way they would up in the office."

"He's getting at Oswald, Auntie Dinah," Beth explained. "And foolscap went out with threepenny bits."

Jonty arched his fierce eyebrows. He had told the young beggar. "You might be my great-nephew," he had said, "but never forget I'm your great-uncle, on your mother's side." Oswald had said that was clever debating stuff and Jonty had tipped the jelly out, not that the young beggar bothered.

Walter struck a random note on the piano, thinking to recall Jonty to duty. "Once more, *Bobby Shafto*," he said, without hope.

"Who's Oswald?" said Auntie Dinah.

"Come come, Auntie Dinah!" said Beth. "He's Casablanca's nephew, remember? Jonathan Casablanca, that is."

Auntie Dinah appraised Jonty. "Jonathan? So that was your name?"

"What about it?"

"To think!" said Auntie Dinah. "You were just an impetuous stranger all those years ago, sweeping into my life with hardly a stitch of clothes on! You've changed!"

"That's enough, missus!"

"You were quite a smart young chap." She turned to Beth. "Well, he wasn't, Beth, but we women have to make do."

Beth sighed. "Yes, Auntie Dinah, the male body's never been anything to write home about. But it's still a woman's job to cover bits of it in sticking plaster when it tangles with a knitting needle."

Walter struck another note, in vain. Jonty had returned to the safer ground of his grievance. "Demarcation!" he said. "The brazen young devil said that adding up the bill for the bunting was an office worker's... I've forgotten."

"He's avoiding your lurid reminiscences, Auntie Dinah," said Beth.

"Prerogative," said Walter.

"That's what I'm saying!" Jonty shouted. "He asked me how I would like it if the office workers came down into the works and enifacted the jumbo thingie's guff-goff rings." He laughed derisively. "D'you know what I said?"

"What?"

Jonty laughed some more, overcome at this bizarre idea.

"What did you say?"

"I've bloody forgotten, haven't I? Listen! Instead of standing there like a tin of mushy peas waiting to be opened, why don't you give me a note and I'll sing *Bobby Shafto!*"

But Walter was forestalled by Beth, who was seeking to cheer her despondent aunt. "Did you ever see Randolph Scott, Auntie Dinah?"

"Is he dead?"

"As a matter of fact, yes. But he'll come to life on Channel Four tomorrow night. He's playing Bat Masterson."

"*He's* not dead?"

"Sadly, yes. He was shot in the back, cheating at poker."

"He should have stuck to patience."

Beth could see that Auntie Dinah was not to be seduced by the Old West. "You're thinking, aren't you?"

Indeed. "You know, Beth, he's not unlike our Dan, that Oswald. He has the same look about the glasses."

"I can't sing while you're talking, missus," Jonty said.

Auntie Dinah said she wasn't all that keen to hear him. She launched into recollections of Dan. "He broke his glasses, you know..."

Jonty found a distant chair to sit on, one which was devoid of knitting needles.

*

Is it possible that you want to know about Mrs Thirlaway? Yes, well, she sits in the alcove of the Nostalgia Centre, making clippy mats, bellowing old street cries and stitching vests with her Victorian treadle sewing machine. The alcove is full of mats and vests. Shouts of "Fresh fish!" greet you as you draw near. The committee keeps hoping that she will retire, or at least get cramp in her sewing leg, but neither seems likely of a hearty woman of twenty-seven.

There is no demand for her vests, which are on sale at 1935 prices, so she cuts them up and progs them into her clippy mats. There is no demand for her clippy mats. In any case, how many people would buy clippy mats (or vests) from a woman shouting "Fresh fish," even if they had one-and-elevenpence (in old money)?

*

"He broke his glasses," Auntie Dinah said, "when they took the school photograph in 1945. The School Board man said I couldn't keep him off for that. By gum, he had a funny look. And a terrible cough."

"Complications brought on by broken glasses, I daresay."

"He didn't have glasses."

"You've been lying all these years?"

"The School Board man, woman! 'You want to watch that cough,' I told him. Oh,

I'd seen plenty TB. But he wouldn't shift until I'd promised to send the bairn back to school in his granny's glasses. She was in bed with her bladder. Well, she was in bed with something."

"Was it something to write home about?"

"It might have been 1946, unless that was a bad year for something else. Have you seen TB?"

"I hear it's making a comeback, thanks to political reforms."

Jonty left his remote chair. "I'm waiting to sing, missus," he said.

Beth would have hit him with her indiarubber plant, but Walter interceded. "Practice, Beth," he said patiently. "For the reception... For the jumbo thingie dispatch... My twenty-first dispatch, you know."

"Your twentieth dispatch!" Jonty shouted.

Twentieth? Twenty-first? Jonty was probably right. Curmudgeons usually were, curse them. But one thing was certain. The dispatch of the jumbo thingie was going to be the last for some time, as far as anybody could tell. It must not fail. Walter moaned distractedly.

After that, there were only a few tiddler thingies on the horizon. Thenceforth, an empty order book. Sir Rodney himself was aware of this, of course; his paternalism could be guaranteed to triumph over his vagueness. The days were gone, however, when he could personally drum up orders on trips abroad by exercise of his absent-minded old English charm.

In any case, acquiring orders was now in the hands of a centralised marketing department. Old English charm was not among its qualities, and would have been pretty useless anyway against the tide of recession. Britain was no longer the thingie provider to the world. Walter's moans became distraught. Most of manufacturing was miserably moribund. (At least he had achieved another alliteration!) What were left? Servicing industries? Micro chips? When the last of Blake's dark Satanic mills was closed, could Britain once again become a green and pleasant land? Well, no. We were still left with a thousand ways to pollute the place. Blake's mills were admittedly mills of the mind, but you couldn't let a literary device divert your distraction.

"I wish you'd stop that distracted and distraught moaning, Walter," Beth said. "Give a bit of heed to Auntie Dinah's maudlin memories."

"I've just remembered," said Auntie Dinah, "what she was in bed with. She locked herself in the backyard one night, letting the cat out. When we found her in the morning, she had complications."

"Aha!" said Beth.

"They couldn't do much for a complicated bladder. If it was your bladder, you had to grin and bear it."

"It couldn't happen now," said Beth. "They have ways with bladders these days. They're disgusting, but they have them."

"Dr. Wrigley got there, on his bicycle. He was tempted to take her pulse, I could tell. But the silly old fool had forgotten his watch."

"Still, he showed willing."

"He said it was what you could expect," said Auntie Dinah, "seeing she was ninety-three. He was wrong. She was ninety-four."

"Medicine's not infallible."

"Mind you, he gave the cat an aspirin. 'Not that it's on my panel,' he said, half-laughing, like. The wind dropped for the funeral. The cemetery was full. They were turning them away. She'd been well-liked, you see, considering she was a nasty old besom. The cat lived to be sixteen."

"Was it a black cat?" Beth asked.

"That reminds me," said Auntie Dinah. "It's Bank Holiday on Monday. I might go round to the cemetery."

"I think I'll just go home," said Jonty sourly, "and bash my head on the back door."

Auntie Dinah stared at him innocently. "I thought you were going to sing, Jonathan." She turned to Beth. "Oh, I love a sing-song, Beth, don't you?" She began to sing in her quavering old voice. "Bobby Shafto's gone to sea…"

"Bloody hell!" said Jonty.

*

Badminton over, Elaine chanced to meet Oswald, who chanced to be near the badminton hall and they chanced to drift into the club together. At the bar, they spied the ruminative Tot, who saluted Elaine with his customary gallantry, but studied Oswald in slightly worried fashion.

"You seem a bit abstracted, my lad," he said.

"What?"

"You sigh and look unutterable things."

"It's all in his imagination," Elaine explained. "He gets fixations about adding up bills for bunting."

"Ah!" said Tot. "A dangerous process, is thought. I'm in favour of it, you understand. Thought changes things. But you see the trouble with change – it shifts burdens without eliminating them."

Oswald sipped his beer and said, "The white collar workers will be behind me in this matter of principle."

"Oh, dear," Tot said to Elaine. "I hope this lad's not going to utter what's better left unuttered."

"The blue collar workers," said Elaine, "will be behind the Unspeakable Uncle."

"I've a feeling," said Tot, "that nobody will be behind anybody. What they'll be following is the sound of trumpets. The principle gets lost amid the battle cries."

"Differentials are not for erosion!" Oswald proclaimed.

Tot sighed and suggested that eroded differentials were the incantation of the departed seventies. His old friend the time warp was at work. Well, we all make use of it. We're obsessed with the best times. Or the worst times. Just as long as they're the old times.

"Differentials have made Oswald eloquent," said Elaine, "which isn't fair when you consider that I have the devil's own job to get him poetic and inflamed on a subject that really matters." She answered Tot's puzzled look by adding, "Sex, Tot, sex!"

"Oh, well, now," said Tot, "there'll be plenty of opportunity for that before you're married, I daresay."

"I haven't asked him to marry me. I haven't even told him I'm going to."

"No, well, he's going through the stage of believing that marriage is an intolerable obstacle to individual evolution. But he'll get over that, poor devil!" By gum, Tot was leaning heavily on Shaw this night and no mistake!

Oswald said he felt like a husband already, with the two of them talking about him as if he wasn't there. "But do me a little good turn, Tot."

"What's that?"

"Please put the question of the red, white and blue bunting on the agenda for the next JUFBAG meeting."

"All right," Tot promised. "unless I forget to send the notices out." Failing that, he would have to hope that the establishing of a quorum would be blighted by the Peter Quirk syndrome.

*

Meanwhile, it had been overlooked by all who mattered – and all who didn't matter, for that matter – that a person with a long-standing grievance had not had it assuaged. Gladys Button, aged 59, who once had to travel down two flights to the ladies', now had to travel down three, slipping knee cartilage notwithstanding. The ladies' which she had been accustomed to using was still fire-damaged and she was obliged to seek another one further afield.

Sir Rodney's board meeting had recommended construction of a new ladies', but new ladies' rest rooms were built rather less quickly than Rome, especially when planning approval was needed from national headquarters. It was a disgrace. But it was not the kind of grievance that got aired, for instance, on Radio Clarts, whose free-for-all 'phone-in, The Rollicking Bigots' Hour, was monopolised by cheerful old folks who advocated chopping off the arms and legs of delinquent school-leavers.

*

What did get aired on Radio Clarts was local lore. Bustling Mel Queasy's guest in Arts in These Parts was Tommy Wrench, the North-East folk-singer, known to some as Charlie Embleton, a name lacking charisma. He sang his newly-minted derivative ballad:

> *"The Thingie Works break! The Thingie Works break!*
> *They're entitled to their break, are the Thingie works mob.*
> *Bank Holiday Monday, they're off the job.*
> *In the recreation park*
> *All day until it's dark,*
> *On the Thingie Works break.*
> *Oh, the Thingie Works break! The Thingie Works break!*
> *Playing bowls and putt in their holiday togs,*
> *Or just lying in the sun like loppy old dogs..."*

"That was Tommy Wrench," said Mel Queasy, "reminding us that Bank Holiday Monday's the big break for the thingie fettling workers. Tommy is, of course, a wodging scurfer in the bock staggling shop. Is that right, Tommy?"

Tommy said Mel Queasy had hit the nail on the head, like, except that he was a straffy hoople fitter. (Truth to tell, he was a zilted spindle spronker, but in a time warp, what does it matter, to those who matter or don't?)

"And what gigs have you got lined up, Tommy?"

Tommy said he was appearing at the Seaton Sluice Culture Fest, playing his bones, along with the Cramlington Kids' Kazoo Band, the Blyth Unmarried Fathers' Poetry Group with some disgusting non-rhyming verse and the Whitley Bay Spray Gun

Graffiti Yobs, who would be giving a demonstration of their art and pissing over the promenade for an encore, like.

"Thank you, Tommy. And is there another verse to your song?"

Like Elsie Pilbury, Tommy Wrench had several more verses.

*

Monday turned out to be one of those halcyon Lastfort days sometimes chronicled by Herbert Mangle, the Tyneside bard, when not a breeze stirred a ripple on the Plodge Burn and a heat haze shimmered over the mini-supermarket and the petrol station.

The Pluvius Works Recreation Park was another legacy of Sir Rodney's grandfather's despotic benevolence. The August Bank Holiday sun shone down on the visiting brass band as it played *Keep the Home Fires Burning*. It shone down on Beth and Auntie Dinah as they sat on a bench near the bowling green. It shone down on Tot as he lay back on a grassy bank and gazed at puffs of white cloud hanging stationary over the factory.

He closed his eyes. The sun was hot on his lids. He imagined time rolling back and saw himself in the same spot a couple of hundred years earlier, a favourite dream of his. It would be a meadow in quiet countryside, he thought, before the Industrial Revolution had blighted the land and men were bludgeoned into hideously uncongenial occupations.

The sun shone down equally on Walter and Jonty, ill-matched as ever as bowling partners.

"Pitch it up, partner!" called Walter.

"Shut your face, partner!" Jonty bellowed.

"Isn't this lovely, Auntie Dinah?" Beth asked. "And aren't you glad you didn't go to the cemetery?"

Auntie Dinah wasn't, but she conceded that it was quite nice.

"It's one of those halcyon Herbert Mangle days," Beth said, "with not a breeze to stir the effluent on the Tyne."

"It's calm," Auntie Dinah acknowledged.

"It's halcyon as well, admit it." Beth sniffed the air. Sitting there by the bowling green, watching Walter fall over the jack, she asked what it was that Oswald's dad's friend William Blake had said about God being in his heaven.

Auntie Dinah inclined her ear towards the band. "Is that *The Desert Song*?" she asked.

"*Keep the Home Fires Burning*."

"Yes, but is it *The Desert Song*?"

"It isn't *The White Horse Inn*."

"That's what I thought. Our Dan was playing *Rose Marie* in the school band when he broke his glasses."

Tot had risen from his grassy bank, having heard a misattribution.

"Good afternoon, ladies," he said. "Excuse me, Beth. It was Browning."

Beth said what wasn't, on a day like this.

"I've been in a reverie," Tot said.

"I see. Did you catch a glimpse of William Blake?"

Tot said well, he had seen Heaven in a wild flower. He had reflected on the effects of the dark Satanic mills. "And now I must go to the gents'," he added.

"Also dark and Satanic," said Beth. "From what I hear."

Tot departed.

Auntie Dinah said she didn't think it would rain and opened the top button of her black mackintosh.

But Beth was contemplating the bowlers. "Would you say that Jonty's game was a bit agitated?" she murmured.

"Pardon?"

"It's just that the bowl he sent up a minute ago went off the green, crossed the dahlia bed and crashed into the bandmaster's ankle."

"You worry too much, Beth."

It wasn't easy, though, Beth thought, conducting *Keep the Homes Fires Burning* on one leg, and smiling. "You know what's wrong with Jonty?"

"He's got an X-shaped burn mark on his bum."

"I was thinking more of his recent troubles – with Oswald. How do you feel about trade unions, Auntie Dinah?"

Auntie Dinah's mind was perhaps wandering. "They should never have done away with the stocks," she said.

"I think I've heard you on Bigots' Hour," said Beth.

"Throwing rotten turnips at villains," said Auntie Dinah. "They should bring it back. Better still, flog them!"

"Trade unionists?"

"Anybody," said Auntie Dinah merrily. She gazed around. "D'you fancy some ice cream?"

Beth was pursuing a theme. "You've got to sympathise with Oswald." She offered a contemporary theory. "He's compensating."

"I never knew."

"That's why he's turning into a fiery agitator – to compensate for living with a cantankerous old devil like Jonty. My word," she said proudly, "psychology! Tot's not the only deep thinker. You didn't know I had it in me."

"Would you like a cone?" said Auntie Dinah. "A choc-ice?"

"And now, whether you like it or not," said Beth, "I'll tell you about sublimation. Oh, well…" This was because Auntie Dinah had risen.

"I think I'll go and sit by the lake, Beth. Near the ice cream man."

"See if I care," said the wounded Beth. "They all laughed at Freud."

*

Walter and Jonty emerged from their bowls match against the foreman debunker and his chargehand, having lost ignominiously.

"That'll be pints you owe us, then," said Jonty to the victors, "when we get to the club tonight."

"We won!" said the foreman debunker indignantly.

"I know you won! Just like a foreman! Too mean to buy the drinks!"

"But we won!" said the chargehand debunker.

"I know! I'll grant you won! You don't have to rub it in that you won! You were lucky, that's the top and bottom! And it's not enough to beat us; you want us to buy the drinks as well. Talk about the lowest of the low!"

The victors withdrew, stunned, leaving Walter to speak up for debunking. "Strictly speaking…" he said, or tried to say.

"Strictly speaking, you played like a right nanny goat," said Jonty. "I've got to carry you around, even on the bowling green. No wonder I'm worn out. And I never slept a wink on Friday night."

"You weren't supposed to sleep on Friday night – you were on nightshift."

"Am I not entitled to a bit of a doss? I mean, just because I nodded off for a couple of hours behind the frame joggler…"

"All right, all right," said Walter resignedly.

"Some folks in this world don't know what it is to work nightshift. There's lords in their mansions would fall off their tiaras if you asked them to work nightshift."

"How many lords in their mansions joggle frames?"

"I'm just saying – there's too many hangers-on. Always knocking the manual workers. Take the bloody schoolteachers."

"Schoolteachers aren't lords in their mansions."

"Why d'you keep going on about lords in their mansions? What I'm saying is, nobody complains about schoolteachers sleeping on the nightshift. Oh. no!"

"Schoolteachers don't work nightshift."

"They couldn't, could they? – bloody namby-pambies!"

"Anyway, *you* were sleeping on the nightshift."

"You can't forget that, can you?" Jonty yelled. "That's what's wrong with this country. Schoolteachers! There's one law for the rich. I've got nothing against schoolteachers. Schoolteachers are all right in moderation. But everybody knocks the working man. Not that you can trust the working man. The working man's his own worst enemy."

"Are *you* not a working man?"

"Well, I'll tell you this! – I'm not a lord in a mansion, am I? But just because I have two minutes shut-eye on the nightshift, what happens? Nobody'll buy me a bloody pint!"

Walter spotted Beth and went thankfully off to join her.

*

Lionel Judge still believed in the efficacy of the telephone call. Not much, but enough to keep trying.

"Hello?" he said. "Is that the Pluvius Works? I wish to speak to Sir Rodney Eames… What? This is Judge! Lionel Judge! I know it's a Bank Holiday!" Good heavens! The work of the world went on, didn't it? "I am Judge, Cost Co-ordinator, speaking from computer headquarters. Put me through to Sir… He's what? Good God! Incredible! In that case, give me the Company Secretary… On holiday too?" Did they not realise that this was precisely why Britain was lagging behind Korea in thingie fettling? Did they suppose thingie fettlers took holidays in Korea?

"I'll speak to the Chief Accountant… Hello? I have sat up overnight with black coffee and have finally uncovered the fault in the Production Incipient Projection Schedule. Did you know that among the input punched in for data processing were the contents of a Newcastle United Football club fixture list for 1992-93?"

Naturally the computer had taken exception to this. It had hiccupped for a while and fallen silent. Oh, he was surrounded by fools, fools! What chance was there in world markets? "Do you imagine the Japanese feed ju-jitsu data into their computers?

What? Of course it has something to do with you! That is the Chief Accountant I am speaking to?"

As a matter of fact, it was the relief gateman. Lionel Judge clashed down his telephone, tugging his ears. And Sir Rodney, it seemed, was sailing his boat on the park lake!

*

Oswald had thought about having a day out in the deep green Northumbrian countryside on his motor bike. Oh, he had a motor bike. He could have afforded a car, but a motor bike was slightly less environmentally hostile. And much less bourgeois. He had even thought of inviting Elaine to sit on his pillion. He had resisted that thought on the grounds that it might commit him to the proposition that he loved the girl and wanted to marry her. He did, but it was rooted in sturdy masculine tradition that you didn't concede emotional ground as easily as that.

He might have tried to treat it as an ordinary matter of boy and girl going out together, of course, and no commitment involved, but his massive honesty precluded that. After all, Elaine wasn't just a girl a boy went out with. She wasn't Mary Tranter, Norma Hartley, Una Lynch, Lois Atkins, Jean Thomas, Alma Charlton, Cheryl Orton, Ursula Niven, Teresa Scott or Denise Embleton – all delightful girls, mind you.

Massive honesty was the devil. So he had left his motor bike at home and was in the recreation ground, walking, apparently unbidden, to the shrubbery behind the tennis courts.

*

Tot had gone in search of another grassy bank on which to dream, but he was unlucky and instead met Charlie Embleton, otherwise Tommy Wrench, zilted spindler, otherwise folk singer. In whatever persona, Tommy/Charlie was an incoherent communicator and wasn't likely to be any more lucid in the heat of a halcyon day.

He asked Tot if he had ever told him the story of how his brother-in-law had fallen down the escalator in Marks and Spencer's and broken a toe. Tot, who had heard the story several times, except for the ending, which Tommy had never been known to reach, politely said of course not.

It wasn't his brother-in-law's toe, Tommy said, but the toe of an old lady, like, who was standing at the bottom waiting to go up. As it happened, like, it wasn't his brother-in-law, but his wife's brother-in-law. There was a difference. And it served her right (the old lady). It served her right for trying to go up a down escalator. Anyway...

"Shall we sit on this grassy bank?" Tot said.

"The band's a bit loud, isn't it?" said Tommy.

"Oh, I don't know," said Tot.

76

Chapter Six

Rumbling At Their Desks

The band was still playing bravely. Its distant strains were wafted to Auntie Dinah as she sat on a bench by the park lake, nursing her terrible ache for the long gone years when her children were growing up and your milk still came from cows and you could get into The Palace Theatre to hear George Formby singing *When I'm Cleaning Windows* for one and threepence, only her husband would never take her. He said he'd rather sit in front of the fire with toothache than hear George Formby singing *When I'm Cleaning Windows*.

She watched the complicated manoeuvres of the unkempt stranger on the bankside.

"It's lovely here, isn't it, hinny?" she said.

Sir Rodney looked up. Oh. Lord! Was this lady addressing him? How could she know that he was agonisingly shy? He could not respond. He was desperately craven. How often had his grandfather's horse's ghost stared up at him reproachfully! "Defend your heritage!" the stare always said. "Remember your grandfather!"

He recalled that other verse, inscribed at his grandfather's bidding above the rough pressing shed:

Of steel we fashion every pressing;
A steely will's an equal blessing.

Oh, he was not defending his heritage very well, but at least he would respond to this lady. Would he?

"Er..." he said.

"It's a bit warm, like," said Auntie Dinah. She undid the second top button of her black mackintosh.

"Very pleasant," Sir Rodney managed. But his total incapacity for small talk had smitten him once more. He cast around for a polite remark. "Ah – built it myself."

"Pardon?"

Sir Rodney indicated his model ship. "She's going to have her – ah – sea trials."

"Fancy!"

"Yes."

"You work in the thingie factory?"

Sir Rodney was nonplussed.

"Do you, well?"

"Well, not exactly," said Sir Rodney. "Yes and no... Excuse me..." He licked his finger and held it up. "See which way the wind's blowing," he explained. "Before I cast her off, you understand."

"It's a nice boat," said Auntie Dinah.

"A tea clipper."

"Oh? It's not unlike a boat." She eyed him keenly. "They still pay rotten wages, I expect." Poor soul! He looked as if he could do with a sausage roll.

"What?"

"In the factory, or wherever you work." Still, it was no excuse for muck on his trousers, or that hole in his pullover. "Where there's muck, there's muddle," her mother had always said, bashing her father's trousers against the backyard wall. The man's wet finger had interested her. "You don't see much of that these days."

"What?"

"Spitting on your finger. All the old customs have died out. Our Stanley used to spit on his boot for luck when he saw a white horse. And many a time he would run in and say, 'Mam, can I go to the cemetery to watch a funeral?' But they don't know how to enjoy themselves these days."

This left Sir Rodney at a total loss, so he merely said, "Ah!"

"Anyway, funerals are not the same without horses."

Sir Rodney saw a theme to grasp at. "Very fond of horses myself."

"Our Stanley broke his glasses at a funeral. He knew how to enjoy himself. Another thing: he loved to watch the butcher cleaving the carcases. How many folks do you bump into today that have seen a carcase clove?"

"Saw the ghost of my grandfather's horse on Friday."

It was very hot. Auntie Dinah undid another button. She was quite drowsy.

"I fear I'm the only one who sees the horse. Symbol of a gracious past. Gone. All computers and suchlike now. No more foremen in bowler hats. No fettling squads paid in gold sovereigns. No diligent apprentices rewarded with salmon taken from the Tyne. No salmon in the Tyne. My grandfather used to organise cricket matches between the workhouse inmates and the chronically sick. They were happy days."

But Auntie Dinah had nodded off.

Sir Rodney held his wet finger up again. The wind was not from the right quarter. Perhaps he should move.

"I say!" Auntie Dinah had stirred and was thrusting a bit of paper at him. "I keep it in my hat."

He took the paper. It had an address on it.

"Why don't you call some time for a sausage roll and a cup of tea?" she asked.

Sir Rodney turned red, mumbled, "Ah, thank you," gathered up his tea clipper and went around to the other side of the lake, beyond the trees.

Auntie Dinah nodded off again.

*

Elaine was walking, apparently unbidden, to the shrubbery behind the tennis courts. She loved Oswald and wanted to marry him, and no doubt she would when they both could convince themselves that it was spontaneous and unpremeditated and not something which they and the entire world seemed to have known from the beginning of time. There was sturdy masculine tradition to be disposed of first, of course. But then, she herself was a vigorous women's libber. It was only fair that there should be a bit of compromise, especially on Oswald's part.

And on reflection, what was wrong with accepting something which had been decreed since the beginning of time? If she was walking to the shrubbery behind the tennis courts knowing that Oswald, also unbidden, would be there, weren't they both conceding that the thing was irresistible?

"Elaine!"

"Oswald!"

So! They had happened to meet in the shrubbery behind the tennis courts, a good place to happen to meet.

"You might say it's a beautiful day," Oswald said.

"And we happen to meet! What can this mean?"

Oswald said he might have to consult his principles.

"I hope you'll hurry up. You won't always be twenty-two. Still, you could start a trend."

"Let's find an even more secluded spot," said Oswald.

"And?"

"I'll consult my principles. Anyway, there are better things to rhapsodise about than a beautiful day."

"Such as what?"

"Well," said Oswald tentatively, "a beautiful young woman, met in a shrubbery, for one thing..." He swallowed. "Hello! Your hand's in mine."

"Start of another trend?"

Oswald was beginning to think, at some danger to his principles, that when the day was beautiful, and so was the young woman – well, who cared about the bill for the bunting? He voiced the thought.

"Hear, hear!" was Elaine's response.

"I could let the whole matter drop." In any case, he had pondered the ultimate possibility of strike action. Was that, as Tot might have said, a viable proposition in the light of current legislation? Of course, a man of principle would be prepared to urge the breaking of a bad law. Still... "Yes, why don't I let it drop?" he said.

"Not a bad idea!" said Elaine. "Good heavens! Your arm's around my waist!"

"Good heavens, so it is!" said Oswald.

Bugger principles!

They reached the lake. A solitary figure sat on a bench, chin on chest, gently snoring.

"Auntie Dinah..." said Elaine. "Yoo-hoo! Auntie Dinah!"

Auntie Dinah started up.

"Come along," said Oswald. "The band's playing the National Anthem."

"I wasn't asleep."

"Of course not," said Elaine. "It was only passing thunder."

Auntie Dinah rose. "I've been chatting to one of the park keepers."

"The what?"

"Funny chap. Posh, for a park keeper. Talked as if he had hot pease pudding in his mouth. I invited him to come around for a cup of tea some time. I hope he cleans his boots, mind."

"Fasten the top of your mac," Elaine suggested. "The sun's gone in." A pity, she thought, because it had clearly gone to Oswald's head.

"Funny chap and no mistake," Auntie Dinah repeated. "From somewhere south of Hartlepool, I'd say." She sighed. "Ah, well..."

"Ah, well, what?" said Elaine, as she and Oswald took an arm each and propelled the old lady homeward.

79

But Auntie Dinah was gazing into the past. That familiar pain was gnawing. She was dreaming that they were all little again – Stanley and Dan and the one she had lost. It was the pain you got lying awake at four o'clock in the morning.

"Here!" she said.

"Hello?" said Oswald.

"I don't half fancy an ice cream!"

*

It was the morning after the holiday.

The ghost of Sir Rodney's grandfather's horse had arrived at the trough. It occurred to him that it was the morning when Sir Rodney remembered that his grandfather hadn't believed in holidays. The horse sometimes met Sir Rodney's grandfather in paradise. The old man wore well. He would have been 131 if he had lived. Not that he had lived much even when he was alive. Always had his nose to the grindstone.

The horse had never understood why Victorians kept their noses to grindstones; it couldn't have done their noses much good. He didn't know that we have a grindstone in the Nostalgia Centre. One of our tasks is to give regular demonstrations on how the typical Victorian would keep his nose to it.

It further occurred to the horse's ghost that Sir Rodney had not yet arrived. Nobody else could see a horse's ghost, so he might as well vanish.

Although perhaps not.

Since he was visible only to Sir Rodney, how did it come that there was now another who could apparently see him? This other was the man Tot Needler. Well, the ghost of Hamlet's father manifested itself to Horatio and one or two others, did it not? We can make that a tenuous justification, or we can plead that Tot, as progenitor of time warp theories, had a certain entitlement to supernatural communication.

At any rate, Tot had been standing at the drinking trough, reflecting on its history, with which, in his character of universal busybody, he was of course familiar, when he realised that he was being addressed by a horse.

"Yesterday," the horse said, "I was talking to Robert Owen."

"Oh?" said Tot.

"He told me," said the horse, "that he had tried desperately in his lifetime to convince his contemporaries that crime, drunkenness and ignorance were the products of social conditions."

"Oh?" said Tot.

"He believed," said the horse, "that the products of a universally civilised educated society would themselves be automatically educated and civilised."

"Oh?" said Tot.

"Poverty and slums were the culprits, not original sin."

"Oh?" said Tot.

"He put these theories into practice in his own factories."

"Oh?" said Tot.

"You see?" said thc horse.

"Up to now," said Tot, "all I've said is 'Oh'. That's because you took me a bit by surprise. May I now add that much of what you've told me I have already derived from Shaw the Sage."

80

"Oh?" said the horse.

"I'll tell you what," said Tot. "If you'll divulge your identity to me – for I'm assured that you are not a horse of the mind – I'd like to further our acquaintance. This could be the first of many enlightening conversations. Tell me, do you ever see Shaw?"

"Only occasionally," said the horse. "He spends much of his time in hell, talking interminably with the devil and Don Juan."

"You don't surprise me," said Tot.

"In any case," said the horse, "it now occurs to me that it would be impossible for us to meet like this again. Already, you must have noticed, we are beginning to attract a crowd, who think you're talking to yourself."

"They know me for an eccentric," Tot said, "but I take your point."

"One thing before I go," said the horse. "If so much wisdom was accorded so long ago to Owen, why has it not become established in practice?"

"I can only say," said Tot, "once more paraphrasing my dear iconoclastic Irishman, that only on paper has mankind yet achieved perfection."

"Of course," said the horse, and vanished.

The crowd dispersed. Tot went on his way. He had a fair idea of the horse's identity. Sir Rodney was known to doubt the perceptiveness of a trade unionist. But Tot was a pretty unusual trade unionist. He could probably talk interminably in hell.

*

It was the morning after the holiday, so it was naturally a glum one. It was a morning when most workers decided that holidays were a bad idea because they only made returning to the factory all the more repugnant, and a cruel clause in the terms of employment ensured that any workers failing to turn up were docked of their holiday pay.

The computer had recovered from its hiccup, but had lapsed into silence, sulking because it had been left unattended during part of the holiday and had languished for a while in semi-darkness. Lionel Judge was trying to cajole it to produce the pay roll, but it was throwing out reams of paper bearing meaningless messages. He had heard of a company which had scrapped its computer and gone back to human beings. It was a trend, he prayed, that would not catch on.

Not that it would, of course. Not until halfway through the 21st Century, when technology would atrophy and Victorian treadle sewing machines would come back into their own. The Nostalgia Centre will be ready. Well, Mrs Thirlaway – she'll be 82 – will be ready.

*

"I wish you'd stand still," said Jonty. "You're buzzing about like a knock-kneed bumble bee."

Walter had been bidden once more to discuss with Sir Rodney the dispatching programme for the jumbo thingie and he had brought Jonty with him in the hope that between them they might achieve some faint understanding with the chairman. The ceremonial part of the dispatch was perhaps in the balance, but the technical work had to go on and Sir Rodney always required to be kept abreast of progress.

Next to being a slifter's toolsmith, Sir Rodney would have liked to be a member of the peccable group of the assembly squad – the one who applied the final lubricant to the connotating gear prior to the ultimate synthesising trial.

There had been an occasion when he enviously watched this job being done and failed to jump aside in time as the connotator began to synthesise. He had to fling himself on his face on the testing floor and the huge peccable whirred and rolled along the culpability bed inches from his prostrate form. Its official designation was Jumbo Peccable 298, but it became known in Pluvius folklore as Rodney's Folly. Little children frightened their grandfathers with the story.

There was no doubt that Walter was fidgeting. He was always overcome by nervousness when ordered to Sir Rodney's presence. They stood in Miss Pilbury's office awaiting the call to the chairman's sanctum.

"Sir Rodney will see you presently, gentlemen," said Miss Pilbury. "He's brushing his trousers." Sir Rodney had come back after the Bank Holiday muttering, "Where there's muck, there's muddle." She excused herself and went into Sir Rodney's office.

*

Sir Rodney really ought to have acquired a wife. Ah, Time! He sometimes asked himself if his life would have been different if a certain Sylvia Pilkington had married him all those years ago instead of taking out an insurance book. An odd profession for a woman, that. "I am going to be an insurance man, Bertram," she had said, laughing.

"My name is Rodney, Diana," he had replied.

"And mine is not Diana," had been her response.

Afterwards, he had felt they had been talking at something like cross purposes. Perhaps her name was not Sylvia after all. It was a long time since those carefree days. But his own name was quite definitely Rodney. It had never been Bertram. He had dwelt in lonely bachelorhood ever since. Sometimes it had been difficult, but he had tried to live up to another of his grandfather's verses, inscribed on the wall of the lintage shop:

> Our lintage bonds and never frays:
> So bind you to abstemious ways.

Ah, well, he was wedded to his Pluvius Works. He sometimes wondered how Sylvia Pilkington – if her name wasn't Diana – was getting along, wedded to Tonti's inexorable Law of Annuities..

"There you are, Miss Pilbury," he said. "I've been meaning to talk to you about that lady."

"That's very kind," said Miss Pilbury. "Which one?"

"The one whose name I've forgotten."

"Could you make a stab at it?"

"I could, but I'd miss."

"Do you mean Gladys Button?"

"Let us, speaking hypothetically, say I do. How is she keeping?"

"Her knee isn't much better."

"Which one is it?"

"It seems to vary. Whichever it is, it incommodes her."

"Has she tried going downstairs backwards?"

"Yes, but strictly speaking we need two office boys to carry her up again."

"Well, then."

"We haven't any office boys; I was speaking hypothetically. And Freddy's on the sick."

"Who's Freddy?"

"The hall porter."

"What did you say her name was?"

"Gladys Button."

"That's the one. If I remember rightly, she has been unable, since the fire, to get to the ladies'?"

"Only, hypothetically, backwards."

"I'm sorry I mentioned that word."

"You can't get office boys these days."

"Why is that?"

"They've gone to be entrepreneurs, most of them."

Sir Rodney decided against asking what those were. "Meanwhile, who's portering the hall?"

"We've managed to get hold of a retired bus inspector. Fortunately, he brought his own peaked cap. Some of them are burglars, of course."

"What?"

"The missing office boys."

Sir Rodney said he might just brush his trousers again.

*

Miss Pilbury returned to the outer office.

"Sir Rodney's brushing his trousers," she told the waiting Walter and Jonty.

"Again?" said Walter.

"The other leg. You must excuse me again." She had to go to sort out some bother in the typists' pool, she said.

"Caught one of them working, did you?" Jonty enquired.

Miss Pilbury attempted to congeal him with a stare, but Jonty had the lowest mortification point since records were kept. She departed.

"Tch, tch!" said Jonty.

"What did you say?" Walter asked.

"It's all very well *you* wasting your time up here, sucking up to the chairman; you're only the foreman. But I should be down at the assembly bay."

"Anybody'd think you couldn't be done without."

"I can't," said Jonty. "That's what I'm saying."

"What you're saying is 'Tch, tch!'"

"Stop prowling about; you'll knock that what-d'you-call-it over." The what-d'you-call-it was Miss Pilbury's photo-copier.

The hapless Walter had already showered carbon paper all over Miss Pilbury's foam rubber seat, and on picking it up had transferred black fingerprints to her chintz curtains.

"You'll be tripping over her Chinese mat next," said Jonty.

"I happen to be highly strung," said Walter. "It's an Indian rug. Sir Rodney picked it up in Calcutta."

"I've seen better mats thrown out in Cullercoats."

"I daresay, but you've got the benefit of ignorance. What can Sir Rodney want? I hope he hasn't heard the white collar workers are rumbling at their desks."

"White collar workers! They're as much use as my left little toe, and I lost that on the champfering machine in 1951."

"Putting your foot in it as usual," Walter muttered.

"Listen! Who keeps your peccable preliminaries right? Who keeps your choir right? Your hardest job's sticking your hand out for your pay packet. And what the hell do you want?" These last words were a greeting to his great-nephew, who had just appeared in the doorway.

"Genteel as ever," said Oswald. "Tch, tch!"

*

"I just have to keep coming back, Elsie," said Gladys Button. "I loved this place."

"I know what you mean, Gladys." They gazed around their dear old fire-damaged ladies'. "Sir Rodney was asking after your leg."

"We came here as girls together!" said Gladys. The place was partly patched-up, but would it ever be operative again? "Sir Rodney? He's a blithering old ninny, Elsie."

"That's unkind, Gladys. He does his best."

"His best's bloody awful."

"You're only saying that because you've got to go down two flights of stairs."

"I was thinking of Sebastian Cabot as I slid down the banisters."

"I thought you were walking backwards," said Elsie.

"Only going up."

"I see."

"I mean, be reasonable. You can't slide up a banister."

"Why were you thinking of Sebastian Cabot?"

"He couldn't have explored the River Plate if he'd had a loose knee cartilage."

"He had a primitive compass."

"It's not the same. I had an ancestor who was an explorer. Sliding down banisters is in my blood. Sebastian Cabot never found the North West Passage."

"Because it was up two flights of stairs and his men cast him adrift."

"Elsie! You'd make excuses for Harry Hotspur's hamshank!"

"Why Harry Hotspur's hamshank?"

"They've got it in the Nostalgia Centre, didn't you know?"

"In that case, let the Nostalgia Centre make the excuses."

"Do you hate me, Elsie?"

"No, but I don't think you should call Sir Rodney a blithering old ninny. He often speaks of the days when you and I were girls with ginger hair down our backs."

"I suppose you think that's nice."

"It is nice. Even if he's thinking of somebody else."

"My ancestor sailed round the Cape of Good Hope."

"That was Vasco da Gama!"

"Vasco da Gama was next."

"I think we're both thinking of somebody else," said Elsie, "I'm going to the typists' pool."

"I'll come with you," said Gladys. "And I forgive you, Elsie."

They went upstairs with linked arms, Elsie walking forwards and Gladys backwards.

"You still haven't said, have you?" said Jonty.

"Said what?" said Oswald.

"What the hell you've come here for!"

"Tch, tch!" Oswald repeated.

"Why's everybody saying 'Tch, tch'?" Walter asked.

"It's Tuesday, isn't it?" said Oswald.

"That'll be it."

"I've come to see Sir Rodney."

"Oh, aye?" said Jonty. "There's a queue, haven't you noticed?"

"He's brushing his trousers," said Walter.

"Strange thing to queue for," said Oswald. "I've brought the Accrued Liabilities Promulgated Assessment."

"We're here about the jumbo thingie dispatch," said Walter.

"We don't know what we're here for," said Jonty.

"That's another way of putting it."

"As long as you don't intrude on white collar prerogatives," Oswald remarked. But it was said off-handedly. If a moral philosopher couldn't laugh at himself, what hope had moral philosophy? As much as it had anyway.

"Now then, Oswald," said Walter, "you and I have no quarrel."

"Of course not, Walter." Not while Walter had a gorgeous daughter.

"No quarrel?" said Jonty. "What about the bill…"

"Shush!" said Walter.

"For the bunting?"

"Jonty…" Walter urged, anxiously perambulating.

But Oswald was not incited. "As I said to Elaine, why should I bother?"

"Fine calculations!" Jonty yelled. "That's what it's about!"

"No argument, please," Walter begged, at which Oswald suddenly leapt towards him.

"Watch it!" he cried, seizing Walter's arm.

But he was merely saving Walter from tripping over Miss Pilbury's Indian rug.

*

At any rate, he had brushed his trousers, Sir Rodney reflected. They were his office trousers, which were relatively presentable anyway; now that they were brushed, he might have passed for one of his own less well-off employees – say, an accounts clerk with six children and a negative equity mortgage.

He gazed around his office. Well, he was spruced up; wasn't there something he should be doing? He had an appointment of some sort, he felt. Not a board meeting; in that case, Miss Pilbury would have been hovering about, thrusting documents under his arm.

He stared out of the window at his grandfather's horse's trough. No ghost there, and therefore no inspiration. He could hear agitated voices from his outer office. Perhaps something was happening there that he ought to avoid. He knew where to go. He opened his side door and went out to the debunking shop.

*

With a grip on a grudge, Jonty was not going to let go. "Fine calculations!" he said.

"I'm the lad for them. That's what you need when you prepare a peccable prior to thingie assembly – fine calculations!"

"That's right, Uncle Jonty," said Oswald cheerfully. "And it's a well-known fact that every peccable you, as chargehand, put on the assembly floor is three feet out of true."

"You cheeky young beggar!"

"Oh, dear," said Walter despairingly, beginning another tour of Miss Pilbury's office. Perhaps he should try to change the subject. "So what about Newcastle United, then? Any chance they'll win the First Division?"

"Not while they're in the Premier," Oswald said.

"I was only one division out, Oswald; that's not bad for a foreman."

"Listen, our Oswald!" said the unshiftable Jonty. "Why should a bolshie like you have anything to do with the red, white and blue bunting? Me – at least I'm a pillock of respectable society! They did a damned good job, did that lot!"

Walter pulled up, puzzled. "What lot?"

"The tsars of all the Russias!" But he was shiftable after all. "Another thing – show me a footballer that's fit to lick Hughie Gallacher's bootlaces."

"You never saw Hughie Gallacher."

"Eh? Never saw Hughie Gallacher! Who never saw Hughie Gallacher?"

"You never saw the tsars of all the Russias," Oswald said.

"When did you see Hughie Gallacher?" Walter asked.

"I'm just saying! – sloshing about in six feet of slush opening the Moscow Ballet wearing one of them ceremonial troikas! Could Trotsky have done that? Where's my glasses?"

"What d'you want your glasses for?" Walter asked.

"I'm not saying I saw Hughie Gallacher! I never saw Hughie Gallacher! I'm not bloody Methuselah, am I?"

"Don't be modest – you're pretty close. What d'you want your glasses for?"

"To blow my nose – what d'you think? Hughie Gallacher was the finest footballer that ever crossed the street. And what was his secret?" He thrust his glasses on his nose, muttering, and dug in his trousers pocket to produce a bit of grubby paper.

"What's that?"

"It's a bit of paper."

"Why did Hughie Gallacher cross the street?" Oswald asked. Perhaps the answer was on the bit of paper.

"He was bow-legged," said Jonty. "That was his secret."

"If you never saw Hughie Gallacher," said Walter, "how do you know what Hughie Gallacher looked like crossing the street? It might have been a bow-legged Tsar of all the Russias."

"Hughie Gallacher could beat six blindfolded men!" Jonty shouted. "He could have opened the Moscow ballet! Hughie Gallacher could have done that!"

"They should have made Hughie Gallacher tsar," Oswald suggested. "A bow-legged tsar who could beat six blindfolded men, crossing the street, wearing a ceremonial troika."

"Listen!" Jonty shouted. He read from his bit of paper. "'Agenda for Joint Unions' Fraternal Branch Action Group. Item Three: Consider alleged unconstitutional behaviour of chargehand of thingie assembly squad, viz Jonathan Theodore

Roosevelt Harwood.'"

Oswald was taken aback. "How did you get hold of that?"

"Aha!"

Oswald had asked for the item to be put on the agenda before his native tolerance (or relaxation of principles) had asserted itself. "It's out of date," he said.

"You see!" said the heedless Jonty. "Not content with flouting my soup and jelly…"

But the agenda had been re-arranged. "That shouldn't be there…" Oswald began.

"Too bloody true it shouldn't be there!"

Walter had been considering the implications. "It's all wrong," he said.

"I can explain," said Oswald.

"All wrong," said Walter. "Your name's not Theodore Roosevelt."

"It is! I was called Theodore Roosevelt because Theodore Roosevelt died the year I was born."

"Don't take all the blame," said Oswald.

"Cheeky bugger!" shouted Jonty.

"Let me explain," said Oswald. "I've asked for Item Three to be deleted."

"Huh!"

"Are you saying you don't believe me?"

"I'm saying you're a cheeky bugger!"

Miss Pilbury was coming back along the corridor. Approaching her office, as she explained afterwards, she heard the rumpus. A voice was saying, "Keep calm, Jonty!" Another was saying, "I am keeping calm!" Then there was a sudden yell of pain.

She opened her door on an indescribable scene, such as you might have found in a Randolph Scott western saloon.

*

No, we do not have Harry Hotspur's hamshank in the Nostalgia Centre. Mrs Thirlaway's antecedence, as exemplified by her Caledonian cries of "Caller hairn!" would have sat very uncomfortably with Harry Hotspur's hamshank. Her grandmother was a Scots fishwife who rode through our cobbled backlanes of long ago on her donkey-drawn fishcart, calling stentorianly, "Get your caller hairn!"

"Caller hairn" meant "Fresh herring." We knew this because our Standard Three teacher Miss Hedger taught us the old folk song "Wha'll buy caller hairn?" instead of arithmetic. She was a collector of street cries and went up backlanes listening to coalmen and greengrocers. Afterwards, she practised the cries in her parlour, saying they would come in handy some day, long after coalmen had died out.

"That bloody woman's off again!" her deaf old neighbour Mrs Wragg used to say, thanking God she had a hearing aid to switch off.

When the fishwife's niece the milk girl married the coalman, there was an arch of churns, scuttles and cucumbers. (The greengrocer was best man). The fishwife threw out coins to us urchins, who were stentorianly shouting, "Hoy oot!" Miss Hedger was there to collect that cry. Her street cries have certainly come in handy for Mrs Thirlaway, although most of us at the Nostalgia Centre wish Miss Hedger had stuck to arithmetic.

*

Well, no. Perhaps not in a Randolph Scott western would you have found such an indescribable scene. A Randolph Scott western was a morality tale. It was a story of

87

good and evil. Good triumphed. Or did it? It was an idealised portrayal of the Old West. There was chivalry. There were decent standards. There was ultimate perfection. Or was there?

Anyway, it was what Beth sought. This was the philosophy she saw shining through the fusillade of bullets, the villainous back-shooting by the bad, the virtuous front-shooting by the good, the lack of doubt, the painless violence, the right for right's sake, the wrong for wrong's sake and no agonising over which was which. It was King Arthur. Almost.

It was *Ride The High Country*. It was on Channel Four. It was the last Randolph Scott movie, filmed in 1962. Of course, it was another 27 years before he was borne off to Avalon. But there we go, confusing the actor with the part, the misconception of the spectator throughout the ages.

Yes, it was on Channel Four. Not that Beth watched it. Instead, in the Lesters' home that evening, she recounted to Auntie Dinah, with amendments from Elaine, the events in Miss Pilbury's office. Walter had gone dismally to the club.

"So, you see, Auntie Dinah," Beth said, "there was blood all over the place."

"Casablanca's?" asked Auntie Dinah.

"Yes," said Beth.

"No," said Elaine.

"No, not Casanova's, alias Casblanca's," said Beth. "It was like this. Jonty punched Oswald in the face and knocked him out. That right, Elaine?"

"In a way," said Elaine.

"In a way?"

"Elsie Pilbury," said Elaine, "got back in time to see it. It was indescribable, she said."

"But she described it anyway," said Beth.

"It seems," said Elaine, "that dad, trying to calm down the Unspeakable Uncle, came up behind him, tripped over Elsie's sumptuous private secretary's Indian rug..."

"Naturally," said Walter's understanding wife.

"Well, he went lurching into Jonty's back," said Elaine, "and Jonty's fist, which just happened to be outstretched..."

"We get the picture," said Beth. "Still, an accident..."

"Don't tell Oswald that," said Elaine. "When he came round, in the Ambulance Room, and had two aspirins, he was raving about the Archduke Ferdinand."

"Then he reached for his union representative's rule book," said Beth.

"And called the white collar workers out on strike," said Elaine.

"Ee!" said Auntie Dinah.

Chapter Seven

How Pythagoras Felt

Lionel Judge had now decided that although personal contact with Sir Rodney might be frustrating, telephone communication was apparently impossible. He had therefore arrived unannounced in Sir Rodney's office. This was hardly fair play, Sir Rodney felt, designed as it was to obviate gentlemanly evasion.

"Three points, Sir Rodney," said Judge, "if I may."

Sir Rodney wandered to his window.

"I have three items to enumerate," Judge persisted.

"Oh, God," said Sir Rodney.

Judge went on to say that his three points or, if Sir Rodney preferred, articles, could be called A, B and C. Or X, Y and Z, if Sir Rodney felt happier with that arrangement.

Sir Rodney said X, Y and Z would be acceptable. It was quite often X, Y and Z, he recalled, who had featured in his old prep school maths.

"Ah! X, Y and Z, then."

On the other hand, Sir Rodney said he liked Smith, Brown and Robinson. They had been his favourites. They quite often filled baths which had holes in them.

"Y was concomitant with X," Judge then said.

"So you've settled for X, Y and Z?"

Z was not literally synonymous with Y or X, Judge added, but was, he believed, circumstantially related.

"Thank you, Mr. Judge," said Sir Rodney. "However, I must not keep you."

"But, Sir Rodney, I have not said what the three items or points are."

Sir Rodney worked at his pullover and said that sometimes they sawed planks of differing lengths. "Robinson and those others."

"If I may…" Judge repeated. X, he explained, was computer ostensible failure. He said "ostensible" because he would not have the computer blamed. Somebody had fed into it the Newcastle United home and away goals tally. It had regurgitated. This brought him to Y, which was that, consequent to the foregoing, there were no labour man-hour schedules for the run-out production cycle.

"What about Z?" Sir Rodney asked.

"What?"

"Are you saving that up for the dénouement?"

"It's just that I haven't finished with Y."

"I think you'd better excuse me," Sir Rodney said. "I have to go to the debunking shop."

"Why is that?"

"Do you mean that is Y?"

"That is not Y."

"Why not?" These exchanges stirred old memories. "Did you ever see Abbott and Costello?"

"Whom?"

"Never mind," said Sir Rodney. A methods co-ordinator would be no more familiar with Abbott and Costello than with Smith and Robinson. "I really must go to the debunking shop. Because it's eleven o'clock."

"It's five to twelve."

"That's just as good."

"Very well," said Judge. "If you insist, I shall come to Z."

"I thought you hadn't finished with Y."

"I can come back to Y. Z is the climax."

"Don't you care for 'dénouement'?"

Point Z, it seemed, concerned the fracas in Sir Rodney's outer office, when blood had flowed, culminating in an ad hoc decision to halt operations pending further discussion on a mandatory ballot for probable industrial action. "The white collar operatives have ceased – ah – operating, you see."

Sir Rodney moved towards the door to his outer office. "Could you hang on?" he said. "Miss Pilbury has the Y."

"You mean the man-hour register?"

"Do I? Yes, that's it." Sir Rodney went out into his outer office, closing the door behind him and said, "Shush!" as Miss Pilbury looked up.

"Pardon?" said Miss Pilbury.

"Hold the fort!" said Sir Rodney. "I must escape that crazed mathematician." He went swiftly out, but immediately popped his head back around the door. "Miss Pilbury! Have you heard of Abbott and Costello?"

"I loved Abbott and Costello."

"Bless you!"

Sir Rodney's head disappeared.

*

Of course, wind of the fracas had already reached Sir Rodney. The rest of Judge's items, articles and points were so much piffle, but this was a matter for genuine concern. Very delicate. So delicate that come what might, he must get away to the debunking shop and forget about it. It was Sir Rodney's view that discussion of vital matters only aggravated them, by encouraging people to find arguments for and against. Leave ill alone, he believed. No less than Tot, he was a fervent advocate of the power of apathy. Well, not exactly fervent; sluggishly eager, perhaps. He wondered, nevertheless, how long he would be able to go on rebuffing Lionel Judge.

*

Lionel Judge wondered how long it would be before he succeeded in pinning Sir Rodney down. Succeed he would, of course. He went through to Miss Pilbury's office.

"Where is Sir Rodney?" he asked. "Where is the man-hour register?"

"Please!" said Miss Pilbury. "One thing at a time!"

"For heaven's sake, there has been a flowing of blood! The debunking shop! Pah!"

"Pah?"

"It's lunch-time. Why should he go to the debunking shop when nobody's there?"

"He likes an untenanted debunking shop."

"But yesterday at lunch-time he went to the rough pressing shed."

"He likes a deserted rough pressing shed."

Lionel Judge harked back to the fracas. "What about the bloodshed?"

Miss Pilbury giggled hysterically at this.

"What has come over you, Miss Pilbury?"

"You made a little joke."

"What?"

Miss Pilbury giggled some more.

Judge stared at her. Did nobody appreciate the gravity of matters? From the moment of the nose-punching, the white collar workers had sat on their hands. "They're sitting on their hands!" he cried. "White collar workers! Sitting on their hands!" As a next move, they might well stop work officially. *De facto* would become *de jure*. "I am going," he said. "Please tell him I shall come back to talk about Y."

"Why what?"

"Not what! Y!"

"Why not?" said Miss Pilbury. "Did you ever see Abbott and Costello?"

Judge uttered one more cry of frustration and stalked out, almost bumping into Gladys Button.

"Now there's a man who'll slip a knee cartilage," Gladys said, "if he really puts his mind to it."

"He's upset," said Elsie, "about the crisis."

"You mean the burnt-out ladies'?"

"Gladys, I don't mean the burnt-out ladies'. You must know about the white collar workers, and how they are sitting on their hands."

Gladys said white collar workers' hands had not bothered her much of late, although in her time she had been acquainted with them, fairly intimately. "In 1961, in the strong room, the chief cashier…"

"There's no need to be disgusting," Elsie Pilbury said.

"Exactly what I told the chief cashier," said Gladys. "But this has nothing to do with Rembrandt."

"Rembrandt? So you've come here to talk about Rembrandt?"

Gladys said yes, she had thought she might. She had been sitting at her desk, ignoring her work, dismissing thoughts of Harry Hotspur's hamshank, and asking herself if Rembrandt could have made a better job of *The Anatomical Lesson* if he had had a loose cartilage.

Elsie said she supposed we were all enriched by suffering, even sometimes our own. "But Rembrandt was a bit obsessed by burghers, wasn't he?"

"Of course! And you can't deny that he anticipated McDonald."

There was a knock at the door. "Excuse me, like," said the entrant.

"What is it?" said Elsie.

"Don't I know you?" said Gladys Button.

The intruder addressed Miss Pilbury. "I'm Charlie Embleton, like. I don't know if you can help me, missus, but I was told that if I came up here, I could maybe use your what-d'you-call-it."

"Who told you that?"

"What-d'you-call-him down in the what-d'you-call-it shed."

"I don't understand this," said Gladys Button.

"Eh?"

"What is it you want?" Elsie demanded.

"I'm saying! I've got this what-d'you-call-it, like, and they told me I could have it copied on your what-d'you-call-it." He produced a sheet of paper. "No offence, like."

Elsie rose imperiously. "I know you!"

Charlie Embleton cowered. "I'm only asking. The thing is, like, I'm going to do a gig at the Nostalgia Centre, to raise funds to re-train redundant corporate consultants, like, in the ancient art of clippy mat making, under Petronella Thirlaway, if you'll forgive the expression, like. I've got the words of my new song, like, and we're going to pelt them at the audience, so they can join in the second chorus, if we last that long."

"So! You want to use my copying machine!"

Charlie Embleton sensed rebuff. "Eh? Oh! It was a rotten idea, wasn't it?" He began to back out. "All right, missus. I'll just go and drop dead in your passage. Sorry I asked, like. Ta-ta, well."

"Stop!" cried Gladys Button. "You're Tommy Wrench!"

"I know I am."

"Have you brought your knackers?"

"Eh?"

"Your bones! I've always wanted to meet you face-to-face! Do you know, Mr. Wrench, that one of the first things my mother taught me was how to handle knackers. I always keep a set of knackers by me." She delved in her bag and triumphantly brought out a pair of bones.

"Fancy that!" said Tommy Wrench/Charlie Embleton. From his hip pocket, he too produced a pair of bones.

And yes, if you had called at the Nostalgia Centre, anybody there would have told you that "knackers" was the colloquial term for the old and honourable musical instrument the bones.

It so happened that Elsie Pilbury had a Jew's harp (which Bacon would have called a "jeutrompe", mind you) in her drawer. It was as well to keep a Jew's harp in your drawer, she had always felt, in case you were called on to accompany a bones-playing duo of folk singer and gammy-kneed matron in your office on an August mid-afternoon.

As it happened, it was indeed consideration of the new ladies' that had been exercising her. There were rumours. There were counter-rumours. Counter-counter-rumours would be available if needed. It was all very well for Sir Rodney and his board to decide that a new ladies' would be built, but had the scheme been approved by headquarters? The time was gone when Sir Rodney in his paternalism could authorise a new ladies' nolens volens. National ramifications came into this. What was government policy on the provision of a new ladies' for an obscure publicly owned minor thingie fettling factory? Would local M.P.s raise the matter in the House and be ignored as was their democratic right? And what would the European Commission say, if stirred?

But to hell with that! In this office of hers, she would let the melody of bones and Jew's harp be unchained!

"I'm not sure, Auntie Dinah," said Beth, "why you want a bath in the middle of the afternoon."

"I've reached a certain age," said Auntie Dinah.

Beth said it was an outlandish idea. "Are they doing it on one of these TV soaps?" she asked.

Auntie Dinah said she was entitled to a few whims. "Will you come up and wash me back while I sing?"

"Do you always sing in the bath?"

"I'd look pretty daft trying to dance. D'you remember Humphrey Bogart in *Casanova*?"

"Only in *Casablanca*. He didn't dance in the bath."

"He said it didn't amount to a hill of beans."

"What didn't?"

"I've no idea. 'Play it, Sam,' he said. He *could* have danced in the bath. They could do anything, the likes of him. They were stars. 'Frankly, my dear, I don't give a damn!'"

"That was Clark Gable."

"I didn't say it was Mickey Mouse. Our Stanley was the musical one in our family."

"*Gone With The Wind*," Beth said.

"He broke his glasses in the school band. He took after his dad. His dad played the buffoon."

"They all do," said Beth. "Even when they're playing the bassoon."

"He thought more of that thing than he did of me – or why did he wrap it in my nightie?"

Beth said it was a pretty pass when you couldn't get into your nightie for a bassoon. She disappeared into the kitchen, confident that Auntie Dinah's voice would follow her.

"*Gone With The Wind*," Auntie Dinah said. She became tearful. "I saw it on my honeymoon, while my bridegroom was at the club. What's that?"

Beth had returned, bearing a tin of emulsion paint. "I'm going to paint the toilet."

"Spring cleaning's a thing of the past for me," said Auntie Dinah mournfully.

"It's late summer."

"Even then." She sensed a rejection. "You'll want me to go home, I daresay?" She nodded resignedly. "My holiday's over – is that it?"

"What are you on about?"

"You'll not want an old woman using your lav while you're painting it."

"Freedom of our lav's written into the U.N. Charter, Auntie Dinah. Besides, you're to stay here as long as you like. Walter loves to have you here."

"He locked me in the cupboard under the stairs last night. Again."

"It's just his way. He locked *himself* in it the night before." She was contemplating her tin of paint. "Oh, no! Will you look at this? They've given me the wrong colour."

"Can't you make do?"

"Walter wouldn't fancy a crushed strawberry toilet. He was brought up a Wesleyan Methodist, you know. I'd better dash back to the shops and change it. I need a new brush anyway."

This was all very well, but wasn't she forgetting something? "My back!" said Auntie Dinah. "You know I like a close relative to wash my back."

"I hope your back's not going to become another Forth Bridge. Ta-ta. Oh, here's Elaine."

Elaine had entered, her usually cheerful mien so palpably overcast that even Hamlet might have commented.

"Auntie Dinah's going to have a bath," said Beth, going out. "I'm off for a paint brush."

"Most of us make do with a loofah," said Elaine.

"You're home sharpish from work," said Auntie Dinah.

"Mass meeting," said Elaine tersely. "Would you believe, Oswald's called his members together. Alleged grievance – the Unspeakable Uncle, aged 73, thumped him in the nose. It's proposed that the company should require the culprit to apologise. Failing that – industrial action."

"Eh?"

"A strike."

"I thought there *was* a strike."

"Sort of."

"Well, then?"

"In the sense that they've stopped work, yes. But now they've got to meet to *decide* to stop work. It would be *ultra vires* not to decide to do what they've already done. That's democracy. It's also trade union practice. Not the same, as Tot would say."

This was cryptic stuff. Auntie Dinah had more explicit tidings. "Your mam's going to wash my back."

"Nero only fiddled while Rome burned," said Elaine. "Mind you, that's a lie. The violin wasn't invented then. Oswald told me that when I still loved him." She was undoubtedly a little vexed. "I'm not very friendly with Oswald."

"I'd give him a penny for his gas any time."

"*I'd* like to thump his other end. Industrial action indeed! If he wants a bit of revenge on his Uncle Jonty, why can't he just put digitalis on his dumplings?"

"Oh, him!" Auntie Dinah made an extravagant gesture of disgust.

"Yes, I know Oswald's Uncle Jonty's the original factory disaster, but a strike'll hold up dad's dispatch, don't you see? Poor dad! You've got to feel sorry for him."

"Well, I must admit, on second thoughts, I wouldn't like a crushed strawberry lav."

"That sums it up perfectly, I daresay," said Elaine. "But could you explain it?"

"Well, *I'm* Church of England."

"That explains it."

"I don't think I can wait, Elaine," said Auntie Dinah. "Will *you* wash me back?"

"Why me?"

"Only because I can't get young Oswald."

"You wicked old woman!" said Elaine. "It would be all the same if he was right here."

"How's that?"

"He's an atheist," said Elaine. "Come along, then."

They went upstairs.

*

94

It was well known in the history of the thingie fettling industry that white collar workers had no tradition of trade union solidarity. The mass meeting called by Oswald was sparsely attended, but he gazed around the hall and went valiantly to business.

"Well, brothers," he said, "we all know the object of our meeting this evening. Our purpose is to take the decision to stop work."

Peter Windsor, estimator, rose and said, "Will you explain that?"

Eric Sampson, purchaser, rose and said, "Point of order!"

Oswald said he would gladly explain. They had stopped work, having demanded an apology. No apology had been forthcoming. And now they must formally decide to stop work.

"Point of order!" said Eric Sampson.

Oswald said he spoke as their shop steward. He could not order them to stop work. They must instruct him to authorise them to stop work. That was the due function of this mass meeting. He surveyed them bleakly. "To which eleven of you, out of a possible 87, have come."

"We *have* stopped work," said Peter Windsor.

"Precisely the point I am making," said Oswald.

Tot Needler, seated beside Oswald on the platform, tugged at his elbow. "If I may intervene…"

"What is it, Brother Needler?"

Tot said that he was present in a strictly advisory capacity, but he felt that Oswald was in duty bound to take the point of order.

"Thank you," said Oswald. "Brother Needler is here," he explained, "as chairman of the Joint Unions' Fraternal Branch Action Group, ex officio."

"Purely consultative," said Tot.

"Nem con," said Mark Tinkler, cost clerk.

Oswald said that the rule book was the rule book.

"It is sacrosanct," said Tot.

"Unimpeachable," said Oswald. He was prepared to take the point of order, he added. There was silence. "Who raised the point of order?" he asked.

"He's gone home," said Mark Tinkler.

Oswald stared at him, stunned.

"He said his tea would be ready," said Mark Tinkler. "It's his wedding anniversary, I think. She's making his tea."

"Of course," said Oswald, with heavy irony. "Where are *you* going?"

Mark Tinkler was making for the door. "I have to get my hair cut," he said. He went out.

Oswald said with even heavier irony that naturally first things must come first. Perhaps they could proceed to lesser business. If the meeting would bear with him, he said, he would be happy to make a short speech.

Tot said it would be a pity to waste a prepared oration.

Oswald thanked him and said he would like to remind them of Wordsworth's words: "England is a fen of stagnant waters." The Pluvius Thingie Fettling Works was just such a fen, in which principle had been swamped.

Not that he sought retribution for personal affront. The white collar workers' prerogative of adding up the bill for the bunting was threatened. Human dignity was at stake. "The meeting will wish to authorise me," he said, "to advise you one and all to stop work." He paused. There was no reaction. The pause lengthened. "Of course, I know we have already stopped work, but…" Confronted by unresponsive faces, he lost his way. "I invite comments," he ended desperately.

There was a long silence. Then Michael Trimble, progress chaser, said, "What about the canteen sausages?"

Oswald was affronted, although perhaps not personally. "The canteen sausages?"

"They're soggy," said Michael Trimble. "If my wife gave me soggy sausages, I know what I'd do."

"You would say they were bloody lovely," said a voice.

"Please!" said Oswald. "Will somebody move that we stop work?"

"Your wife's eighteen stone," said the voice.

"We *have* stopped work," said Peter Windsor.

"It must be formally moved," said Oswald, in growing despair.

Peter Windsor rose. "The point is, Oswald," he said apologetically, "my tea'll be ready." He went out.

"So'll mine," said Mark Tinkler, following him.

Oswald found himself addressing departing backs. "If we do not have this motion," he called, "we shall not be able to go on not working."

"Okay! We'll start working again tomorrow, then," said cheerful Michael Trimble, last man out. "Tomorrow. Ta-ta, Oswald."

"The club'll be open," said the voice, from outside.

Oswald miserably gathered his papers. "It's no good, Tot," he said. "We'll never make genuine trade unionists out of white collar workers. I've failed."

"You haven't failed," said Tot. "You know just how Pythagoras felt."

"When?"

"When they all scoffed at transmigration of souls. And remember the time warp."

"What?"

"The one *you* told *me* we were living in."

"I thought you told me."

"I know, but neither of us was listening."

"I've failed."

"We constantly re-live the past," said Tot. "What did Hegel say?"

"He said that history teaches us that people have never learnt anything from history."

"Did Hegel know that the logic of that doesn't bear examination? No. It was something that Hegel didn't learn from history."

"I've failed."

"Oswald!" said Tot. "You sounded the feelings of your members. You took cognizance. Your members' decision not to withdraw their labour in the face of extreme provocation demonstrates a magnificently unselfish sense of responsibility in the current economic climate. You've succeeded, lad, you've succeeded."

*

If you drop in at the Nostalgia Centre, we might tell you about Harry Hotspur's hamshank. But first we'll tell you about old Tom Postle who, when he was the last lamplighter in Lastfort, used to say to us youngsters, "If a lamplighter gets £2 a week for lighting lamps, what does he get for putting them out? A long pole with a hook on the end." What a forbearing lot we youngsters were, not to tip the old bugger into the Tyne!

If you drop in at the Nostalgia Centre, we'll tell you more than that about old Tom Postle. We stand on our own two feet, you know, unpropped by the Heritage Department.

*

The sound of singing had reverberated around the canteen, but now the choir was taking a break from rehearsal. Walter was happy. They were coming along a treat. Happiness was relative, of course.

"You're looking pleased with yourself, Walter," said Hubert Clarke.

"You are that, dad," Elaine chipped in from the piano. "Up to now."

Walter grinned and sat back. Things were working out remarkably well. The white collar workers had simmered down. So there would be no hold-up to the jumbo thingie's last-minute preparations. His grin widened. "Everything's on schedule," he said.

"And you've forgotten it's mam's birthday tomorrow," said Elaine.

"What!" Walter leapt up in frightful panic. "Oh, no! What'll I do? I never even sent a card! Shurrup, you lot! It's not a laughing matter."

It was, if they were cruel.

"All right, dad," said Elaine. "Just my sadistic joke."

"There's a nasty streak in you, our Elaine." He sank back, relieved. "I've a fair idea where you get it from."

"Where's Jonty, by the way?" asked Alfie Yates.

"Aye," said Fred Itchen, "where is he – the leading tenor?"

"He'll be along later," said Walter. "He's working a half-shift on the peccable drubberdrogs."

"Half-shift?" said Hubert Clarke. "He puts in more hours than the mice."

"Are you sure he's not doing a bit of sparring practice," Alfie Yates asked, "for his return bout with young Oswald?"

"Don't go into that," said Walter hastily.

Elaine agreed. Poor Oswald (whom she now almost loved again)! Red hot he had been to lead his troops into battle and he was now, she was pretty sure, sitting at home feeling like the grand old Duke of York.

Walter had been thinking. "It's in February, your mam's birthday. Isn't it? Or is it on March the 19th?"

"It's on September the 22nd."

"Pretty close to an equinox, anyway."

"Mind you," said Fred Itchen, "Oswald had no call to insult old Jonty."

"Who says he did?" Elaine asked indignantly.

"Oh, aye," said Neddy Scranton. "Scoffed him about the manual workers being inferior to the office staff. That's why Jonty hit him."

"Rubbish!" cried Elaine.

"Are you sure it isn't April the 23rd?" Walter asked.

"September the 22nd!"

"You're right. I was mixing your mam up with St. George."

"You never sent a card to St. George." Elaine returned to correcting Neddy Scranton. "You should get your facts right, Neddy."

"Only saying what I heard," said Neddy.

"So should you, Fred Itchen!"

"Sorry I spoke, Elaine," said Fred.

"Say no more," said Elaine. "Keep your vocal cords for singing. Ready, dad?"

"Aye. Shall we strike up again, then, lads?" Walter asked. But he was still troubled by recollections. Happiness was indeed relative. "I say, Elaine…"

"Hello?"

"I'm sure it's somebody's birthday tomorrow."

"Of course it is, dad," said Elaine. "It's yours."

Striking up was delayed. It was a laughing matter.

*

"'Tis all a chequer board of nights and days," said Miss Pilbury, "Where Destiny with Men for Players plays…" (Pieces)

"That was Elsie Pilbury," said Mel Queasy, consulting his script, "reading from Fitzgerald's Omar Khayam."

Miss Pilbury was the latest guest in Radio Clarts's series, *Heaven Knows Why They Do It*, in which citizens with bizarre interests were brought to the microphone to be interviewed by the mercurial Mel.

"Oh, yes, very bizarre," he said. "Tell me, Elsie…"

"Yes?"

"Why do you do it?"

"It is not bizarre," Elsie stated.

"It isn't?"

"It is not grotesque and outlandish."

Mel was puzzled. "Then what are you doing here?"

Elsie said that her friend Gladys Button had a bad leg.

Mel Queasy was sorry to hear that. "But you are reciting Omar Khayam every week from now until Christmas in the Lastfort Social club?"

Miss Pilbury said that was because she felt she had so much in common with Edward Fitzgerald, and indeed might have suffered rather as he did.

"Oh," said Mel Queasy.

"Yes."

"Well, well!"

"Did you know," said Miss Pilbury, "that he had a mole on his chest that prevented him from swimming in the nude?"

"Is that so? But you are here because you are standing in for Gladys Button's bad leg?"

"I am not. I am here to say that if we permit Gladys Button to have a bad leg, what has happened to life as we know it?"

"For yourself, however," said Mel Queasy, "it's your thwarted ambition to swim in the nude?"

"Certainly not," said Miss Pilbury.

"But you have a mole on your chest?"

"Not on my chest."

"Er…" said Mel Queasy.

"But I'll tell you this," said Elsie. "In 1961, in the strong room, Gladys Button and the chief cashier…"

"Yes?" said the eager Mel.

"Never mind. Not that Gladys Button was the only one. My word, no!"

Mel Queasy was at something of a loss. He was at a loss once in every programme.

"My mother's father," said Elsie, "was Irish, like his."

"The chief cashier's?"

"Edward Fitzgerald's."

Mel Queasy decided to touch on her career. "You are a secretary?"

Rather more than that, she would have him know. "I am private secretary to Sir Rodney Eames, chairman and managing director of the Pluvius Thingie Fettling Works, Established 1891."

"And you find release from the humdrum workaday world in the great verses of the *Rubaiyat*? Of the *Rubaiyat*," he repeated, mispronouncing it bravely.

Humdrum? Miss Pilbury exploded. "My work is not humdrum! Oh, you wouldn't think that if you'd seen the blood!"

"The blood?"

"On my Indian rug!"

Mel Queasy had been hoping for something like this, failing nudity or excitingly placed moles, neither of which came over well on radio. "Ah!" he said.

"Oh, yes. A stand-up fight between…" Miss Pilbury paused. She must be discreet; it was incumbent on a private secretary. "Well, between a grizzled member of the thingie assembly squad and a certain representative of the white collar workers. 'You're a cretinous bigot!' he shouted. 'And you're a stuck-up nincompoop!' he shouted back."

"Who shouted this?"

"I'm telling you," said Miss Pilbury vexedly.

"But which was which?"

"You might well ask, because they're related, you know. Then it came to blows. There was an ugly encounter over the photocopier, then he punched his nose, and he retaliated… Well, he didn't actually retaliate because… And it's not quite true that there were loose teeth in my electronic typewriter…"

"You witnessed all this?"

"Pardon?"

"You saw it happen?"

Miss Pilbury began to suspect that discretion had departed after all. This was what occurred when people sat you down in front of a microphone. They led you on. "The point is, I was out. It happened in my absence. Perhaps I'm wrong. Perhaps it wasn't quite like that." She wished she could recant. "Shall I recite another stanza?"

But they had reached the end of their time. They had to make way for an hour of Northumbrian Quoits, which came over even worse on radio.

"Thank you, Elsie Pilbury," said Mel Queasy. "Well, I think we can claim that Heaven Knows Why They Do It always comes up with something new and thrilling. Tonight we brought you Edward Fitzgerald's Irish grand-niece. Goodnight, Elsie."

"I could tell you – just as surely as Gladys Button – where the chief cashier had a mole," said Miss Pilbury.

"Goodnight," said Mel Queasy.

*

"I've discovered treasure," said Avril.

Tot was sitting comfortably in the living room of his daughter's home when she entered, carrying a book. He did not mind the interruption. He had been dreaming, but his dreams these days tended to be rueful; it was the curse of advancing years. "Treasure? What treasure?"

"*The Apple Cart*," said Avril.

Oh, dear! She had been among his books, and no doubt they were now symmetrically rearranged. The first rule about books was that you left them as untidy as you found them. "All right," he said. "Break it to me."

"It's all here," she said. "Your chocolate cream society. Written in 1929."

Exactly! That was when Shaw envisaged the era they were now approaching.

"Manufacturing industry is dead," said Avril, fingering through the pages.

"Yes, and the Industrial Revolution has drawn its last breath," said Tot.

"Is Britain in ruins?"

"Certainly not! Our society is pronounced prosperous by our ruling politicians." He took the book, but did not read from it; he knew the passage by heart. "Birmingham has four square miles of confectionery works. In Christmas crackers we are the workshop of the world. Gateshead and Middlesbrough have not known a day's unemployment in five years; their daily output of chocolate creams adds up to 20,000 tons. There is no equal to the English golf club. Our chinaware and tapestries are universally envied. There is no livestock to beat the English polo pony. What a consoling thought it is that if we are ever blockaded we can live for at least three weeks on our chocolate creams!"

He handed the book back to Avril. "Put it away, love."

"What?"

"We are both being corrupted," said Tot, "by the ravings of a genius."

*

Walter gazed around him, again a relatively happy man. "Mind you, the working men's club's a wonderful institution," he said.

"It is," Beth agreed. "Where else could you sit with your family in an overcrowded room, having ale slopped over you and listening to raucous voices racketing on about football, football and more football?"

"It's not that perfect," Walter said, "but it's nice to know you're enjoying yourself."

"Walter, dear, it's *your* choice. This is *your* day."

"Thank you," said Walter. "It's not every day I'm forty-eight."

"Or forty-seven," said Beth. "which you are."

"Am I? I could have sworn I was forty-eight. Or forty-nine. On the eleventh."

"The thirteenth! You're forty-seven! Today! The thirteenth!" It was her own fault, of course. Walter got things wrong only because she expected it of him and he didn't like to disappoint her. She kissed him. "Many happy returns, my love."

Walter beamed. Things were going rather nicely. The jumbo thingie dispatch preparations, the choir... Oh, he felt quite blissful. Well, relatively.

100

The bliss had not gone unnoticed by Tot Needler, wearing his club chairman's hat. "Ladies and gentlemen," he said, "I crave your indulgence. Some of you may have witnessed some disgraceful sex play just now. The respected foreman of the thingie assembly squad has just been kissed in public by his own wife."

This was greeted with cheers. But Tot, wily trouper, was softening his audience up for an unexpected pay-off line.

"There's no reason at all for this disgusting licence," he said, "except that it's the said foreman's – viz, Walter Lester's – birthday."

There were more cheers and a chorus of *Happy Birthday*.

Tot waited. When the atmosphere was sufficiently euphoric, he selected his moment for high drama. "It behoves me now, ladies and gentlemen, to make a grave announcement. News is just coming in that the final assembly and subsequent dispatch of the jumbo thingie are to be postponed."

There was a startled silence, followed by uproar, during which Walter knocked over his beer.

"Please, please!" cried Tot. "I gather that industrial action is being taken. Not by the white collar workers, as was feared. I've received a message from the shop steward of the thingie fettlers' branch." He paused and gazed around. "The whole of the thingie assembly squad is coming out on strike."

Walter knocked over Beth's gin and orange.

Chapter Eight

———————"What Is Your Irrelevance?" ———————

Lionel Judge had an office in the Pluvius Works. It was too small, of course, but when he had demonstrated his indispensability to headquarters, matters would change. To this tiny retreat, on the morning after the thingie assembly squad made its melodramatic decision, he urgently invited Tot Needler.

Tot had been glad to leave the interior of the jumbo thingie. Not that it was different from any other jumbo thingie. Not bad to work in. Not bad at all. Sometimes sub-contract work had taken him into shipyards. "Shipyards": now there was a word that would be archaic in a very few years. He thanked heaven that he had never had to work again on one of those million ton tankers they had once built on the Tyne. The newspapers had been full of "the romance of the giant tankers." The giant tankers were hideous monstrosities.

Besides, anybody who talked about romance should have tried working on a ship on a January morning when the steel deck was like a skating rink and the plates were so cold they took the skin off your fingers. Not much better in August, come to that. Down in the tanks, you boiled for eight hours and when you came up for air all you smelt was the open sewer that in those times was the Tyne on a hot day in high summer.

Perhaps the shipyard workers had had the right idea, going on strike from time to time. If it came to that, perhaps the thingie assembly workers were not all that misguided. Everybody should withdraw his labour now and then, as a matter of principle, just to get away from the hell of industry, and to remind the world that you were a free man. It was a principle, sadly, that applied only as long as the industry existed. When it ceased to exist, where was your alternative hell?

Even so, "The right to work includes the right not to work," he was telling himself as he entered Judge's office.

"Thank you – er – Tot," Judge said, "for coming for immediate consultation. This really is most baffling and frustrating."

"Baffling and frustrating it is," Tot agreed. "That's the human race for you."

Judge tugged his ears agitatedly. "But how... how?"

"Ah, well, you see, the lads in the thingie assembly squad have a grievance."

"They have no cause for grievance."

"I didn't say they had *cause* for grievance, Lionel." Really, it seemed that Lionel Judge, for all his claims to have sat in on his share of industrial disputes, was hardly familiar with the niceties.

"What is this grievance?" Judge asked.

"Violence."

"Violence?"

"Violence. In Miss Pilbury's office. A horrifying story."

"And inaccurate."

"Ah!" said Tot.

Lionel Judge, with great restraint, refrained from scratching his knees. "Tot!" he said. "As I understand it, one blow was struck. One blow. That blow was delivered by the chargehand of the assembly squad."

"Well..." said Tot, conceding nothing.

"Since any aggression that occurred emanated from an assembly squad member, how can the assembly squad regard themselves as aggrieved?"

"That's one version," said Tot.

"There is no other version. That is what happened."

"There are twenty-seven versions going around the factory," Tot said, "most of them colourful variations on the one told by Miss Pilbury on the wireless."

"Fiction!" said Lionel Judge. "That woman!" Restraint was impossible. He scratched.

"An inventive lady, I'll grant you. Shall I tell you the version accepted and acted on by the assembly squad?" As Judge had yielded now to mixed ear-tugging and knee-scratching, Tot proceeded. "Their ancient and revered chargehand, Jonathan Harwood, was insulted in Miss Pilbury's office by his insolent nephew, white collar worker Oswald Gorman."

"No!"

"Goaded by jibes about the inferiority of the manual workers, he defended their reputation. This gave young Oswald the excuse to threaten a brutal attack on the benign old gentleman."

"No, no!"

"As it happened, the wizened saint held his own and, they aver, flattened the young upstart."

"So why..?" said the puzzled Judge.

"Ah! But a principle was at stake. The historic dignity of the assembly squad was affronted. There was only one course open to proud tradesmen."

"Strike!"

Tot winced. "Withdrawal of labour."

"But the consequences! Did they not pause to reflect that the current jumbo thingie is the last one on order?"

No trade union official would miss the implications of such a question. "Is the chocolate cream future upon us?" Tot asked.

"What?"

"Are you saying that we face closure? Are you in fact spelling that out?"

No employers' representative would acknowledge such blatant implications. "All I am saying is that, bearing in mind the circumstances, these men are a cussed, infuriating, wrong-headed mob!"

Tot said he could not but agree again. "And they're the same lads, I seem to remember, who gave two days' pay last month to the handicapped bairns. That's the human race for you."

*

The news of the withdrawal of labour had hurt Sir Rodney abominably. He felt sure that if he went out to the chaps and said, "Look here, you're all my men, all members of my family. Just for me, will you go back?" and appealed to their *esprit de corps*, they would return at once, for hadn't he known their fathers? Through fair times and foul, hadn't they all put shoulders to all the wheels on all the shop floors in this dear old Pluvius Works?

But his dismal inability to communicate kept him pinned in his office, gazing down at the trough. The ghost of his grandfather's horse was drinking there now. "Show your mettle," its stern eye was saying. But he had no mettle. He could not live up to the verse that his grandfather had had engraved in the moulding shop:

As these firm laths are moulded true,
In such strong mould be all of you.

He turned away. Why was he unable to talk to the individual man? He had a wonderful access of fluency when he was addressing the Lastfort Model Boat Society, or delivering a lecture on Old Drinking Troughs in North-East Factories to the Antiquarians.

The happiest night of his year was when he was guest of honour at the foremen's dinner. Plied with lime juice, he would launch into a splendidly witty speech crammed with fantastic puns on all the foremen's names. He could communicate to an anonymous blur of faces, but when he came upon one specific model boat builder or antiquarian or foreman, the most he could manage was, "Ah, yes."

He moved to his work bench. Perhaps if he concentrated hard enough on his model tea clipper, it would turn out afterwards that the strike had never really happened.

He concentrated for twenty minutes. Then it occurred to him that it might also help if he asked after that woman's leg. That was communication of a sort, wasn't it? He went into the outer office, where Elsie Pilbury and Gladys Button were both typing.

"Sir Rodney?" said Miss Pilbury.

"Yes?"

"Did you want something?"

"Only a firm resolve," he mumbled sadly to himself. He then acknowledged Gladys Button. "Ah – Mrs – er…"

"Mrs Button is helping me with the Board minutes," said Miss Pilbury.

"Of course. Well now, Mrs Button. The old leg? Still playing up? It's your right leg, isn't it?"

"Yes, Sir Rodney," said Gladys.

"I thought so." He took an aimless turn about the office. "And what about your left leg?"

"Fairly intact," said Gladys. "But a right leg is only a right leg, Sir Rodney, however afflicted."

Miss Pilbury felt constrained to explain this noble sentiment. "Mrs Button is a woman who has lived with a ruptured spleen, Sir Rodney."

"I see."

"Suffering enriches, of course," Miss Pilbury added.

"Does it hell!" said Gladys Button.

"I thought we agreed."

"I can change my mind."

"All right."

"What about Rembrandt?"

"I thought we'd finished with Rembrandt."

Sir Rodney paused in his aimless wandering and repeated, "I see. And how long?"

"Pardon?" said Gladys.

"How long did you live with it?"

"It wasn't *her* ruptured spleen," said Miss Pilbury.

"That makes a difference."

Gladys Button was not willingly going to relinquish Rembrandt. "Would Rembrandt's chiaroscuro," she asked, "have been improved by a loose knee cartilage?"

"It was her late husband Alfie," Miss Pilbury pursued, "who had the ruptured spleen."

At this, Gladys Button relinquished Rembrandt after all. "He loved me utterly," she said tenderly.

"Ah!" said Sir Rodney.

"But I was too dear for his possessing and he died, probably of a broken heart."

"The doctor diagnosed a ruptured spleen," said Elsie Pilbury.

Sir Rodney said that on reflection he didn't think Rembrandt should be belittled.

"The fact that I loved him as only a passionate woman can," said Gladys, "would hardly rupture his spleen, would it?"

"And yet you claim," said Elsie, "to have lived with his ruptured spleen."

Sir Rodney said he conceded that Rembrandt didn't invent a bicycle, like Leonardo, or sit in a bath, like Archimedes.

"But he is no less an example," Gladys Button contended, "of what you can do if you don't have a loose knee cartilage." She turned to Elsie. "The ruptured spleen I claim to have lived with was a ruptured spleen of the mind. The doctor's mind."

Sir Rodney said that he for his part had once loved an insurance woman.

Miss Pilbury knew this. She said, "I never knew that, Sir Rodney."

"I do not belittle Rembrandt!" Gladys Button cried.

Sir Rodney said it was the old old problem. He wanted a firm resolve. He took out a handkerchief.

"Rembrandt was a good enough painter," said Gladys Button, "even though he had a lump on the side of his nose."

Elsie Pilbury said Gladys was too sceptical of the medical profession.

"I have every reason to be sceptical of the medical profession. I'd like to see one of *them* die of a broken heart!"

"Gladys! Gladys! This kind of talk won't bring back your Alfie!"

True, true! It would not bring back her Alfie! Nothing would bring back her Alfie. Gladys Button began to sob, very unpleasantly.

Sir Rodney returned to his office. This was a woman, he recognised, who could summon up the mighty dead and demolish them by demonstrating that they were no mightier than they ought to have been. He dabbed his eyes. He felt a little better now.

*

Oswald was not at all pleased with the turn of events. Neither was Elaine, and she was signalling this by being not very pleased with Oswald.

"Say what you like, Oswald..." she said.

Oswald had said nothing, but no doubt Elaine would goad him.

"To be fair to Elsie Pilbury..." she said.

Oswald had not mentioned Elsie Pilbury, and fairness had always been his undoing.

"When Elsie said what she said on Radio Clarts (and incidentally, damn Radio Clarts)," said Elaine, "she knew the office workers had decided against strike..."

"Yes?" said Oswald.

"So what are *you* stiff-necked about?"

"Me?" said Oswald. "That is, I?"

"Why are you annoyed? Only because your lot wouldn't come out when you asked them."

"That might be so if I were, but I'm not."

"Of course you're annoyed."

These seemed to Oswald to be fiendishly unfair tactics. "*You're* annoyed," he said, "so you accuse *me* of annoyance, to disguise your own annoyance."

"I'm not in the least annoyed."

"Good! Nobody's annoyed."

Elaine controlled herself for ten seconds. Then she burst out. "You had a cheek! Threatening to bring out the white collar workers! You didn't care about upsetting my poor old dad's thingie dispatch."

So that was it! He had a perfectly good defence. "It was a matter of principle."

The noise Elaine made did not become one whom he had thought to be exquisite, elegant, gorgeous, lovely, graceful and sublime. "Another thing," she said. "When Elsie said what she said, she couldn't possibly know that the assembly squad *would* strike."

"I don't think you understand."

"So now I'm stupid."

"Only partly."

"What!"

Oswald was still perplexed. "In any case, the white collar workers didn't come out."

"No thanks to you. You and your stiff-necked principles!"

"Stiff-necked I am not."

"Stiff-necked you are. And pompous."

"Thank you," said Oswald. "Besides, there's a strike anyway – and it's your dad's own assembly squad."

"That's not the point."

"Oh, of course not. Because you can't blame me for that, much as you'd like to." Really, it was impossible to understand the girl. She'd had sympathy with him when he might conceivably have been culpable, and now that he clearly wasn't, she was attacking him. "I daresay you think it was my fault that my face got in the way of Uncle Jonty's fist?"

"The point is," said Elaine, "that I'm still annoyed..."

"Ha! Exactly!"

"I mean, I would be still annoyed – if I were annoyed – because you're still as stiff-necked about what would have happened if things had turned out as you hoped they would, except that they didn't."

They had reached Elaine's gate. She swept up her garden path without a "Bye-bye."

Oswald stared after her. Then he went on his way, reflecting. "Oh, she understands," he told himself.

*

The ghost of Sir Rodney's grandfather's horse had arrived invisibly at the trough. It occurred to him that recent developments in Lastfort had recapitulated a morsel of plot and inserted a bit of conflict. Conflict, he had been told by William Shakespeare, who had occasionally held his head in heaven, was necessary to drama.

As for Sir Rodney, the horse was not after all much worried about the chairman's lack of mettle. "Odd, isn't it," he told himself, "how guilt makes people think we're thinking what they don't want us to think, and having assumed we're thinking it, they explain their failure to act on our assumed thoughts by claiming they don't have the courage, as though admitting their weaknesses excused them?" Oh, yes, he had been talking to Shakespeare.

Shakespeare had told him that he wished he had never said "Thus conscience doth make cowards of us all," because people had been using it ever since to rationalise their cowardice.

The horse had said to Shakespeare, "But you didn't say it."

"What do you mean, I didn't say it?" Shakespeare said. "I said it *Hamlet*, Act Three, Scene One."

"You didn't say it," the horse said. "Hamlet said it. You can't be held responsible for what your characters say."

"By gum," Shakespeare said, "I never thought of it like that."

It hadn't made Shakespeare happier. A pessimistic sort of man.

*

"A sorry day, Mr – ah – Lester," said Sir Rodney, so little himself that he got Walter's name right.

"A sorry day, Sir Rodney." Walter was in Sir Rodney's office to make his customary progress report. There was no progress. As there was therefore nothing to report, they mourned the sorry day.

"Yes, a sorry day," Sir Rodney repeated.

"A sorry day, yes," said Walter.

Sir Rodney plunged his finger in the hole in his pullover. "I am hurt devilishly by strikes. Devilishly."

"The dispatch of the jumbo thingie," said Walter. "Delayed indefinitely."

Sir Rodney said it had never happened in his grandfather's day.

"And the choir singing at the post-dispatching reception," said Walter. "I mean – no reception, no choir…"

"A sorry day."

"That's what I thought," said Walter. He could not contain his bitterness. "It's not fair. My twenty-first dispatch! The twenty-first reception I've conducted the choir at! How I look forward to that! That glorious choir in full song!"

There was no escaping it – he was a man for whom things were always going

107

wrong. Objects fell on him or he fell over them. He was like his father before him. As a young man, his father, obsessed by the fear of standing on people's feet, had thought of stopping at home instead of going to dances and probably would have done if a certain young woman, captivated by his curly-haired bashfulness, had not taught him to foxtrot as a preliminary to marrying him and becoming Walter's mother.

Sir Rodney toyed with his tea clipper and refrained from saying that there might never be a reception at all if there was too much delay in resuming work; so that fellow Judge was forecasting. Computer printouts indicated that costs would have got out of hand. "Escalated" – that was the word.

Walter was continuing to dream. "And Jonty Harwood!" he said. "Dear old Jonty! – stepping up to sing tenor solo. The finest tenor in the six-and-a-bit northern counties!" ("Tyne and Wear" – ridiculous name! – was only a bit of a county). And it was all threatened by the anarchy and chaos stalking the factory. "D'you know what I think, Sir Rodney?"

"What's that, Mr Lester?"

"It's a sorry day," said Walter.

*

Old Tom Postle wasn't the only old Postle, you know. We can also tell you, at the Nostalgia Centre, of old Tom Postle's grandfather, old Sam Postle, who sixty years earlier was the last wainwright in Lastfort, and sat on the roof of his workshop on the village green, wrighting the very last wain in Lastfort.

He sat on the roof so that he could watch the last square riggers (all of them Postles) plying up and down the Tyne, rigging their squares. How they plied and rigged at the same time was a family secret. No Postle ever gave away the mysteries of his calling, except to his uncle, which was why it was called cozenage. If he told his cousin, God knows what they called it.

Sam Postle's old grandfather, Jack Postle, was the last ostler in Lastfort. Ostler Postle, they called him. He used to wait for the coaches, with a long pole with a hook on the end, at the Coach and Horses inn, and what an infernal fool he felt when they turned up, as they frequently did, at the Jolly Sailors because the drivers liked the beer better there.

*

This was another, and different, mass meeting. These were men who were used to attending mass meetings. These were practised trade unionists. They knew what mass meetings were about. The atmosphere proclaimed as much.

"Brothers!" said Tot. "Members of the assembly squad! You have now been taking industrial action for two days. As chairman of JUFBAG, I have convened this meeting, with the agreement and concurrence of your shop stewards, to sound your opinions. I speak myself not as a thingie operative – rather as a thingie inspector – so my position is non-committal."

A voice called, "Point of order!" There was always a voice calling "Point of order!" and introducing an irrelevance. "I speak as the smooth strokers' shop steward," the voice said.

"What," Tot enquired, "is your irrelevance?"

"I'm authorised to state," said the smooth strokers' shop steward, "that the smooth strokers might be prepared to come out in sympathy."

"Why?"

"You may say 'Why?' But why not?"

As it happened, the smooth strokers were not completely aware of the rights and wrongs of the dispute, but it was well known that they were the most sympathetic trade in the thingie fettling industry.

Tot expressed weary thanks for this fraternal offer.

"Brothers!" he went on. "I have been in touch with the management…" This was greeted with catcalls. "I have also had contact with union headquarters…" This was greeted with some cheers and even more catcalls. "I have sought ways and means of clearing the air. Beside me on the platform, you will have observed, is your alleged victimised brother, chargehand of the assembly squad, Jonathan Harwood."

There were wild cheers, which Jonty acknowledged by glaring fiercely around the hall.

"Also present," Tot continued, "we have his alleged assailant, Oswald Gorman…" The rest of Tot's remarks were punctuated by jeers. "Brother Gorman wishes to make a statement – in the interests, he claims, of verisimilitude – and I know you will be prepared to give him a fair hearing, because a fraternal delegate will always be welcome… And we are not ones to stifle free discussion. I call on Brother Gorman."

Oswald mounted the platform and said, "Brothers…"

His voice was drowned in boos, catcalls and a certain number of regrettable curses. He left the platform and resumed his seat.

"I take it," said Tot, "that the wish of the meeting is not to hear Brother Gorman. Well done, democracy. Without further ado, then, let me call on your alleged victimised chargehand. Brother Jonathan Harwood!"

Jonty rose and as the tremendous cheers subsided, said, "Mr. Chairman! Brothers! You're a lot of stupid sods!"

*

"Did you get your paint, Beth?" asked Auntie Dinah. "For your lavvy wall?"

"I did that," said Beth. "Tomorrow morning I start, at the crack of half-past ten."

"Elaine's quiet."

"She is. But she always tells me about her troubles when she's ready, which is sometimes never."

Elaine, sitting thoughtfully in a corner, said, "All right. If I'm to be talked about, I'll join in. If the strike lasts – and you never know – dad might be laid off, and he'll be able to help you decorate."

"Heaven spare us that!" said Beth. "When your dad decorates, he's like a cow handling a gun." A simile culled, we may assume, from Randolph Scott.

Auntie Dinah assumed her self-pitying voice. "There's nobody to paint *my* lav. When you're old, not a soul cares."

"I wonder how long it'll last," said Elaine.

"Eh?"

"The strike, Auntie Dinah!"

"Oh, that!"

"Yesterday, a demonstration," said Beth. "Tonight, a mass meeting. Tomorrow, a protest march." She gazed around the room. "Sometimes I think Nature intended me

109

to be an interior decorator. Either that or a night watchman."

"You used to be a vet's receptionist," said Elaine.

"True. Shall I tell you what I learnt at school? It won't take a minute."

"You're not built like a night watchman."

"The teacher told us one day that Dr. Johnson wrote: 'If a man who turnips cries / Cries not when his father dies, / 'Tis a proof that he would rather / Have a turnip than his father.'"

"Why did Dr. Johnson assume that the man's father would want to have a turnip?"

"He wouldn't if he was dead," said Auntie Dinah.

"Look!" said Beth. "I'm no literary critic. I'm only explaining why I don't have a job."

"Not very well, though," said Elaine, "as that blasted Oswald would say."

"But people wonder," said Beth. "I'm fit and not much over forty."

"What did this man die of?" Auntie Dinah asked.

"It was a long time ago," Beth said.

"Nobody asked why you don't have a job, mam," said Elaine.

"He's dead for all that," said Auntie Dinah.

"Oh, they wonder," said Beth.

"No, they don't, mam."

"They're not to know that all I learnt about at school was turnips."

"H'm. It doesn't equip you to be an interior decorator or a night watchman, I'll grant you that."

"Death's death," said Auntie Dinah.

"Not that there's much demand these days," said Beth, "for somebody to go around the streets after dark with a big bell, shouting, 'Nine o'clock and all's well!'"

"He'd be telling a lie if he did," said Elaine. "And somebody would pretty soon have his bell. But you were the right build for a vet's receptionist."

"I'm not so sure."

"You were! The vet never lost a single hamster the whole fortnight you were there."

"Our Stanley could have done it," said Auntie Dinah. "He could have rung a big bell. Another thing: he could have painted my lav. Why did he have to run away?"

Elaine had gone quiet again. She had been rude to Oswald. But she'd forgiven him for that. She hoped he was having a good time at the mass meeting.

Auntie Dinah was reflecting that the turnip man would have died, no less than his father. They all did in those days.

*

Whatever differences he might have had with his Uncle Jonty, Oswald told himself, he had to admire the old warhorse. His ability to browbeat a gathering of assembly squad workers extorted wonderment.

Years of practice as chargehand of the squad had probably helped. Bawling instructions at a gang of men, above the row of the factory and very often in the teeth of a north-east gale, was as good a schooling as any for cowing a mass meeting. Heckled continuously, he had not hesitated to develop his theme that they were a lot of stupid sods, those of them who were not barmy buggers.

It was fifty-nine years since he had started in the works, a raggy-arsed lad. He had a question for them. "What the hell are you on strike for?" he demanded. "For me? I don't want you on strike for me, you useless crackpots!"

This was not what the assembly squad had expected to hear. Dougal Claypole, the squad strong man, rose and said mildly, "Listen…"

"*You* listen!" said Jonty. "Nobody's going to shout me down!"

"I don't want to shout you down," said Dougal.

"Shut your face, then!"

"Sorry I spoke," said Dougal, resuming his seat.

Just why had they come out on strike, Jonty wanted to know. They were doing him no favours, he could tell them. "Another thing – I didn't punch the daft young beggar in the face."

There were cries of "Shame!"

"At least, I did, but what I mean is, I didn't mean to. Not that I couldn't take the clarty young nannyhammer on, and knock hell out of him, or any other sodden penpusher."

Cheers.

"If it comes to that," Jonty shouted, "I can take on any bugger in this hall, and I'll be seventy-four on Pancake Tuesday."

There was now considerable bewilderment on assembly squad faces. A certain amount of impatient muttering began to be heard.

Jonty said he needed nobody – nobody! – to come out on strike for him. "D'you think I can't look after myself? Is that it?"

The muttering swelled. Jonty raised his voice to counter it and went ferociously on with his tirade. It wasn't war, but it was magnificent.

*

Walter arrived at his back door, stumbling routinely over the step. As a foremen, he was not allowed at the mass meeting. He would wait at home, he had decided, until it was over.

As he entered the living room, Auntie Dinah was saying, "Mind you, it might have made him sick."

"What was that?" Beth enquired.

"Our Stanley, woman! If he'd painted the lavvy."

Walter sighed and sank back on the sofa. "This'll kill me," he said. But nobody asked him what.

"He didn't like work?" Beth asked Auntie Dinah. "Your Stanley?"

"Naturally not! But it wasn't that! His sensitive skin! Painting brought him out in a rash."

"Hello, dad," said Elaine, joining Walter on the sofa.

"So did plumbing," said Auntie Dinah. "Made him all blotchy. And joinerwork. It wasn't just that he didn't like work…"

"No, no," said Beth.

"But work always made his eyes water."

"Twenty-one jumbos I've dispatched, Elaine," said Walter. "Every one on schedule. And now – a strike!"

"A shame," said Elaine. "I hate him."

"Allergic," said Auntie Dinah. "That's what he was. A martyr to rashes. I remember once I pulled on my goloshes and went to fetch Dr. Wrigley."

"Twenty-one dispatches," said Walter. "Twenty-one receptions I've conducted the choir at! Well, it might be twenty. And now – anarchy!"

Auntie Dinah enunciated her reproachful reminiscences of Dr. Wrigley. "Just keep him warm, missus," he had said. "Warm!" she had retorted. "His little head's boiling!" "Then keep him cool," he had said. "Or lukewarm. Keep him anything, but keep him away from me!"

"Oh, he wouldn't come," she said, as tears prepared to flow.

Beth patted her hand, but changed the subject. "Is anybody sitting on the *Radio Times*?"

"Why?" asked Elaine. "What else should we do with it?"

"Anarchy and chaos…" Walter ventured, as Beth eased him up and retrieved the *Radio Times*.

"Rashes!" said Auntie Dinah. "A martyr to rashes!"

"*Tall Man Riding*," said Beth.

"What?" said Elaine.

"Randolph Scott," said Beth. "Channel Four."

Walter sighed again, rose, left the room and went on a sad perambulation of the house, thinking it might relieve his tension. It didn't. What a terrible dilemma this was for a man who enjoyed misery! Here he was getting a surfeit of it, and he couldn't bear it.

*

Jonty had bellowed, "And that's all I've got to say," and had gone on to say a good deal more, when big Dougal Claypole managed another interruption.

"Just a minute," said Dougal.

Jonty paused, partly for breath.

"Who gave you the right to call me a daft bugger?" Dougal enquired, somewhat less mildly than before.

"Speak through the chair, brother," Tot advised.

"Through the chair, Brother Chairman," said Dougal, "is the speaker or is the speaker not calling me a daft bugger?"

"I am!" shouted Jonty. "I'm calling you a daft bugger!"

"Speak through the chair, brother," Tot reminded him.

"To hell with the chair!" Jonty cried. "You're all daft buggers!"

Several assembly squad members were now on their feet, shouting and waving arms.

"Speaking of Pancake Tuesday," said Dougal, "any more of that kind of talk and you mightn't live to see it. Through the chair, that is."

"And who's going to stop me?"

"Any seven-stone weakling in this room," said Dougal.

"Hear, hear!" said many voices.

Jonty leant forward from the platform and thrust his face towards Dougal. "Come outside, then, and put your fists up!"

Dougal regarded him scornfully. "I wouldn't hit an old man," he said, "not even an obnoxious bloody blatherskite like you."

"You're a yellow-bellied sod, then!" shouted Jonty. "You're all yellow-bellied sods!"

Tot gave up all attempt at control and the meeting was enveloped in uproar, Jonty yelling hoarsely through it all.

*

Walter's perambulation had brought him back to the living room. He lurched through the door, bumping into Beth's chair.

"Walter, Walter," she begged him, "come to rest. You're like a granny at a christening."

"Go to the club, dad," Elaine suggested.

"I've been to the club. I was forcing myself after the first pint." He flung himself disgustedly into his chair. "Demarcation! Talk about man's inhumanity to man. Young Oswald started this, our Elaine."

"It's his inhumanity to woman that bothers Elaine," said Beth.

Elaine made her second unladylike noise of the week.

Auntie Dinah had been silent for too long. She delved in her bag, brought out a snapshot and said, hauling the discussion back, she hoped, to a historical plane, "It's our Dan."

Walter groaned dementedly.

"He was sitting on the backyard wall in his combinations," said Auntie Dinah. "Unless it's the little lass from next door." She delved again. "And this other one's our Dan."

"At that age, they're all alike in a drizzle," Beth said.

She passed the snapshot to Walter, who stared at it perfunctorily and handed it to Elaine, saying it was a good likeness of a backyard wall.

"I'll never forget," said Auntie Dinah, "the day he gave up combinations. He came into the kitchen and said, 'Mam, I'm not going to wear them no more.' I knew then my little lad had grown up."

Walter rose. Double negatives notwithstanding, he had decided to go back to the club after all. He would force himself to another pint. If that didn't produce oblivion, he would throw himself in the Plodge Burn, although with his luck he would probably miss.

He was halfway to the backdoor when Oswald burst in, shouting, "It's finished!"

"Eh?"

"The mass meeting!" said Oswald. He took Walter's arm and propelled him back into the living room.

"What happened, then?" Elaine wanted to know.

"Talk about excitement!" said Oswald.

"What happened?" asked Beth.

"Believe me, Walter," said Oswald, "this is a tremendous hour."

"What happened?" screamed Beth, Elaine and Walter.

"Uncle Jonty shouted non-stop for seventy-five minutes. What eloquence! What rhetoric! What loudness! It was overpowering! The assembly squad came unanimously to their decision."

Elaine thumped his arm. "What decision?"

"That (a) if Uncle Jonty had been six months younger, they'd have knocked his block off, and (b) they're going back to work. The strike's over!"

Walter beamed.

"And where is he?" asked Beth. "Where's the stone age tub-thumper?"

"Yes," said Elaine, "where is the Unspeakable Uncle?"

"On his way," Oswald assured them.

Walter found delirious tongue. Was this happiness? It was almost as satisfying as grief. "We'll be able to carry on with the dispatch, then!"

"As scheduled," said Oswald.

"And the choir," said Walter. "We'll be able to sing our hearts out at the reception! Dear old Jonty – the finest tenor since Gigli hung up his decibels! I'll have him practising the minute he walks through that door!"

"Well, you can't do that," said Oswald.

"Why not?"

"He's lost his voice."

Chapter Nine

Hurtling Into Orthodoxy

Bearing in mind... One moment. There is something not unlike a crowd outside the Nostalgia Centre. They have heard that Mrs Thirlaway is about to turn out a batch of toffee apples...

Yes, bearing in mind that Elaine and Oswald were in love with each other, there would have been no reason in natural life (than which nothing is more irregular) why they should not have progressed through the normal routes of courtship towards marriage. That would have been regrettable, of course, from the point of view of purists who require that a story should have prescriptive complications. They had jointly done their best, be it said, to raise a few contrived obstacles to the story's course. There was Elaine's disaffection, for instance, over Oswald's idealistic preoccupations.

The fact that they had not even been out together on a formal date was Oswald's contribution to the contrivances. It derived less from his proclaimed diffidence than from his reluctance to do what everybody expected of him. That was an honourable enough stance for a self-respecting idealist. When all was said, they both anticipated the inevitable. But inevitability would have to hang around a bit, while intransigence had its brief day.

Enough of this pedantry. While Mrs Thirlaway dispenses toffee apples, let us go on to say that when Oswald re-visited the Lesters' on the night after the one on which even Randolph Scott found himself shoved aside by wanton events, his cheerful mien was a facade and his "Hello..." was tentative.

Elaine's reply was "Get lost!" Admittedly, it was not spoken aloud. But she glared at him and that was eloquence enough.

Walter merely said, "Uh," Auntie Dinah uttered a mournful "Hello, son," and Beth contributed an abstracted "It's you, Oswald."

Oswald refrained from inquiring if this was indeed the Lesters' living room, famed as the jolliest emporium in the partly civilised world.

As it happened, Elaine appeared to expect a question of this kind. "Aren't you supposed to have a conscience?" she asked.

"Yes."

"So what right have you to be breezy?"

"Now, now, Elaine," said Beth.

Walter spoke up. "This will go down as the bitterest hour in the history of the Pluvius Thingie Fettling Works."

"Just trying to convince myself," Oswald said, "and failing even to convince myself that I can convince myself."

"I don't say it's your fault, Oswald," Walter said.

"I will, if asked," said Elaine.

"Elaine!" said Beth.

"I don't say it's your fault," said Walter, "that the assembly squad went on strike and then came off strike."

"Thank you."

"Or that the choir's leading tenor has lost his voice."

"Thank you."

"But the human race always needs somebody to blame, you see, and you're the one that comes to mind."

Oswald said he had believed he was acting for the best and Elaine said so had Attila the Hun. Oswald said he knew that "All men mean well" was the ultimate indictment of the aforementioned human race. He added that he had come to report on his Uncle Jonty's voice. It was still lost. Elaine asked, this time aloud, why he didn't follow suit. Beth said, "Elaine!"

"Fat bacon," said Auntie Dinah. "You should try fat bacon, Oswald."

Beth said that in her experience the human race needed more than fat bacon; perhaps the U.S. Cavalry, led by John Wayne, in default of Randolph Scott. Walter said, "I had a dream last night."

"I mean for his throat," said Auntie Dinah.

"It was the same dream that I've dreamt umpteen times," said Walter.

Auntie Dinah said she was talking about Casablanca's throat. "Hang fat bacon round it, Oswald."

"What for?"

"Shall I tell you about my dream?" Walter inquired.

"It'll bring his voice back," said Auntie Dinah. It was what Dr. Wrigley had recommended when her Stanley had lost his voice and broken his glasses playing the triangle in the school pincushion band in 1948. "It didn't work," she added.

"Why not?"

"It's the same dream that I have for weeks before a dispatch."

"We had no bacon, that's why not," said Auntie Dinah. "Bacon was still rationed in 1948."

"How could he lose his voice playing a triangle?" Elaine asked.

Beth said that only Euclid knew the answer to that.

"In this dream, what happens is this…"

"Dr. Wrigley said our Stanley was what he called unique in medical history."

"I'm not surprised," said Elaine. "The cymbals I could have understood."

Oswald thought of encouraging Walter to talk about his dream, but he had to justify his presence here. He couldn't let it be known that he had arrived in the hope that somebody would be kind to him. Saints never defended themselves, it had been established, but surely they aspired from time to time to receiving a welcoming smile? Well, no. You didn't get many welcoming smiles on your way to being burnt at the stake. He would encourage Walter anyway; that was how saintly he was.

"Why don't you tell us about your dream, Walter?" he suggested.

"Crawler!" said Elaine.

Walter said he had been trying quite hard to do that. In this dream, the bells rang, as they always did to signal a dispatch, the champagne bottle smashed against the side of the jumbo thingie, the chocks were knocked away, the crane jib came down to

116

lift the thingie on to the big transporter, the thingie was secured to the transporter under Walter's personal supervision, the transporter moved off and the thingie which, heaven help him, had not been properly secured, lurched sideways and plunged into the Plodge Burn. He dreamt that next morning he was dismissed with ignominy. It was the Pluvius equivalent of John Wayne having his epaulettes ripped off.

And on top of that he had a voiceless leading tenor.

"I feel sorry for bachelors," said Auntie Dinah.

"How's Jonty taking it?" Beth asked Oswald.

Oswald said, "He takes the popular view – he blames me. He isn't speaking to me. That's frustrating for a man who can't talk."

"I could roast your joint one weekend, Oswald," said Auntie Dinah. "Life's hard for bachelors."

Walter had retired to a corner to brood over his troubles. What had he done to deserve this? Of course there were other tenors in the world. There were other tenors in the choir. He could promote Ivan Williams, Tommy Offord or Clive Paxton. Indeed, he would have to promote one of them. Any one of them would do a good job. But it was Hamlet without the prince. It was Elaine's scrambled eggs without pepper.

There was also Charlie Embleton in his Tommy Wrench persona. He was a sort of tenor leaning unsteadily towards baritone. He was neither one thing nor another. They didn't have one thing or another singing Pagliacci at La Scala, did they? And Tommy Wrench wouldn't recognise a simple passage in a major key with a modulation into the fifth key above it if he fell over one outside the club. This was a consideration that lay heavily on a conductor.

"A man misses a woman," said Auntie Dinah.

Walter groaned deeply.

"I feel sorry for you, Walter."

"He's got a woman, Auntie Dinah," Beth assured her.

Walter rose. "I think I'll go and have a lie-down," he said with infinite sadness.

"That's right," said Auntie Dinah. "And Walter…"

"Eh?"

"Pleasant dreams."

*

"All right, dad?" said Avril. She had brought him a cup of tea.

"All right, Avril." Tot switched off Mozart. "Are the bairns in bed?"

"Oh, yes. All's peaceful downstairs. Unnatural, isn't it?"

"I'll pop in and say goodnight to them."

"You don't have to switch Mozart off for me."

"Enough's enough, even of Mozart, especially when half of my mind's on Jonty – and jumbo thingies in general."

"Dad! Jumbo thingies – and tiddler thingies for that matter – will still be here when we're all in paradise with Mozart."

"They won't, you know. Have you forgotten what you and I decided the other day? The Industrial Revolution's being laid to rest. Next stop: the chocolate cream society."

Avril asked if the old goat had found his voice yet.

"No sign of it. Poor old Jonty!"

"Poor old obstreperous nuisance."

"Yes, but aren't they the very ones to feel sorry for? I'd develop that noble theme, but I know how trying it must be for you, living with a philosopher. Anyway, thanks…"

"What for?"

"You know."

"No."

"You and Arthur – giving a home to an old windbag when your mam died."

"We had only one reason for that – so the bairns would grow up sick of the sound of Mozart."

*

The bill for the bunting was quite far from Jonty's glum thoughts. He had gargled with salt and water, he had had his stomach rubbed with camphorated oil by the short-sighted woman from next door, he had slept on his face and he had tried his own more congenial remedy of large whiskies. He could still raise no better noise than a fingernail on a window pane.

His gestures were becoming more violent. Rage, said Beth, was rendering him permanently pop-eyed. He had taken sick leave and Walter was left to cajole the assembly squad by his own diffident methods.

Let it be said that the squad worked pretty hard for Walter, because of his unfailing good nature and hesitant politeness. A man can become a foreman and remain a decent human being. Once in a while.

*

Mrs Thirlaway has added to her street cries. The Nostalgia Centre is now ringing to shouts of "Fresh fish and toffee apples!" This is a travesty of tradition, but we are helpless. We are at the mercy of a zealot.

*

Lionel Judge had prevailed on Tot to come to his small office again, but this time his greeting was a merry one.

"Gratifying, Tot, gratifying – that the assembly squad strike is over!"

Tot could bear that word no longer. "Industrial action! That's what you mean, Lionel!"

"You don't care to call it a strike?"

"We prefer the euphemism. Only history can get away with the stark words, because nobody heeds history."

Lionel Judge said that at any rate common sense had prevailed.

"Oh, the workers can be relied on," said Tot, "to arrive by wise judgment at a rational decision following, of course, the recognised procedural channels."

"Of course."

"Which is the cosmetic explanation you and I will agree to give," said Tot, "whereas the truth is vastly more romantic, and also unrepeatable."

"I did hear," said Judge, "that Jonathan Harwood's rhetoric persuaded a return to work."

"Human nature," said Tot.

"What?"

"Complex, lovable, bloody-minded! – in short, normal. During the first forty

118

minutes of his speech, Jonty invited each interrupting member of the assembly squad to step outside and take his coat off. The final interrupter was about to be castigated as either a barmy bugger or a silly sod when suddenly Jonty stopped, clutching his throat."

"His voice – will it be a long time returning?"

"There are those who hope so. As chairman, I plunged thankfully into the hush. It was from the subsequent discussion that the formula for peace emerged. The meeting agreed to deplore the episode in Miss Pilbury's office when nephew Brother Gorman had disgracefully provoked Uncle Brother Harwood, but were prepared to return to work as a gesture of good will, having accepted uncle brother's apology. The bill for the bunting was to be regarded as a *nolle prosequi*."

Judge said there were certain matters he did not understand. "If Mr Harwood hit Mr Gorman," he said, "how could Mr Harwood be the aggrieved party?"

Tot said, "Ah." Judge was proving himself to be indeed a tyro. He was apparently experienced in neither real life nor its trade union equivalent.

Tot could have understood his ignorance of real life; he shared that with the rest of humanity. But damn it! – the man might have made the effort to show some appreciation of the trade union afflatus. After all, trade unionism was fantasy. What kind of man was he who had no feeling for the fantastic? Ah, poor innocent Tot! The man Judge's feeling was for computerisation, the arch-fantasy of the age. And he was married. Did Tot not know that? Well, no. Who knew? Who knew that his marriage was worth a story of its own?

In the present story, however, Judge's next speech was: "And if the assembly squad struck – I beg your pardon, took industrial action – on behalf of Mr. Harwood, their chargehand, why should Mr Harwood denounce them as..."

"Daft," Tot supplied, "and stupid."

"Why should they return to work when, as I understand it, the original grievance remained?"

Tot said, "Ah," again, for the same reason as before.

"And why should they accept Mr Harwood's apology?" Judge asked.

"Which he hadn't made, mind you."

"What? But you said..."

"I said that was what the meeting agreed to agree on," said Tot. "You see, Lionel, it comes back to human nature."

"Which is incorrigible," said Judge.

"Not quite. Perverse, spiteful, petulant. But redeemable, I think. If you and I didn't believe that, why are we carrying on?"

Judge didn't answer that.

But he had every hope that the day would come when he would inhabit a very large office at headquarters. He would have private, personal and immediate access to the computer's deepest secrets. By such means, he would climb to power. He would be an international tycoon. Not merely in thingie fettling. In a multiplicity of enterprises. Meanwhile, he would make do with this small office in this small factory. But he would bend this small factory to his will.

He scratched his knees. "Well, we must not be Utopian, but it seems the dispatch preparations for the jumbo thingie can go ahead."

"Exactly!" said Tot. "Because we recognised that productivity should not be made to suffer by further absence from work."

"We did?"

"Of course."

"Oh."

Did they understand each other? Not quite. But at least there was tacit mutual approval for that word "cosmetic".

*

"Sir Rodney!" said the man. "Are you all right, like?"

Sir Rodney was taken aback. Here he was, returning from one of his heart-warming visits to the debunking shop, pausing briefly at the drinking trough to gaze at it rapturously, and he was being addressed by a worker. "Well…" he said.

"Can I help you, or something, like?" said the man. "I've seen you many a time standing here, like, and I thinks to myself, thinks I, I wonder if Sir Rodney would mind, like, if I went up and had a word with him."

Sir Rodney was not displeased. Not displeased, but hopelessly embarrassed. "Well…" he repeated.

"I mean," said the man, "I don't want to be cheeky, like. It's just that I'm a bit doo-lally, you know. Anybody'll tell you that Charlie Embleton's doo-lally."

"Well…" said Sir Rodney.

"Or Tommy Wrench. With a name like that, I'm bound to be barmy, eh? They laugh at me, you know. I don't mind, like. They all laughed at Charlie Chaplin. They all laughed at Fattie Arbuckle. And I mean, if they can laugh at them buggers, they'd laugh at anybody. You're sure there's nothing I can do for you, like?"

"Well…" said Sir Rodney.

"That's all right, then. I'd better get back to my spronking. We don't want to hold the job up, do we? You know the Nostalgia Centre?"

"Well…" said Sir Rodney.

"I've seen you there, like. I've done a few gigs there. There's nothing wrong with nostalgia, is there? It's the coming thing, is nostalgia. I'm playing my knackers at a funeral tomorrow. There's no organ in the crematorium, you see. That's the pass we've come to. Eh? Eh? Ta-ta, well."

Charlie Embleton went back to the zilted spindling shop. Sir Rodney stood for a few moments. Then he proceeded blissfully to his office. He had communicated with one of his men.

*

If Elaine and Oswald happened to be walking home together again, it was entirely accidental; both of them were quite certain of that. But it had come about, and the burden of making conversation seemed to have fallen on Oswald.

"Walking home with you, Elaine," he said, "I never do say very much, even in a drizzle."

Elaine didn't answer.

"And now that you're not speaking to me…"

Elaine was silent. She didn't even comment on the drizzle. Drizzles belonged in Auntie Dinah's snapshots.

"It looks as if we're going to have some pretty wordless journeys."

120

A minute-and-a-half later, Elaine said, "Who says I'm not speaking to you?"

"Well, are you?"

"I'm not friendly with you. It's not the same."

"What's the difference?"

"If I weren't speaking, I shouldn't be able to tell you what sort of rotten skunk you are."

"That's all right, then," said Oswald. It probably wasn't worth while defending himself, even if he hadn't yet been canonised. "I'm the one who got punched, you know."

"Serves you right."

"I'm the victim, so you blame me. Just what I'd expect. Logic."

"That's twice in a week you've called me stupid."

"Not exactly."

"Oh, well…" said Elaine, inclined to soften.

"It's three times. I should do it more often," said Oswald, and having outraged her anew, he added, "How many sorts of rotten skunk are there?"

Elaine, having lost her inclination, launched into a catalogue. "Look at poor old dad," she said. "First his thingie dispatch was threatened. No sooner does that get put right than his leading tenor loses his voice in a fracas."

"More of a mêlée."

"Shut up!"

"And of course it's my fault."

"Well, who started this silly business of who adds up the bill for the bunting?"

Who knew? That was last week.

"But do you think I haven't suffered?" Oswald asked.

"Not enough."

"*My* uncle hit *me* in the face! Not that he meant it. And how did it happen? Because your fatheaded father pushed him."

Elaine gasped. This was a remarkably aggressive Oswald.

"Not that *he* meant it," Oswald conceded. "He tripped. He's one of nature's trippers. Two left feet – and he fell over Elsie Pilbury's Indian rug with both of them. Put his knee through her typewriter. And his elbow in her Wedgwood teapot. But that of course was *my* fault. The wonder to me," he went on, "is that he's got such a beautiful daughter. Or that she's worth getting upset about, even in a drizzle."

Elaine paused in second mid-gasp. "You can't get round me like that."

"So now you don't like the truth."

Elaine went back to her earlier claim. "Suffered? You?"

"Suffered," said Oswald pitifully.

"My foot!"

"You may think your foot covers it, but haven't I suffered? I got a poke in the nose, didn't I? That was nothing. But what do you think it's like at home? It was bad enough living with the neolithic ancestor when he was just his lovable bigoted old self. But now he's got a grievance against me – and that's the classical case of hating the one you've wronged. And after all, I've told him I forgive him."

"He would appreciate that."

"His eyes watered, veins bulged in his neck, his nostrils flared, he bared his dentures... The words he couldn't speak I couldn't repeat to a lady, let alone your dad's beautiful daughter."

Oswald paused for breath. He seemed to be damaging his reputation for being reserved. Well, his reputation for rectitude had already been buffeted. Before long, his reputation for resistance to romantic convention would crumble. And he was only twenty-two! Tot had told him (not once, but too many times) of the Shavian axiom that every man over forty was a scoundrel. Merciful heaven! Here he was eighteen years short of the threshold, and already hurtling into orthodoxy. Still, native reserve was an expendable characteristic. Its loss didn't imply any compromise on politics, philosophy or morality. If he could talk dementedly about those, romantic convention might still be kept at bay.

Elaine said, "H'm." She had always felt that Oswald could talk dementedly – about politics, philosophy and morality. It was the important items he had been bashful about, like saying the right things to a girl.

"Oswald..." she said.

"Hello?"

"Say some more."

But Oswald had had a relapse. "The drizzle's stopped," was the bashful best he could manage.

Not just the drizzle. Also the flood, it seemed to Elaine. Lucky girl, though. She was walking home with a near-paragon.

*

Tot had spent rather less time than usual with Mozart in his little room in his daughter's home. He had now been sitting in silence for a while, holding a debate with himself in his head; it was another form of recreation he and Oswald had in common.

He was reflecting on how the world misunderstood the simplicity of genius. Lionel Judge had spoken of Utopia. Utopia was More's panacea (hadn't Shaw said?) for what he regarded as a rational and balanced system of society. Ever since, the world had used the word as though it meant something hopelessly unattainable.

He went downstairs for his supper. "Have I told you what Salieri said about Mozart?" he asked his daughter.

"Only three hundred times," said Avril. "He said: 'If this young man is to go on, what is to become of the rest of us?' Would you like some cheese?"

It wasn't Utopia. What was?

*

Impervious though he was to social niceties, Jonty had not been unaffected by the breach with Oswald. The pollution in the domestic atmosphere had filtered through to him. They normally went their separate ways for the great bulk of their lives, but at certain times they had to meet, especially on Saturdays and Sundays.

Oswald, as it happened, had been away for a couple of weekends with the harriers and the footballers. It would not always be so. Still, whatever was wrong was the cheeky young beggar's fault, Jonty told himself.

The doctor had put him on the sick. It had seemed the easiest way out for a weary G.P. Jonty had stood in front of him, squeaking, grimacing horribly and turning puce. The doctor had handed him a prescription and said, "Take one of these when your back's bad."

The receptionist said, "I don't think he was saying he had a bad back, doctor."

"Neither do I, Doris," said the weary G.P., "but you know the rule – when in doubt, it's a bad back."

The receptionist ushered Jonty out. "Come back in three years," she said, "unless it gets better. If it gets better, shoot yourself. Without suffering, life's useless."

Jonty went to the club.

*

Walter brought a small whisky from the bar. Jonty's eyes bulged and he emitted a squeak, perhaps of astonishment or gratitude.

"Don't try to speak," said Walter. "Just lubricate your larynx with that. I mean, I invited you to the club, hoping to take you out of yourself."

"And into something warm and lovable," said Beth.

Walter gazed anxiously at his suffering chargehand. "Sup up," he urged.

"He doesn't need that kind of encouragement," said Beth.

"Those capsules I got you from the ambulance room, Jonty," said Walter. "What did you do with them? Pardon?"

"I think he's trying to suggest, Walter," said Beth, "what *you* can do with them."

Walter sat back glumly. It was Providence at work, he believed. Just when he was savouring his imminent triumph, fate had laid a stultifying hand on Jonty's vocal cords. "It's my twenty-first assem…" he said, and was interrupted by another vehement squeak.

"Your twentieth, I think he's saying," said Beth.

"Oh, dear," said Walter, "I fear nothing'll bring that voice back in time."

It seemed to Beth that Jonty was being very inconsiderate. If he had to be incapacitated, why couldn't he simply have sat on another red hot primus stove?

Walter was pondering his own rotten luck. His leading tenor had let him down. What a pity the dear old chap hadn't kept his damned silly mouth shut. The stricken foreman groaned.

Jonty squeaked.

"Pardon?" said Walter.

Jonty squeaked again.

"Voice or no voice," said Beth, "there's certain information that Jonty can always get across."

"Eh?"

"He wants another whisky. Large one this time."

It was her turn to sit back, but in contemplation. She was thinking about emulsion paint.

The toilet, she had decided, would have to be painted apple green. She reasoned that since it faced east and caught the morning sunshine it would benefit from a delicate pastel shade. Her start was delayed, however, until her stock of toilet rolls, which were mid-blue, ran out. Clearly a mid-blue toilet roll would clash with an apple green wall.

The next question was: What colour would she paint the kitchen? She hadn't intended to paint the kitchen, but it was an established principle that when you started decorating, you didn't know when to stop.

And she couldn't paint the kitchen, of course, unless she painted the lounge first. But there was no problem there. She would paint it Marigold Ecstasy. Or Pink Surprise. Or Lilac Dream. She had discussed it with Auntie Dinah, who said that in her day nobody had a lounge. You had a front room. And that was only because you had to have somewhere to lay out your corpses.

*

The ghost of Sir Rodney's grandfather's horse had still not composed a verse about a horse. He reflected on this as he stood at the trough. Perhaps he would never write the verse. Not in heaven. The place was already over-full of poets. He had thought they would all be in hell. Only the other day, he had looked in Chapman's Homer, having borrowed John Keats's battered copy. What it said about horses was: "We have watered our horses in Helicon." He had never himself had that sort of advantage; nobody had ever taken him to the home of the Muses. Still, people didn't want to bother with a horse that wallowed in self-pity. People all had their own self-pity.

He gazed up expectantly at Sir Rodney's window, but failed to be noticed. He wasn't to know that Sir Rodney was composing a sea shanty.

*

How often had Gladys Button bewailed the unsatisfactory provenance of her knee injury! She unburdened herself to us in the Nostalgia Centre, hoping we might find a place for her elastic bandage alongside the Emperor Hadrian's toga.

In the years of her girlhood, few women had played football. Nowadays, of course, you couldn't fall down twice without bumping into women footballers; it was the natural progression of sex indiscrimination. In her twenties, she had pined to be a centre-half, but there was no place for a female centre-half in a male football world.

She burned her bra at Wembley Stadium.

"What's that woman up to?" the President of the Football Association asked.

"She's burning her bra," his secretary said.

"What's a bra?" he asked, blowing up a ball. "The Cup Final's kicking off in twenty minutes," he added testily.

If you were a centre-half, there was quite a good chance you would damage a knee in making a fearful tackle. Your cartilage might slip out in truly heroic circumstances. All those years ago, she had watched Newcastle United. They had a centre-half named Frank Brennan. What a magnificent man he was! She could have been a Frank Brennan! He was an exponent of the fearful tackle. As it was, she had to slip her cartilage getting off a bus at the age of fifty-nine. Heroic it wasn't. Vasco da Gama wouldn't have applauded. Nor Galileo.

We might accept her burnt bra at the Nostalgia Centre. It'll be a bit more authentic than the Emperor Hadrian's toga.

*

Walter safely negotiated the geography of the main building and arrived in Sir Rodney's office. Sir Rodney beamed at him and said with strange accuracy, "Ah, Mr Lester!"

"Yes, Sir Rodney?"

"What?"

"You sent for me, I believe?"

"What for? I mean, did I? Yes, I suppose I might well have done." Sir Rodney

124

fiddled with his tea clipper and collected his thoughts.

As was well known, Sir Rodney had affected absent-mindedness for so long that it had become part of his character, just as the great comedians of the past – the Will Hays, the Robb Wiltons, the Harry Tates – so often found their private personas assuming the mantles of their public lives.

He had retained sufficient grasp, however, to have continued prospering in the rôle of paterfamilias to the Pluvius Works as long as the old order remained unchanged. Aye, there was the rub! Changed it had, and the only response he could manage was to cling more achingly to the romantic trappings of the past – the bunting and the receptions and the noblesse oblige of paternalism.

He turned back to face Walter.

"I'm a bit of a Will Hay figure, you know."

"Pardon?"

"Or Robb Wilton."

"Pardon?"

"Still! To the point! Thingie dispatch reception!"

Walter sighed. Surely Sir Rodney had heard?

"I relish the works choir's contribution, you know. A pity about your leading tenor." Of course Sir Rodney had heard. He seldom missed vital matters.

Walter permitted himself an emotional "Ah!"

Sir Rodney for his part was also undoubtedly moved.

"Family!" he cried, in a sudden burst of near-hysteria. "What about my Pluvius family?" He controlled himself. This would not do. "Yes, well," he said, and then embarked on a theme which Walter found mystifying even by Sir Rodney's standards. 'Heave-ho, my hearty Mrs Green.' Not eponymous. No Mrs Green in the song. Symbolic, that's all."

"I see," said Walter. He always said "I see." It was always a lie. He hoped desperately that unravelment would emerge.

Sir Rodney had taken up a stance behind his desk and begun to recite:

"Oh, I sailed one fine day out of Hartlepool town –
Heave-ho, my hearty Mrs. Green!
And my eyes they were blue and my hair it was brown –
Heave-ho, my hearty Mrs. Green!"

He paused expectantly. Walter coughed and said, "Thank you."

"I used to sing from time to time when I was younger," said Sir Rodney, with a certain meaningfulness. "A bit of a compulsive warbler, I seemed to be. You'll not have heard, I shouldn't think."

"Pardon?" said Walter.

"No, no, of course not."

"Er – of course not, Sir Rodney." Walter shifted feet.

Sir Rodney said that the second verse spoke of the girl who was left behind. "She sits on the quayside at a bit of a loose end. But when he comes back, heartache is his lot."

"Is it?" said Walter.

"Oh, yes."

"I see."

"She has run off with a bespoke tailor, dull but available. What do you think?"

Walter was unable to think anything.

"As I was saying," said Sir Rodney, "I was something of a tenor myself... A tenor... I could... At a pinch..."

Walter gazed at him uncomprehendingly.

"Perhaps you're right," said Sir Rodney ruefully. "Ah, well! Never wrote the last verse anyway." He retreated to his model tea clipper and added despondently, "Well, if that's all, Mr – ah – Lester..."

Walter, who had been standing stupefied, roused himself. "What? Oh, yes. Thank you, Sir Rodney. Good morning."

He went out through Miss Pilbury's office.

"Cheerio, Walter!" she said.

"Eh?"

"This is me, over here. You have a glazed look."

Walter leant earnestly over her desk. "Take care of Sir Rodney, Elsie," he said earnestly. "He may be cracking up."

*

Sir Rodney had sunk back in his seat. The choir was in desperate trouble. He had half-written a sea shanty. He had been half-prepared to sing it to his foreman thingie assembler, by way of demonstrating something, he wasn't quite sure what. His foreman thingie assembler had seemed not to understand him. He apparently hadn't even heard of Will Hay. Was the poor chap cracking up?

Chapter Ten

Dislodging Oswald's Glasses

That evening, Beth contemplated her husband's dismal face and said sharply, "Walter!" The urgent tone aroused Walter from his torpor, but had no effect on Auntie Dinah, who was snoring gently on the sofa.

"It's no good sitting there, Walter," said Beth, "with your face blacker than the tunnel of love."

Walter said that as far as he remembered it wasn't black in the tunnel of love.

"You've never been in the tunnel of love."

"I was in the tunnel of love with Selina Gowke."

"So you sit there thinking about Selina Gowke, when all the time I thought you were just in a torpor."

"I *was* just in a torpor. Selina Gowke was nothing to me."

"Then what were you doing with her in the tunnel of love?"

"What do people usually do in the tunnel of love?"

"I know what people usually do, but you never did it with me."

"I was never with you in the tunnel of love."

"Why do you keep going on about the tunnel of love? You feel guilty, don't you?"

Walter said he hoped so. Next to feeling nervous or despondent he liked to feel guilty. He added, "Peacock!"

Now he was talking in code. There were supposed to be no secrets in their marriage, apart from the necessary few thousand.

"My poor old Peacock," said Walter. "The jumbo thingie, Beth – that's its name. It's painted on the casing, ready for the ceremony." He moaned softly. Dispatching ceremony! And no solo singer for the reception! He would almost settle for one of those punk rockers. "If only he had a bad back!"

"Who?"

"Jonty! He could sing with a bad back."

"Not if he was touching his toes."

"You're getting ridiculously hypothetical, Beth."

"You're talking like Tot! But then, why not? We're interchangeable – you, me, Tot, Gladys Button, all of us." She turned to the sofa. "Auntie Dinah, please!" The snores had begun to rattle the ornaments on the sideboard.

"Eh? What?" said Auntie Dinah, starting up. "Did you speak, Beth? Is it raining?"

"Not enough to snore by."

"In that case, I think I'll get on with this jumper. I mean, I don't want to nod off." She took up her knitting. "Aren't you going to your choir practice, Walter?"

Walter uttered a short wail of agony.

"Walter's going into one of his torpors, Auntie Dinah," said Beth, "to dream of Selina Gowke."

"I have no dreams," said Walter, "of Selina Gowke. Selina Gowke was little more than a plaything of the moment to me. But Selina Gowke would have married me."

"She would have married anybody to change her name from Gowke."

Walter sat back, but what he dreamed about was tradition. It was a precedent set by Sir Rodney's grandfather that every time a jumbo thingie was dispatched, there was a naming ceremony. It derived from shipbuilding. Sir Rodney's grandfather had wanted to be a shipbuilder, but had set up in thingie fettling instead when his mother left him a secret new thingie fettling formula in her will, wrapped around her rhyming dictionary, in which she inscribed the words:

This new thingie fettling formula's now your own to cherish,
Guard it closely, you young sod, or may you bloody perish.

"We never had lounges in my day," said Auntie Dinah. "Don't answer that. You didn't last time I said it."

"Did you ever foxtrot, Auntie Dinah?" Beth asked.

"Why do you ask?"

"For ridiculous hypothesis."

"Lounge, is it? When I got married, you were lucky if you had a coal bucket. What? Foxtrot? In 1941? There was a war on, you know. When I got married, we lived in with my mother, and we had to share a frying pan. Have you any idea what it's like to share a frying pan? As a matter of fact, we did foxtrot in 1941, until the dance hall was knocked down during an air raid, by the fire engine. I foxtrotted at least twice with my late husband. He was alive then. Quite alive. I loved him, Beth. I loved him. It was a pity we never got on together. Lounges? Lounges didn't come in until after the war. There would never have been any lounges if Stafford Cripps had got his way. He had the right idea."

"What was that?"

"Nobody was entitled to be happy. That was Stafford Cripps's motto."

"Did you ever tango?"

"French windows. You had no French windows before the war. When I set up house, I had a coal bucket, half a pair of sheets, no bed, a cake tin and no coal. But he died."

"Stafford Cripps?"

"My late husband. Stafford Cripps as well. Oh, Stafford Cripps died. And what happened? People started going in for happiness. Tango? What? I tangoed with my late husband the night they bombed the chip shop. The fat was running in the streets. We tangoed the night away. He tangoed like a dream."

She rose, seized Walter and began to tango with him, but not for long, because the door was flung open and a whirlwind entered.

"A fine bloody thing!" said Jonty. "I go down to the club looking for you, and you're cavorting about here, doing the hokey-cokey with Whistler's mother-in-law!"

"Jonty!" cried Walter.

"I'm standing at the bar like an idiot. 'What's wrong with you?' Charlie Embleton said. 'Buying your own beer? Are you not well?' Cheeky beggar!"

"There's people here trying to tango," said Auntie Dinah.

"It's the last tango in Lastfort," said Beth.

Walter found words to address Jonty. "You're talking!" he said.

"Why aye, I'm talking! You know that linctus the doctor gave me? I threw it in the backyard. And what happened? A sparrow supped it and dropped down dead. So what did I do?"

"Fat bacon!" said Auntie Dinah.

"Eh?"

"You hung fat bacon around your neck."

"I hung fat…" He paused, astonished. "How did you know?"

"Dr Wrigley."

"Eh?"

"Dr Wrigley was your doctor when you were a lad."

"He wasn't!"

"Eh?"

"Dr Drabble was our doctor when I was a lad."

"But they shared the same bicycle," said Beth. "They worked in the same clinic, anaesthetising toothache sufferers with the same half-brick."

Walter was still gazing at Jonty in amazement, but Jonty ignored him and proceeded. "I said to myself: 'They'll miss me. They'll miss me if there's no bugger to sing *Bobby Shafto* at the reception. They might appreciate me then,' I said. They can't manage without me. Look at the last dispatching ceremony. Sir Rodney shook my hand. The works manager shook me hand. But what have I got to show for all that?"

"A handful of crushed fingers," said Beth.

Happy thoughts were crowding in on Walter. Jonty was talking!

He was. "It all started with that bloody bill for the bunting. I could add up that bill on the back of a matchbox while the daft bloody penpushers are breaking their fingers over their fancy little calculating machines."

"Jonty…"

"I mean, they started a nasty rumour that I was colour blind, and couldn't even see the red, white and blue bunting. Oh, they'll not get me down, bugger them! I'll tell you this…"

"Jonty!" Walter shrieked.

"Eh?"

"This is marvellous! Now that your voice has come back, you'll be able to sing at the reception."

"I'll tell you this," said Jonty. "I went to the doctor. 'Well, Mr. Harwood,' he said, 'it's come back, thanks to my linctus. How's your back?'"

Walter's gaze was now ecstatic.

"'I haven't got a bad back,' I said. 'There's time yet,' he said. 'Mind you,' he said, 'I forbid you to take chances. No singing! No singing for a long time yet!'"

Walter cried out again in pain. "No singing?"

"No singing. 'But you can talk,' the doctor said. 'You can talk in moderation.' So here I am. I mean, I was at the club, but where the hell were you? Get your coat, then! I mean, it's typical. The world's full of people thinking of nobody but Number One…"

Walter went for his coat. The voice pursued him. It was considerably worse than sitting about in a torpor.

*

Sir Rodney was thinking about his Pluvius family, bracketed with his eccentricity. He had decided early in life to cultivate eccentricity. Probably it was now out of control. His housekeeper had tried to break him of it. An ill-disposed woman, he thought. No, no, that was cruel. She meant well. Ah! Why was it that meaning well turned out a damned sight worse than meaning ill?

But he had been thinking of his Pluvius family, bracketed with something. What was it? Redundancy! That was it! It was in the air and no mistake. Tradesmen unemployed: it shocked him. Some had accepted redundancy payment and left: the older chaps, that was. Well, good luck to them – they would have a bit of extra leisure to swill their backyards and help their womenfolk to polish the brasses – all those dear old customs so beloved of gritty northerners!

But what of the younger fellows? Would they be able to handle redundancy if hit them? Satan found work for idle hands, didn't he? Still, it might not come to that. He would keep the old Pluvius Works going one way and another, wouldn't he? Wouldn't he? H'm.

Sir Rodney sighed and went down to the debunking shop.

*

In the outer office, Elsie Pilbury said to her friend Gladys Button, "Oh, he's acting in a peculiar manner, Gladys, is Sir Rodney."

"There's been talk," said Gladys.

"Very strange behaviour. Apart from staring out at the trough, I mean. And apart from statistics that are not to be sneezed at. He's even odder than usual, if you can believe that. More and more he's coming to the office in his gardening trousers and old rugby boots."

"There's always been talk," said Gladys. "You can't stop talk. You wouldn't want to stop talk, if you're healthily inquisitive."

"Peculiar's not quite the word."

"Barmy?"

"I prefer idiosyncratic."

"Well, it's got six syllables."

"He's gouging more and more holes in his pullover. Yesterday, he was shouting, 'Heave-ho, my hearty Mrs. Green!' and dancing something that looked not unlike a hornpipe. Not that I could claim to recognise a hornpipe. You're a woman of the world, Gladys. Have you ever danced a hornpipe?"

"I hornpiped intermittently in the Brownies."

"I didn't think Brownies hornpiped."

"That's why they threw me out. Another thing – you're overlooking my bad leg."

"And the fact is," Miss Pilbury sighed, "there's no noticeable Mrs. Green in his life. Nervous debility. I like to think it's nervous debility."

"That's got a nice ring to it. And if he had a secret Mrs. Green, Elsie, I'm sure you'd be the first to know."

"Now that the factory's no longer his own private property, there's a bit of what you might call deprivation syndrome. Do you like the ring of that, Gladys?"

"You're impeccable. Elsie. You're a woman without a stain on her Indian rug."

There was a clumping of boots in the corridor and a voice was heard singing, "Oh, I sailed one fine day out of Hartlepool town..." Sir Rodney, halfway to the debunking shop, had lost his bearings and put about.

130

Gladys Button prepared to leave. "Cheerio, Elsie," she said. "I shan't tell anybody what you've told me."

"Of course you will."

"And another thing…" said Gladys.

"What?"

"I meant to talk about homoeopathy."

"You will next time."

"You bet I will. Plus several more reasons why they threw me out of the Brownies."

*

Sir Rodney stalked back into his office. He was thinking again about his eccentricity. The gardener at his country home in the Coquet valley hadn't tried to break him of it. In fact he positively encouraged it. A good chap, that.

Old age. Time perhaps to consider that. Yes. His old age, he supposed, would probably be given over to an orgy of idiosyncrasy in that idyllic Northumbrian retreat. He thought a good deal these days about that retreat. Was that, he wondered, why he was wearing his gardening trousers?

*

"They say," said Oswald firmly, "that you should never explain and never apologise. Still…"

"Who says that?" Elaine wanted to know.

"The kind of people who are always saying things like that." If he could find it in his dictionary of quotations he would spring it on her. She would like that, although not much.

"It doesn't matter, really it doesn't," said Elaine. "I think I've decided to forgive you."

"Thank you. Not that I've done anything wrong."

"Then what were you going to apologise for?"

"I didn't say I was."

"Oh."

"What were you going to forgive me for?"

"For all the things you said to me yesterday."

"I didn't mean them," Oswald admitted. "For that I do apologise."

Elaine considered this for several moments and said, "All right." She considered it some more and added, "You didn't mean any of them?"

"Not one."

"I see."

Several more moments elapsed during which Oswald did his share of considering. Then he said solemnly, "Except one. I refuse to take back what I said about your dad having a beautiful daughter."

They turned into Elaine's street. "Hello!" she said. "My hand seems to be in yours again."

"Good heavens!" said Oswald. Then he decided to explain after all. "About the threatened strike action that you blamed me for…"

"I didn't blame you."

"You did."

"All right, I did."

131

"Well, you didn't really."

"Mercy!" said Elaine. "Your arm's round my waist again."

"Are you sure you want mercy?" This was beginning to look like a standard love story. Good God, that would never do! "Well, anyway, here's my explanation. It's all to do with society."

"I thought it might be."

"No, listen! It's this totally unnatural existence we all lead."

"Oh, there's nothing more unnatural than falling in love."

"You've noticed that? Falling in love was invented by romantics."

"The fools."

"But I was going to talk about industry."

"That's better, blast you."

"Industrial and urban life," said Oswald. "It's unsocial, noisy, degrading... We should all abdicate from it now and then to preserve our sanity. The irony is that the one thing that's worse than work is not having work." Oh, this young man was Tot's heir-apparent.

They were almost at Elaine's gate. "Say it again, Oswald," she said.

"I'm glad you like it," said Oswald. "It's unsocial, unsalubrious..."

"Not that, you swine! You know what I mean."

"I'll say it on Saturday," Oswald suggested.

"Saturday?"

"Well, I was thinking... In this urban hell – it would be altogether unbearable if we couldn't flee to the countryside once in a while."

"So?"

"So, will you flee with me next Saturday on the back of my bike for a day out in the hills?"

Elaine considered this for less than several moments and said that would be lovely. "Just one condition, though."

"Oh?"

"I refuse to wait until Saturday for you to say it again."

"Stand by, then." He swallowed. "Your dad has the most beautiful daughter in sixteen counties. Seventeen, if I stretch to hyperbole."

Reciprocation seemed not unreasonable. "And the Unspeakable Uncle," Elaine said, "has a scrumptious nephew. Bye-bye." She plonked a kiss on his nose, dislodging his glasses, and ran up her garden path.

Oswald went on his way. Scrumptious he might be, but this yielding to romance had just committed the damned fool to missing Newcastle United's home match on Saturday. That was the trouble with the Oswalds, the Tots and the Thomas Mores: they were unworldly. Why Thomas More? The man had his head chopped off, didn't he? It happens to romantics.

*

The female staff had returned to using the fire-damaged ladies'. Fortunately, its plumbing was still intact. The decor had suffered rather badly, but joiners and painters had worked two weekends patching it up. It was now not too far from its pristine seedy best. The rest room's sofa and two armchairs, drenched by the firemen, had been thrown out and replaced by six deckchairs from the summer house of Sir

Rodney's country retreat.

Of course, Sir Rodney, as a man of honour, stood by his promise to provide a new ladies', but that matter was in the hands of headquarters, which tended to grind rather more slowly than the mills of God.

*

"Only two of them work," Gladys Button stated.

"I know, I know, Gladys," said Elsie Pilbury.

"It's musical deckchairs, that's what it is. You never know which one's going to pinion your bum. Who wants an uncartilaged knee aggravated by bum-pinioning?"

"It is your right leg, isn't it, Gladys?"

"That's what I've put about. Really, it's a bit of both legs, depending on whether I'm going up, down or sideways. Anyway, homoeopathy…"

"What?"

"That's what I've come to talk about, isn't it?"

"Well, between deckchairs, yes. Is homoeopathy good for both legs?"

"One at a time, until you learn to pronounce it."

"Could you tell me how it works?"

"I'll tell you what I've found out, Elsie, and we'll both be none the wiser. The principle is that the homoeopath treats you by giving your leg just about as much of the bad leg therapy as would bring on a bad leg if you didn't have one."

"That's what I thought. Are there any side effects?"

"That's where it started: in my side. And when he treated my side, that's when I began to get the leg effects."

"By the time he treats your feet, the pain should drop out through the floorboards. You're looking all right in yourself."

"I'm always all right in myself. It's outside of myself that's entirely unsatisfactory, from my point of view. Still, there's always somebody worse off than yourself."

"Yes, and long may it last. Take my mother."

"How long did she last?"

"Not long after she fell into her poss tub. Not that there was any truth in that."

"No, but there's not much fun in the truth."

"There wasn't much fun in that poss tub."

"I don't understand that."

"No," said Elsie. "A bit like homoeopathy, isn't it? Ta-ta, Gladys."

*

Well, she had arranged for two good-looking young draughtsmen to help Gladys up and down the stairs as long as she had a bad leg, and even afterwards as long as Gladys liked the idea.

There was, however, a matter over which Elsie felt guilty. She had perhaps been rather incautious on a certain occasion. She went in to see Sir Rodney. It might be as well to explain herself.

"Sir Rodney…" she began.

"Mm?" He picked at the hole in his pullover.

"I wonder if I might have a word with you?"

"Of course, Miss Pilbury. Any time. Any time tomorrow."

"Tomorrow?"

133

"I mustn't keep you now. It's five o'clock."

"It's twenty-five past twelve," said Miss Pilbury.

"Is it? I'll never get used to this Daylight Saving Act. What did I want to say to you?"

"*I* wanted to speak to *you*."

"So you said. But why wait until tomorrow? Out with it!"

"I just wanted to say I'm sorry."

"That's all right," said Sir Rodney. "It wasn't your Daylight Saving Act. Somebody called Willett was behind it. A builder, I believe."

"No, no."

"It was. In 1908. Nobody can save daylight, you know, not even a builder. There's the same amount, no matter what you do with your clocks. Anyway, he died before it was implemented. One dark night, no doubt."

"I know," said Miss Pilbury, "but I wanted to explain about my appearance on Radio Clarts last week."

"Who?" said Sir Rodney.

"Radio Clarts," said Miss Pilbury. "If I seemed to give away company business, and if that contributed to the industrial dispute, I didn't mean it. There! I felt I had to get that off my chest. It's that Mel Queasy."

"Where's that?"

"*Heaven Knows Why They Do It*."

"Exactly."

"So there we are."

"Indeed."

"Is that all right?"

Sir Rodney regarded her earnestly. "Miss Pilbury," he said, "I must say this, and I must say it with all the force I can muster. I haven't the faintest idea what you're talking about. And that's a state of affairs with which I am sure you and I are both completely happy." He made for the door. "I'm going now. Get somebody to look at that clock. A clock-repairer, for instance. I appear to have no letters to sign. Goodnight. And I hope you have a pleasant weekend." He went out.

"All's well," said Miss Pilbury. She spoke truth. It was mid-day. On Tuesday.

*

Lionel Judge had consoled himself for the smallness of his office in the Pluvius Works with the conviction that he would one day have a large one at headquarters. Now it seemed to him that he must strive towards a medium berth. He must press for the broadening of his brief at Pluvius. It was not going to be enough to try to inject efficiency into the Pluvius system. He was probably going to have to take over the running of the place. Sir Rodney's developing idiosyncrasies were making that imperative.

Yes, he must aim to sit in Sir Rodney's chair. Then, if the big office at headquarters proved not to be forthcoming, he would at least have a fairly big one at Pluvius. It was what was called a fallback situation, he believed. He was calling it that, anyway. Meanwhile, he must lean a little more heavily on Sir Rodney.

Oh, poor Lionel Judge! He was as liable as anyone to be the victim of headquarters' covert decisions. But perhaps he already suspected as much. Perhaps he was preparing a further fall-back. And that perhaps was why he had been in touch with Q.Q. Who was Q.Q? Was he another caricature executive? And was that why he and L.J. addressed one another in initials?

*

It was on Wednesday that Oswald arrived home to the smell of cooking, something he had almost learnt not to expect.

"What's this, then?" he said. "Preparing a meal?"

Jonty glowered at him from the table. "No. Just burning the house down. Rice pudding," he added. "I've put a rice pudding in the oven. You can take it. Or you can turn your toffee nose up. Please yourself."

What was happening? For two weeks, Oswald had come in each evening to nothing but a flinty stare. Now it was rice pudding.

"Rice pudding!" Jonty repeated. "The thing is, I'm not one to hold a grudge. So there it is. Rice pudding."

"Well, well," said Oswald. Everybody was forgiving him. There must be a moral here. The whole world was prepared to forgive a man who hadn't sinned. "Rice pudding?" he said. "Good! And what else?"

"What else? What else? Talk about greedy guts!"

"All right…" said Oswald hastily. Better not break the truce, if that was what it was. "We'll start off with rice pudding. And follow it with rice pudding."

"Always the same," said Jonty. "Stuck-up sods that work in the office! Mind, I don't forget whose fault it is – me with this horrible handicap. I mean, not being able to use my voice."

This was more like it. Uncle Jonty was making Oswald feel guilty again. And just when he was beginning to feel heroic. After all, he was missing next Saturday's football match. This put him in the same legendary class as Gerry King, who missed the 1955 Cup Final to go to a funeral. It was his own, but even so… "Is it ready?" he asked.

"Eh?"

"Is the rice pudding ready?" Oswald went to the hand-basin to wash.

"Ready? That's the thanks I get! I work both of my socks off to cook a rice pudding. I mean, I know you like your rice pudding. Your mother told me how you liked your rice pudding. Before she ran away, leaving you helpless in your cradle, she said: 'Don't forget to stuff the poor little bugger with rice pudding.' So I fall over backwards to get you a rice pudding. Are you grateful? Some bloody hope!" He proceeded to the oven.

Oswald said he was sorry.

"Another thing," said Jonty. "I cut my finger opening the tin."

"Is that somebody knocking at the door?" Oswald asked.

"No, no, it's not somebody knocking at the door. It's the death watch beetle."

"I'm washing my hands and face," said Oswald.

"And I'm looking after the rice pudding!" Jonty licked his finger. "You'll not mind a drop of blood in it?"

The knock was repeated. Oswald went to the door with soap in his eye.

"Useless bugger!" Jonty called after him. "And look at the plight you've got me in! Lost my voice, haven't I? Can't sing at the reception, can I? I don't hold a grudge, mind!"

Oswald opened the door.

"Well, let me in, then," said Auntie Dinah. "And what are you winking at me for, you young devil?"

"There's soap in my eye."

"There's a twinkle in your eye, that's what! Still, a wink and a twinkle always got a kiss in my day." She kissed him and preceded him into the kitchen/diner.

"You're a forward minx, and no mistake," said Oswald.

Auntie Dinah dumped her bag on the floor, ignoring Jonty's open-mouthed gaze. "I was sitting there doing my knitting and I said to myself: 'Dinah,' I said, 'why don't you go along and make a meal for them two hopeless men?' So I got this half-pound of bacon from Beth and picked up some sausages on the way. Have you got any eggs? And tomatoes? Oh, and I've brought a bit of black pudding. I thought I'd do you a nice mixed grill. Where's your frying pan? What's this in the cooker?"

"Rice pudding," said Oswald.

"Rice pudding! Rice pudding! What sort of grub's that for a lad with a twinkle? Next time, there'll be rhubarb roly-poly."

"Next time?" Jonty muttered. Better the death watch beetle!

*

Why should Charlie Embleton, whether in his own guise or that of Tommy Wrench, have called on Tot Needler and Avril? Nobody could have answered that, including himself – even if he had tried, which he would have done if pressed. Tot avoided pressing.

"Come in and have a cup of tea," Avril said.

So Charlie sat over his cup of tea and sat and sat and eventually said: "I've been thinking, like, there's not much time left to find out which direction we're all going in, the way I see it is this, though, mind I'm not at all sure I've got it right, like, but take all of us, you and me, Tot, and you, Avril, and all them what's lives is wrapped up in ours, like, but I look around and I ask myself, when it's all added up, what does it amount to, what we're doing, d'you never have the feeling that it's nowt more nor less than something that's all been done before, like, your story, my story, the story of all them that's what we call our friends and acquaintances, like, I mean, the way I look at it, you've got to ask yourself whether you do this or that, what's the difference when it comes down to it, like, I mean, take all your great men, or all your great women, if it comes to that, they're all dead, aren't they, or if they're not, they're all going to die, like, aren't they, I mean, what's the point in asking, when you're never going to find out, the way I see it, like, what's thingie fettling to you and me, or what's you and me to thingie fettling?"

When he had left, Avril said, "Well!"

"I know," said Tot. "But Hamlet got away with it, by saying it in blank verse."

*

As far as we know, no visitor to the Nostalgia Centre has asked why an ostler would have a long pole with a hook on the end. Nobody, for that matter, ever asked Ostler Postle and he went a bitter and unfulfilled man to his grave, dug incidentally by his cousin, Jim Postle, not quite the last gravedigger in Lastfort. Jim Postle had always wanted a long pole with a hook on the end, but had to make do with corduroy trousers tied up with string.

Jack Postle's old grandfather, Joe Postle, was the last fletcher in Lastfort. He claimed to be a veteran of Agincourt, but of course he was a liar, unless he was 413 when he did his last bit of fletching. His arrows never flew very straight and Nelson refused point blank to use them at Trafalgar, saying that since he was reduced to one eye already he wasn't taking any chances.

"Look what happened to Harold at Hastings," he said to Hardy. (Mind you, in view of what happened to Nelson at Trafalgar, the last laugh certainly wasn't with him).

"The question of using arrows doesn't arise, admiral," Hardy responded. "We've got guns, you know."

But Nelson was holding his hearing aid to his good ear in addition to his telescope to his blind eye, not easy with one arm. How they won at Trafalgar God knows, but there you are. We respect the Henry Ford view of history at the Nostalgia Centre.

*

Sir Rodney was in his office. He was pretty sure he had got the day right. He was pretty sure he knew what he was doing. Still, he had an uneasy feeling. It turned to downright discomfort when Lionel Judge walked in.

Lionel Judge had thought to have the building to himself. But he had heard the clumping of boots in the executive corridor and followed the noise to Sir Rodney's office.

"Sir Rodney!" he said. "I didn't expect to see you."

Sir Rodney merely gazed back dejectedly and said, "Oh, God!"

"I'm glad, however," said Judge, "to find you here."

"Mr Judge," said Sir Rodney, "there's something most peculiar going on."

"Oh, I do agree."

"I don't really see how you can agree. I haven't said what it is."

"In that case, what did you mean?"

"The question is: what did *you* mean? I'm fully entitled to be in my own office. But it's very peculiar."

"Exactly," said Judge.

"So you've noticed?"

"Of course."

"That's good," said Sir Rodney. "I thought it was something to do with me." After all, it usually was. "The point is, I seem to be the only one here. Unless I count you. The whole works is deserted."

"It's Thursday evening," said Judge.

Sir Rodney permitted himself a smile. "You mean, the calendar's wrong? As well as the clock? Aha!" He nodded sagely and decided to set Lionel Judge a taxing question. "Can you think of a rhyme for 'spinnaker'?"

"I'm sorry?"

"That's all right," said Sir Rodney. "Neither can I."

"Sir Rodney," said Judge, "you might wonder why I'm here."

"Frankly," said Sir Rodney, "it has sometimes occurred to me that you're a rather unusual chap. It's Thursday evening. Surely you know it's pay day. Nobody works evenings on pay day."

"I could not rest. I had to come in to check the computer input for the pre-calcs of the non-classifiable trade report alignment."

"It's for my shanty," said Sir Rodney.

"What?"

"There aren't any rhymes for 'spinnaker'." He had consulted his great-grandmother's rhyming dictionary and he knew.

"Sir Rodney, the pre-calcs input..."

Sir Rodney had decided that on a Thursday evening this was really not good enough. "Mr Judge..." he began.

"This trade report alignment is not conduc..."

"Mr Judge!" And as Judge pulled up short in mid-"conducive", Sir Rodney permitted the ire of months to spill out. "Don't tell me about the trade report alignment. I don't wish to hear about the trade report alignment."

"Sir Rodney..." said Judge.

"If I may say so," said Sir Rodney, "bugger the trade report alignment! Confronted by you and your everlasting computer jargon, how can I, in the privacy of my office, on a supposedly quiet Thursday evening, sing the second verse of my sea shanty?" He paused. Damn it all – sing it he would!

He sang.

"Oh, the sadness of love is the lot of the sailor –
Heave-ho, my hearty Mrs. Green!
For it's nothing but blubber aboard a fine whaler –
Heave-ho, my hearty Mrs. Green!"

And as Lionel Judge reeled in astonishment, the chairman of the Pluvius works went on, "As I see it, Mr Judge, relic that I am of a freebooting era, and trammelled as I am by the electronic age that now envelops my beloved factory in my dear town of Lastfort, the only release I can contemplate is to burst out singing. Or, if frustrated in that, to put my head out of the window and scream. And come to think of it, I shall now do precisely that."

And he did.

Chapter Eleven

Nothing More Basic Than Nature

Lionel Judge was prepared to say that he was nothing if not tenacious. He arrived back in Sir Rodney's outer office the following morning, having searched his soul overnight and decided that he must begin to assert himself. Sir Rodney's concentration, always insubstantial, was now, he was convinced, fast disappearing.

Tot Needler had also arrived and Judge seized the opportunity to unburden himself.

"This may surprise you, Tot," he said, "but I have begun to have a feeling of being rebuffed."

"Is that so?"

"However, I am nothing if not tenacious."

Tot said he sympathised.

"What?"

"I used to believe," said Tot, "that I was nothing if not altruistic. Now I know I'm nothing."

Judge said he wasn't a man who needed sympathy and Tot said that in that case he sympathised again.

They entered Sir Rodney's office. Sir Rodney was gazing out of the window.

Judge coughed. Sir Rodney turned and bade them an abstracted good morning.

"Good morning, Sir Rodney," said Judge. "I have searched my soul."

"You have?" No time at all since breakfast, and the man was soul-searching! Merciful heaven!

"What I have to say is that we must regard Mrs Edgefield as a political opportunity."

Sir Rodney viewed him gloomily and said, "Whom as what?"

"Please! I have mentioned her several times."

Tot intervened to point out that Mrs Edgefield's husband was Minister with Responsibility for Phosphor Bronze in the Department of Trade.

"Poor devil!" said Sir Rodney.

"Somebody has to be," said Tot.

"So! Shall we consider the lady?" Judge persisted.

Sir Rodney said something like "Humph!" It was clear that this fellow Judge was not going to go away. Was the rôle of bizarre old stick, he began to ask himself, coming to the end of its usefulness? But he said nothing (apart, that was, from "Humph"). A pity, because Tot, whose day it was to feel sympathy, would have sympathised, having begun to question his own rôle in the continuing farce.

"Her impending visit here to name the jumbo thingie," said Judge, "is an event that we must take advantage of."

On the whole, Sir Rodney was slightly relieved to hear that subject mentioned, even by a philistine who ended a sentence with a preposition. He had someone in mind to perform the naming ceremony. He said so.

"But, Sir Rodney! – her husband is a man to watch," said Judge. "He may be the next Secretary of State but six."

"As soon as that?" said Tot. "God help us!"

"One of our own people, that's what I thought," said Sir Rodney. "To name the thingie, if you see what I mean."

Judge was revolted. "No, no!"

Sir Rodney grew a little testy. "Pluvius Works," he said. "Family affair. Keep it like that, I say."

It was becoming a trial of wills.

"I took it upon myself," said Judge, "to confirm Mrs Edgefield's invitation. Her husband, you see, is a man we might do well to impress, indeed must impress."

"Why?"

"Keeping in with the politicians," Tot inserted.

"Why?"

Tot had no idea, unless it was Judge's rôle in the farce.

Took it upon himself, indeed! Sir Rodney was appalled at this effrontery. He was also taken aback. Nevertheless, he knew he was not on firm ground. He muttered something about having always deplored political intervention.

"Precisely."

"What?"

"It's from the agenda of the past. But Michael Edgefield is a man for the unbridled market place. What's the next political scenario, we should ask?"

Perhaps they should. But would the thingie fettling industry in general, and the Pluvius Works in particular, be privatised? Those thingie fettling companies which could count on Ministry of Defence contracts might be sold off (or might not, given the growing scarcity of such contracts), but where stood the Pluvius Works in that respect? If history was any guide, probably filed away in a damp vault in the Duchy of Lancaster.

"It will never," said Sir Rodney, "be like the old days." When at a loss, fall back on legend.

"I take your point, believe me," said Judge, tugging his ears, "but we must be realists. There might even be a change of government. We can safely say that a socialist government will never privatise us."

"A Labour government might," said Tot.

"In any case," said Judge, "doors open, you know."

"They do what?" said Sir Rodney.

Judge fixed him with a steady eye. "Propitiate the politicians," he stated firmly. "Appease the Edgefields. Doors open to those who keep their noses clean."

He opened the door and went boldly out.

Sir Rodney slumped into his chair. A misplaced preposition followed by a mixed metaphor! Good God!

"We know what we must do, Sir Rodney," said Tot.

"Must? Must? We must do nothing!"

"Exactly! And do it to the best of our ability."

Tot went out and through Miss Pilbury's office. He noted that she too had slumped.

*

She had indeed. It was not a characteristic pose, but she was dispirited. Things were not what they once had been. They never had been, of course. That much she had gleaned from Omar Khayam. But that reflection didn't help. It never did. Omar was a thousand years old. A thousand years in which the world had learned nothing.

She shared Sir Rodney's conviction that the Pluvius Works as he and she had known it was sadly moribund. Or would Sir Rodney have said "in extremis"? Either way, their tears wouldn't wash out a word of it. So what must they do? Tot and Sir Rodney would have said, "Nothing." They would have said that doing nothing had worked for a thousand years.

"Bugger it!" said Miss Pilbury. Not a phrase she would normally have delivered. More characteristic of her old friend Gladys, really. But she was dispirited.

She was dispirited enough to suspect that the stars were setting and the caravan was starting for the dawn of nothing.

*

Jonty rose from his rickety sofa. He went to the kitchen sink and gargled. But not for long. He was wasting his time. He essayed a scale. "La-la-la!" He abandoned it. The sawbones had told him not to sing. So why was he singing? The sawbones could be wrong, couldn't he? They were always wrong. He tried again. "La-la-la!" But suppose the sawbones was right? Suppose he forced himself to sing? All right, he would force himself. But suppose he dropped down dead in the middle of *Bobby Shafto*"? Bloody hell! He went back to his rickety sofa.

*

There was one man who was fit to sing. Tot introduced him in the club that night, saying he was a man who needed no introduction, but he would introduce him anyway. He introduced him. Then he said he had introduced him. Oh, Tot had read his Public Speaker's Manual.

The man was Charlie Embleton, appearing in the guise of Tommy Wrench, who announced that he would sing the what-d'you-call-it song, which he had never sung at a gig, like, but here it was anyway: the what-d'you-call-it song, otherwise known as *The Thingie Fettler's Ditty*. He sang it. It went:

> *"Now I want to say this plainly so it's settled:*
> *When it comes to thingie fettling I'm the top,*
> *And I've turned out many a thingie finely fettled*
> *In the twenty years I've fettled in this shop.*
> *I started fettling thingies as a very callow lad.*
> *My dad before me fettled and I loved my fettling dad –*
> *A thingie fettling champion and the only dad I had.*
> *When a thingie's firmly fixed, you can't detach it,*
> *For a truly fettled thingie's there for life.*
> *It can't even be unfettled with a hatchet –*
> *And your fettler loves his thingie like his wife.*
> *Oh, there's more to fettling thingies than meets the layman's eye;*

141

> Your thingie man's a fettler till the very day he'll die –
> And then he'll go on fettling in that workshop in the sky."

He was grateful to the two ladies who accompanied him on the knackers and Jew's harp.

*

No, the Nostalgia Centre does not house Harry Hotspur's hamshank. It's not that we doubt the importance of Harry Hotspur's hamshank. After all, if Pascal was right and Cleopatra's nose might have influenced the entire earth's physiognomy, why not Harry Hotspur's hamshank? But we don't want to frighten Mrs Thirlaway, only to get her to shut up now and then. We don't think she would mind a ghost. Yes, we might advertise for a ghost.

In any case, try as we would we couldn't get Harry Hotspur's hamshank. Somebody mislaid it on the way back from the Battle of Shrewsbury. Are you familiar with the legend of Harry Hotspur's hamshank? If there's a sequel to this story, we might find room for it.

*

Beth laid down her brush and inquired if Walter was quite at ease. "Sprawled in that armchair, dear lord and master, in your socks, with your feet up on the sofa…"

Walter gazed at her sombrely, but did not respond. Another sorry week had drifted by. Surely a loving wife could manage to be understanding when her husband was heavy laden? It was bad enough that half of the room was swathed in sheets. It was a pretty chaotic scene to have to gaze on. A man liked to be heavy laden in comfort.

"You'll have to touch up that cornice," said Auntie Dinah.

"That's what I was thinking," said Walter. "You'll have to touch up that cornice, Beth." Not that he knew how she had the heart to paint the ceiling. First there was the toilet. Then the hall. Now she had arrived in the lounge. All this when she should have been solacing him in his despair.

"It's right mucky," said Auntie Dinah, "is that cornice."

"I know, I know," said Beth. "Just above where Walter used to smoke his pipe, before I dragged it away from him, for his own good. He still breathes there, mind you. Still, breathing's one pleasure I won't deny him. All right, I'm an artist who heeds the critics. I'll give it another coat."

"My twenty-first dispatch," Walter moaned. "The twenty-first reception I've conducted the choir at. And no leading tenor! Oh, dear! Oh, dear!"

"I wish you'd gone to a football match, Walter," said Beth. "At Borussia Mönchengladbach, for instance. It's unnatural having you sitting about the house on a Saturday afternoon." She moved his legs while she shifted her bucket of paint.

Walter found another resting place. Anybody would think, to hear his wife, that he was useless. "I'm not just sitting about," he said. "I'm sitting about and worrying. You forget that worrying's meat and drink to some of us. We can't all find fulfilment in a bucket of paint."

"It's not like you, Beth," said Auntie Dinah, "to have a mucky cornice."

"Give me a brush," said Walter, "and I'll touch up the cornice."

Beth declined with thanks. Besides, she knew it was a rhetorical offer, designed only to unleash some of her extravagant reminiscences. "I'll never forget, Auntie

142

Dinah, when he promised to block the bath in."

"Fancy!"

"I did block the bath in," said Walter.

"Across the top."

"She tells that lie," said Walter, "to everybody that still remembers unblocked-in baths."

"Without lies, domestic harmony would fly out of the window," said Beth. "You can fetch the stepladders in for me, there's a good lad."

Walter could do that fairly well, he was sure. "Why not? I fetched stepladders for you on our honeymoon." He went out.

"Why did he fetch stepladders on your honeymoon?" Auntie Dinah asked.

"We went to Tenerife," said Beth.

"I might have known."

Walter's voice was heard calling. "There's just one small matter, Beth. Where are the stepladders?"

"He'll find them in a minute," Beth predicted.

"I thought you went to the Scilly Isles."

"You don't need stepladders on the Scilly Isles."

Sounds of a crash proclaimed that Walter had found the stepladders.

"Something else I'll never forget, Auntie Dinah – the night he proposed to me. Stood at our gate in the moonlight for forty minutes. Couldn't tear himself away."

Walter laboured in with the stepladders. "How was I to know your dad had just painted it?"

"Ah!" said Beth. "Another of those whoppers we tell about each other."

"That's right," said Walter. "It was your mother." He set up the stepladders. "Will it be all right if I sit down now and worry some more?"

"I never had a honeymoon," said Auntie Dinah. "I never even had a pair of stepladders."

"Neither of them's what they're cracked up to be," said Beth, "except possibly the stepladders."

Unrest was in the air. Hence the compensatory extra-mural waggishness. Beth reflected that Randolph Scott would have said there was a wind blowing from the Rio Grande. Damn it, he did say it in *West of the Pecos*. Would they all one day fettle thingies in heaven with Tommy Wrench? It was a consummation not to look forward to. What were pecos?

"I'll have to tell him, you know," said Walter. "Sir Rodney – he doesn't know that Jonty's still got no singing voice." He groaned. "And the dispatching platform's erected, did I mention?"

"In your sleep," said Beth.

"The signwriters have painted the name on the side of the jumbo thingie."

"You didn't mention that," said Beth.

"Peacock," said Walter.

"What's that?"

"That's what they're calling it. I've said."

"What?"

"The jumbo thingie, woman! And Mrs Edgefield's naming it."

"What?" said Auntie Dinah.

"Peacock! I said!"

"Did she live in Stackpool Street? I thought she was dead."

"I keep saying! She's the lady who's naming the thingie!"

"I thought you said it had a name."

"It has! But she's naming it officially!"

"I thought you said she was naming it Peacock," said Auntie Dinah.

"We'll thank you to leave the badinage to us, Auntie Dinah," said Beth. "Anyway, take no notice of Walter. He's making it all up to confuse you."

"Mrs Edgefield," Walter explained doggedly, "is the wife of the Minister with Special Responsibility for Phosphor Bronze in Thingie Fettling."

"See what I mean?" said Beth.

In the years since 1891, several hundred jumbo thingies had been dispatched. Sir Rodney was in danger of running out of birds' names. The last three had been Pochard, Dunlin and Hoopoe. The practice of naming them all after birds meant that thingies' names were becoming ever more esoteric. The newly-fettled Peacock was being so called only because the original Peacock, back in 1923, had been named by a lady ornithologist, who insisted on calling it Phasianidae. The signwriter who painted it was on the sick for a fortnight.

"But the whole thing'll be a fiasco," said Walter. "No tenor for the choir!"

"Worse things happen on the recreation ground lake," said Auntie Dinah.

Walter had no time to ponder this profundity before there was a hesitant knocking at the front door.

"You wouldn't call that a ready money knock," Auntie Dinah said, as she went to answer.

In a moment, there were excited cries from the lobby. "Speak of the devil!" Auntie Dinah was shouting. "It's that old gadgie!"

"Now she's lapsing into the vernacular," Beth said. "Heaven knows what next."

"We should never have let her out of the cupboard," said Walter.

But Auntie Dinah had returned, regally ushering in the visitor.

"Ah, Mrs – er…" said Sir Rodney, bowing to Beth. He turned to Walter, who was up and hopping agitatedly in his socks. "And good afternoon to you, Mr – er – Lester…" He eyed Walter gravely. "So! It seems you've been keeping something from me."

"Oh, my God!" Walter said.

*

There were those, mind you, who would have claimed that the best place to be on such a day was the deep green countryside.

"A gorgeous September afternoon," was Elaine's opinion, as they dismounted from Oswald's proletarian motor bike a few miles beyond Bellingham.

"Idyllic," was how Oswald put it.

Well, it was all right. They were agreed on that.

Oswald could have afforded a small car, it might not be worth repeating. But it's repeated now. He had once come fairly close to buying one, but had resisted the craven surrender to convention.

"Just the faintest of breezes," Elaine murmured. "Lovely."

"And the ground's soft enough for a good studhold," Oswald said. They would be kicking off just about now, he knew, at St. James's Park in the Newcastle United-Sheffield Wednesday soccer match. Surrender? Wasn't he yielding a huge chunk of principle? Wasn't he placing this beautiful young woman ahead of a game of football?

Elaine knew. "What a sacrifice you made!"

"My word! I feel noble!" He felt treacherous.

"No regrets?"

"No regrets," said Oswald. He had terrible regrets. "They melted away," he lied, "when you turned up in that most frugal of T-shirts and those jeans that flirt with indecency."

"Don't talk like that," said Elaine, "within earshot of a herd of frisky young bullocks."

"Can't shock them," said Oswald. "There's nothing more basic than nature."

He wheeled the bike through a gate. "Dump your helmet and anything else here," he said. "Don't worry," he added, as Elaine hesitated. "They'll be here until those cows come home. We're not in the heart of civilisation, where somebody's liable to take your eyeballs and come back for the sockets."

"I've a feeling nothing has stirred here for a hundred years."

"Two hundred years ago," said Oswald, "there was plenty a-stirring. You know – border skirmishes with the Scots. Hard to believe, isn't it, that this place's history is soaked in blood? You can't turn round twice in Northumberland without getting dizzy on the site of a battle."

They crossed a rustic bridge and Elaine gazed down at the waters beneath. "That's the North Tyne, isn't it?"

"Yes. Odd how for some folks the word 'Tyne' just means a mucky industrial river."

"Well, part of it is."

"Only the last few miles. The rest of it's a beautiful stream flowing through marvellous countryside." That was the end of his commercial for the Northumbrian Tourist Board. "Shall we climb up on to that fell to have our picnic?"

Elaine put her hand in his. He was reading her script, but might still need some prompting. Mind you, women too made sacrifices. Didn't they? What were they?

*

Lionel Judge was in his tiny office at the deserted Saturday afternoon Pluvius Works. He was making a telephone call, speaking in initials.

"Yes, yes, C.H., I know it's Saturday, but there's always work for a chap like me... Yes, a workaholic, you could say that. I hear you're no longer at HQ? What? Oh, well, the grapevine, you know... I've heard from QQ at HQ... Set up a consultancy, I hear, right? That's the game these days... Oh, things are fine here. Well... I'm licking them into shape. That's not to say I don't keep my eye peeled for openings... Well, consultancy, for instance... Yes, well, C.H., I'm not tied hand and foot to the Pluvius Works... What? Rumours? Closing? The Pluvius Works? Well, it's an unstable world... I keep my options open... Now that you're running your own consultancy business, C.H... Thingie fettling could be a dying industry. Nothing lasts forever... Anyway, I'm pleased life's treating you well... As I say, I'd be more than keen to try my hand at consultancy... Yes... I'll be in touch, C.H... 'Bye for now."

*

"Mind you, I do feel a bit guilty," Oswald said…

One moment. You may have inferred that we at the Nostalgia Centre eschew references to sex. Not at all, as long as Mrs Thirlaway, our arbiter in these matters, is not too offended. As it happens, censorious termagant though she is, she finds the following scene acceptable. Here goes, then…

"I do feel a bit guilty," Oswald was saying.

"M'm?" said Elaine.

"Out here enjoying myself. While your dad's back home, worrying over his thingie dispatch."

They had found a picnic spot looking down on the valley.

Elaine squeezed his hand. "That's his way of enjoying himself. It's hot. Let's just rest for a while before we eat."

Oswald spread a rug and they sat.

"And then there's Uncle Jonty…" he said.

"Oh, him!" Elaine echoed Auntie Dinah.

"Yes, but it's a shame about his mislaid singing voice. And the union – I feel I should be worrying about that as well. Why was I cursed with a conscience?"

"It's not your fault you're a saint. Nobody's imperfect." She contemplated the dozing valley below. There was not a soul in sight for miles. Oswald had said the T-shirt was frugal, so what was the difference if it came off while she sunbathed?

All very well, but this was further taxing a peerless conscience.

Elaine stretched out, face down. "You can cream my back if you like."

"Well, all right." But he would have to force himself.

"The lotion's in my bag."

It took him a moment or two to find it. When he turned back, her bra was mysteriously unfastened and lay discarded. He knew about bras. He was not the President of the Football Association. But she was face down. Decorum was uncompromised.

He creamed her back. He didn't really mind.

"Oswald," Elaine murmured presently, "are you going to stay in thingie fettling or something like that all your life?"

"It depends on how unambitious I turn out to be."

"I seem to see you as more of a great outdoors sort of man. Felling trees. Building dams. In your glasses."

"Like one of Auntie Dinah's long-lost lads, I always wanted to shoot rapids."

"You don't get rich shooting rapids. Just pneumonia. Not that I want you to get rich."

"Nor I. But as long as I don't want to get rich, I might as well languish in thingie fettling."

"That won't do. If you're going to be unambitious, you might as well be unambitious at something you enjoy."

"That's all very well, but I can't rub your back for the rest of my life."

"So you've stopped loving me already?"

"It's not that, but my glasses are steaming up. Anyway, thingie fettling might collapse and shrivel into dust."

"You sound like dad's nightmare," said Elaine. She wriggled ecstatically. "You've

146

got a lovely touch."

Oswald rubbed lightly on. "If it does survive," he asked, "can you see me escaping from the grip of industry? Or can you see me, thirty years from now, still in the Estimating Department, if it's still there – Chief Estimator, perhaps... Fat. Bald. Defeated."

Elaine groaned slightly at that.

"So we'd better escape?" said Oswald.

"Yes! Tomorrow!"

"Well, the day after." He stopped rubbing. Elaine didn't move. "Your back's done," he said.

"Then you know what to do," was the barely audible reply.

"What?"

"You're a cook, aren't you?" said Elaine. "Turn me over, you fool."

*

Walter was casting feverishly about for his slippers. Beth swept his newspaper aside, moved sheets from an armchair and ushered Sir Rodney into it. Sir Rodney was muttering that he hoped his visit was not – er – inconvenient.

"Auntie Dinah," said Beth, "do you know who this is?"

"I've just said," said Auntie Dinah. "He's the recreation park groundsman. Mind, he's cleaned his boots."

"What! Oh, dear!" Beth decided to complete the introduction. "It's Sir Rodney Eames, the company chairman."

Good heavens! The man had come up in the world in a few short weeks. Auntie Dinah shook Sir Rodney's hand. "Pleased to meet you again, I'm sure."

Beth turned to Walter. "This is nice, isn't it, Walter?" Sir Rodney had never been under their roof before. What could possibly be the reason for this visit? "Isn't it nice, Walter?"

Walter was under the table. "Oh, it's nice," he said. "Very nice."

Sir Rodney had taken note of the stepladders. There was a bucket of paint on top of them. It seemed he had called at the wrong moment after all. He half rose. "Perhaps I'd better..."

"Please make yourself at home," Beth urged him.

"You're very kind. I couldn't resist your invitation to tea and sausage rolls." He thought for several moments, bidding some small talk to spring to his tongue. None emerged. He decided to come to the point. "As I was saying, Mr – er – Lester..."

Walter had come out from under the table with one slipper. "Yes, Sir Rodney?"

"You've been keeping something from me."

"Oh, dear."

"About the choir."

"Have you seen my left slipper, Beth?" Walter asked desperately.

"We shall have to have a chat," said Sir Rodney.

"Shall we?"

"The leading tenor of the works choir, which you so worthily conduct..."

"Thank you," said Walter miserably.

"The leading tenor, Montague Harebell..."

"Jonathan Harwood."

147

"Who?"

"The leading tenor."

"That's the chap – Montague Harebell," said Sir Rodney. "He still won't be able to sing his customary solo at the dispatch reception, I gather."

Walter ought to have known. How foolish to suppose Sir Rodney would have missed those abysmal tidings!

"Because his voice is still lost," said Sir Rodney.

"Not entirely," Walter amended. "He did lose it, but he found it again. In the backyard."

"Found it?"

"Yes."

"Ah."

"But not enough to sing," Walter mumbled.

"Exactly!" said Sir Rodney, adding a strangely triumphant "Aha!"

Life was unfair, Walter felt. He was at sufficient disadvantage without being reduced to one slipper. "I was going to tell you, Sir Rodney," he said.

"You were?"

"He was, Sir Rodney," said Beth, "but I hope you'll understand what it's like to be a coward."

That was something Sir Rodney understood very well.

"Mind you, it's not Jonty's fault," said Walter.

"Whose?"

"The leading tenor."

"You mean Montague Harebell?"

"I suppose so."

"That's what I thought. So the position is – we must find a tenor from somewhere."

Walter said yes, that was the position. Beth rose. Auntie Dinah, who had kept wonderfully silent, sat on the sofa, preparing herself to talk, when the opportunity arose, about her scattered progeny.

"And have you, as conductor, any ideas?" asked Sir Rodney. "Or are you bereft?"

"That's what I am," said Walter.

Sir Rodney leaned forward, conquered diffidence, and spoke with the practised authority of the paternal employer. "In that case, *I* have something to say. You and I, Mr Lester, are going to have a very serious talk."

"I'll put the kettle on," said Beth, "and we'll have a cup of tea."

She went kitchenwards.

"I could darn that for you, Walter," said Auntie Dinah.

His big toe was sticking out of his sock.

*

Elaine and Oswald had walked on and reached the top of the fell.

"I know you're an anti-romantic," Elaine said.

"Oh?"

"So I'll go along with you on that. Let's say that I'm just an ordinary girl."

"Fine," said Oswald. "You're just an ordinary girl."

Elaine hoped the fool wasn't always going to be as agreeable as that.

If this were romance, of course, she would be the archetypal juvenile lead. That "if"

148

may seem a bit indefinite, but it leaves the options open, to purloin some of Lionel Judge's jargon. We who superintend nostalgia centres must borrow a bit of that commodity from time to time. Besides, we all have our own ideas of archetypes. So Elaine would be entirely gorgeous to those romantics who expected it of her, and her gorgeousness would be of the kind they relished. For the realists, she would be just another young woman.

As for her character, she would be generous, forbearing, affable, considerate, beguiling, niggardly, impatient, unprepossessing, thoughtless and disconcerting – depending on what we were looking for.

And Oswald? He was just another young man. Except to a romantic.

"You see," he said, voicing the realism. "it all depends on what we're looking for."

"Oh."

"Then again, we might be in love, which happens even to anti-romantics."

"I bet you wish you knew what you were talking about," Elaine said. She conventionally hugged him. Then she gazed down the fell. "Is this about as high as we can get?"

"Probably," Oswald said. "We've got the rest of our lives to find out."

"Mm."

"But yes, this is the top of the fell. If we shout like mad, we'll hear the echo roll magnificently."

Embracing, they shouted for joy. The echo answered. Magnificently? Or was it just another echo?

*

Avril fanned herself. "Hot, dad," she said.

They were sitting in the recreation park. The children played close by.

"It is that," said Tot. "And yet – it feels a bit autumnal."

Symbolism? Good grief! Was he succumbing to the malaise that seemed to be settling on Sir Rodney and Miss Pilbury? Not he, surely? – the old warrior who had finessed his way to a few dozen victories, and no wounds inflicted. Well, not many.

"I had another letter from Arthur this morning," said Avril.

"Oh?"

"I'm pretty sure this'll be his last voyage – if he can find a shore job."

"Ah, yes."

"Well, he wants to watch the bairns grow up."

"Quite right."

Victories? What victories? It had all been mock warfare, followed by mock peace. "Peace," he mused aloud, "is not only better than war, but infinitely more arduous."

"When did Shaw say that, dad?"

"Don't be cheeky, young woman. Preface to *Heartbreak House*, as it happens."

The ritual dance was beginning to pall, even though it belonged to the dear old time warp he'd enjoyed living in. He had always practised a healthy scepticism, but avoided incredulity. "Believe what you can, disbelieve what you must," he said, "and I forget where Shaw said that." Perhaps somebody else would take over and leave him to Mozart.

They called the children and wandered off.

*

149

If Sir Rodney hoped to embark at once on his serious chat, he reckoned without Auntie Dinah who, having prepared herself, had decided that her opportunity had arrived.

"Been a funny kind of day," she said, "as they used to say in our backlane." Indeed. It was the immemorial conversational opening.

Sir Rodney was not disposed to disagree.

"September," said Auntie Dinah. "The nights are putting in. Or the days are cutting off. Take your pick. Oh, there was a lot of funny things said in our backlane. Would make your hair curl. For a start, plenty was said about me and my late husband."

"Is that so?"

"It wasn't true, not more than half of it." She surveyed Sir Rodney. "Tell me, have you ever grown, or have you ever considered growing, a short clipped moustache?"

"I grew a beard."

"Where was that?"

"In minesweepers."

"You have a look of my late husband, before he died. Or would, if you had a short clipped moustache. He hated combinations. Do you wear combinations?"

Sir Rodney had no idea. "I could ask my housekeeper."

"Hated them, he did. It was because I always used to clap the bairns into thick combinations on the 31st of August. I mean, take our Dan."

"During the war," said Sir Rodney.

"Pardon?"

"I grew a beard."

"Excuse me, I'm talking about our Dan. Delicate, he was." She turned to Walter. "It's on the sideboard."

"What is?"

"Your slipper. I lost one, you know," she informed Sir Rodney.

"Where was that?"

"I think you mean when."

"What?"

"Please yourself. One of my bairns: I lost one of my bairns. Dr. Wrigley used to say, 'Missus, your bairns are between you and your wits.' Oh, he had a clever way with words, the doddery old fool. Take the time when our Dan caught his knee in the park railings. They brought him home with his elbow like a pudding."

Sir Rodney was puzzled. "His knee, you mean?"

"Eh?"

"You said his elbow."

"I said his knee."

"So you did," Sir Rodney conceded. "What about his elbow?"

"Excuse me," said Auntie Dinah. "Is it you or me that's telling this story?"

Heaven forbid that they should return to the subject of the choir, Walter felt, but Sir Rodney seemed in some need of rescue. He put on his recovered slipper and said, "I don't like to blame young Oswald, Sir Rodney."

"Er..?"

"Oswald Gorman."

"I don't suppose this has anything to do with the knee in the railings?" said Sir Rodney.

"I don't think you follow me," said Walter.

"My point exactly," said Sir Rodney.

"The lost tenor, Sir Rodney. All that business of the bill for the bunting."

"Ah!"

"You see," said Auntie Dinah, "when he wrenched his knee, out of the railings…"

"This Oswald person?"

"Our Dan! I'm telling you! He fell sideways and caught his elbow in the fireman's back. Black and blue, it was. Up like a pudding."

"What fireman was this?"

"He didn't give his name. Dr. Wrigley wouldn't come. He said his bicycle was punctured."

Walter inserted some more exposition. "That's where Jonty lost his voice. Er – that's Montague to you."

"Not in the park?"

"At the union mass meeting. Shall we have a short rest?"

They sat back for a moment or two. Then Sir Rodney said, "Opera!"

"Pardon?"

"I'm a bit of an opera buff, you know."

"I knew for a fact it was a lie," said Auntie Dinah.

"What?"

"About his bicycle, what else? His bicycle was outside the Conservative Club that very night. It was a nasty injury. Affected his kidney."

"The knee injury?"

"Eh?"

"Or the elbow?"

"No, no, I'm talking about the fireman's back! His name was Phipps, now I come to think. He couldn't use his hose for a fortnight. Well, he wouldn't, with a bad kidney." She sat back and began to nod.

The serious chat was clearly slipping away from Sir Rodney. He made a firm effort to retrieve it. "About the choir, Mr – er – Lester…" He pronounced sternly. "A tenor soloist. You will have to find a tenor soloist."

Walter braced himself. Retribution was at hand. Auntie Dinah snored gently.

"Mi, mi, mi," said Sir Rodney.

"Pardon?" said Walter.

But Sir Rodney had merely been striking a note. This was preparatory to bursting into song, which he now did, in a very fine tenor voice, while Walter gazed at him in astonishment.

"Your tiny hand is frozen," sang Sir Rodney.

"It would have been "Heave-ho, my hearty Mrs. Green," but he never did find a rhyme for "spinnaker".

Chapter Twelve

The Last Quill Penpusher

The ghost of Sir Rodney's grandfather's horse materialised beside the trough and gazed up at Sir Rodney's window. Sir Rodney wasn't there. He wouldn't be. It was Saturday. The horse reflected that he was growing as absent-minded as Sir Rodney. Well, he supposed anything was possible in the time warp that man Tot Needler was always talking about.

He had been thinking about Shakespeare again. A remarkable fellow, that. A poet who didn't need a rhyming dictionary. Truly eminent. The horse swished his tail, for want of something better to do. Time seemed to be running out. He probably wouldn't make many more non-appearances at this old trough. Well, not in this story. He would be back on the day of the jumbo dispatch, of course, It would be raining. It always rained on jumbo dispatches.

After that, what? He might haunt the Nostalgia Centre. Surely a Nostalgia Centre ought to have a ghost? He would watch the Sits Vac in the *Celestial Gazette*.

*

When he had finished *Your Tiny Hand is Frozen*, Sir Rodney demonstrated that the popular ballad was as much in his repertoire as the operatic aria and sang movingly, *Macushla, Macushla*, in the direction of Auntie Dinah, who slept on.

Beth had paused in her tea-making and was framed in the doorway.

"Walter," she said, "you're in the presence of not quite Jose Carreras."

Walter knew. After a suitable deferential delay, he got around to asking Sir Rodney if he would – could he possibly? – please! – sing solo at the dispatch reception. Sir Rodney refrained from saying, "You booby! Why else do you suppose I've paid this melodramatic visit?" He merely smiled and nodded. And Auntie Dinah sat up and said why didn't he sing *Macushla*? Her late husband had often sung *Macushla*, after closing time.

Then, of course, nothing would do but that Sir Rodney should sing the song that dominated every dispatch reception – the incomparable, irreplaceable *Bobby Shafto*. And Walter, overcome with joy and tears, rushed across the room to embrace Beth, tripped over Auntie Dinah's feet and stumbled into the stepladders.

So the bucket of paint teetered, discharging half of its contents, and Sir Rodney – at the point where Bobby Shafto was combing down his yellow hair – was covered in white emulsion. Sir Rodney assured them that it was as nothing to what went on in mine sweepers during the war. Hands were shaken all round and Sir Rodney and Walter clutched each other in a paroxysm of hysterical mirth.

*

Lionel Judge stood upon a small gangway which commanded a view of the bay in which Jumbo Thingie Peacock was cradled. There he was joined by Tot Needler. They both gazed at the resplendent casing. The day of the dispatch was close at hand.

"Another monument to man's labour," Tot suggested.

"All shoulders to the wheel," said Judge.

"Every man to his platitude," said Tot.

"Yes, we've got through," said Judge, "in spite of dislocations, delays and threats of – er…"

"Industrial action," said Tot. Every man to his euphemism. "Not in spite of them," he continued. "Because of them." And he answered Judge's quizzical look by adding, "It's the sheer quarrelsomeness of human nature that ensures its survival. Anyway, you and I have jointly won the ultimate accolade."

Oh, yes, they had appeared on television; the icon of the late twentieth century had embraced them. They had been jointly interviewed in a documentary entitled *The Fettling of a Thingie*. They had been filmed, mouthing those platitudes and euphemisms to which a man is entitled, to an inserted backdrop of the Plodge Burn as it gently lapped effluent over its tiny jetty.

"It's not all roses, you know," said Judge.

"It certainly isn't."

"I mean, Tot, that Jumbo Thingie Peacock is now 27.13 per cent above estimated total cost. Today's computer reports are not sanguine."

Those latest ill tidings, tossed off by the computer during a rare coughless spell, had caused him to lock himself in the data stationery cupboard for half-an-hour with tranquillizers while he darkly contemplated giving it all up. If he had been a son of Auntie Dinah, thoughts of seeking bliss in Grimsby might have occurred to him.

But not very earnestly. The 21st Century would require men like him. In consultancy. It seemed to him that the less work there was, the greater would be the need for consultants. Besides, he had a wife to think of. His own, yes. We have established that he was married? It's not germane. Let it go.

"There will be those advising and those receiving advice," he told Tot, "in the new era."

"I see," said Tot. "And where will the wealth come from?"

"Where does wealth always come from?"

Tot said that, unless Marx was right, there was no answer to that.

"Precisely."

"What a deeply religious man you are!" Tot said. "By the way…"

"Yes?"

"When will the works be closed?"

Judge was taken aback. He had not expected such bluntness from this gentle diplomat.

"When?" Tot persisted.

Judge drew breath. "I can only reiterate," he said, "that there is no official proposal – to my knowledge – to that effect."

Tot said, "H'm."

"In any case," said Judge, "we still remain publicly owned, do we not? And even though I abhor socialism… No offence."

Tot was not offended. "In any other case, Lionel," he said, "public ownership is not necessarily socialism. It has done nothing, for instance, about stratification of income, which has frustrated every government for as long as I can remember; and I mean all income, not just wages."

"So! You advocate egalitarianism?"

"Though cowards flinch and traitors sneer."

"It doesn't work." Any more than his tranquillizers.

"Would you like to hear what a great socialist pioneer once said?" Tot asked.

Judge couldn't think of anything he would like less, but he listened with remarkably good grace.

"He pointed out," said Tot, "that we've got economic equality between captains. We've got economic equality between cabin boys. What we need, he propounded, is economic equality between captains and cabin boys."

Lionel Judge said, "God save us!" to that.

*

"You'll be making a Yorkshire pudding, will you?" said Jonty. "I say you'll be making a Yorkshire pudding?"

It was Sunday. Oswald invariably made a Yorkshire pudding on Sunday. "You'll be going to the club?" he asked, from behind his *Observer*.

"Eh?"

They had established that it was Sunday. If Oswald stayed in and made a Yorkshire pudding on a Sunday, Jonty always left him to it and went to the club, returning, brown ale replete, for Sunday dinner. With Yorkshire pudding.

"I'm not going to the club!" Jonty barked.

"Good heavens!" said Oswald. "That I should live to hear those words!"

"Do I have to go to the club? There's no law that says I have to go to the club!"

"Hear, hear!" said Oswald.

"What d'you mean – 'Hear, hear'? I don't need 'Hear, hear' from you. Not you and all the penpushers."

They were speaking to each other again.

Jonty peered at the oven. "Put the joint in, have you?"

"No."

"You should put the joint in. I mean! You'll have to put the joint in. Here! Shall I put it in?"

"Why don't you just go to the club?"

"I'm not going to the club! I'm going to stop here and put the joint in."

"Ah!" said Oswald, "There's a special arrangement for the joint this week. Not to mention the Yorkshire pudding."

"Off his rocker! The useless beggar's off his rocker!" Jonty muttered. He took a turn around the room. Bloody penpusher! Now he hadn't the sense to put a joint in. "By gum," he said, "I've put some joints in in my time. I've won medals for putting joints in. Yorkshire pudding! Green peas and custard! I could do the lot! And for why? I'll tell you for why!"

Oswald was sure he would.

Jonty plunged into a maudlin catalogue. "Because it was every soul for himself! Those were the days when there was nobody without a raggy arse! None of your namby-pamby modern rigmarole like canteens! No first-aid! No toilets! Toilets! What? If you wanted a run-off on a winter's day, you had to go behind the fettling shed and make piss-holes in the snow." He wept. "How many of the young 'uns in this day and age could do that?" Very few. And it was the kind of superannuated anecdote that we at the Nostalgia Centre strenuously resist. "Sixty years! And now I cannot even sing at the dispatch reception. The bloody doctor says I've got to rest my bloody voice. What the hell's that?"

It was the back door opening and a voice crying "Yoo-hoo!"

"It's that old woman!" Jonty said.

Auntie Dinah entered and kissed Oswald.

"I told you, Uncle Jonty," Oswald said, "that there was a special arrangement. Now listen! On Tuesday, Auntie Dinah vacuumed all the way through the house. Right?"

"That's right," said Auntie Dinah. "I bottomed your muck."

"On Wednesday, she changed the curtains."

"On Thursday, I did the washing," said Auntie Dinah.

"Aye, and on Friday," said Jonty, "you chucked out my underwear."

"And now," said Auntie Dinah, "I've come to cook your Sunday joint." She bound on a pinny. "Where's your roaster, Oswald? I hope you've got the taters peeled."

"Bloody hell!" said Jonty.

"And *you* can keep out of my way!" said Auntie Dinah. "A woman likes a kitchen to herself. You'll find that out when you're married, young Oswald."

"Married?" said Jonty. "Who's getting married?"

"It's another of those rumours," said Oswald.

"Oh, I'm not as young as I was," said Auntie Dinah, "but I can still see a thing or two without binoculars."

"Married!" said Jonty. And the young numskull was standing there looking pleased about it! Anyway, what was so special about getting married? Any daft beggar could get married. He, Jonty Harwood, had never got married! What!

"Oh, aye," said Auntie Dinah. "Our Elaine's not barmy. She's like me; she knows a nice randy lad when she spots one." She pointed at Jonty. "Mind you, Oswald, fifty years ago, even he wasn't bad-looking, you wouldn't believe." She dumped a parcel on the table. "And you owe me for these," she told Jonty.

"Eh?"

"Three new sets of vests and pants."

"Listen, missus!" said Jonty, growing red and preparing to assert himself.

"Give over!" said Auntie Dinah. "You're cluttering up my kitchen."

Her kitchen! "Listen! Listen!" Jonty shouted.

Auntie Dinah quelled him with a look. "*You* listen, Casablanca! I'm used to handling crabby old buggers like you. I mangle them with the washing." She started pulling open cupboard doors. "Where's all the pans, then?"

"Tell you what, Uncle Jonty," said Oswald.

"Eh?"

"We'll both go to the club."

*

"So that's my news, Miss Pilbury," said Sir Rodney. "It was half-expected, you know."

"But, Sir Rodney..." said Elsie Pilbury.

"No more palatable for that, be it said."

An offer of sorts had been made to him. It had come from headquarters. It was the kind of offer that had been likely ever since the confusing changes had begun to be

155

made at the Pluvius Works.

"You haven't actually told me," said Elsie. "You haven't given me any news."

Well, no. But he would quite possibly get around to it, given patience and coherence on their respective parts. The burden of the offer was that in the light of certain recommendations – from an undisclosed source – it was suggested that Sir Rodney might consider relinquishing his chairmanship. The reason? It was something to do with alleged mountainous costs of Jumbo Thingie Peacock and various extravagances incurred in lavish dispatch ceremonies.

"It's good of you to confide in me, Sir Rodney," Elsie said. She meant it, even though he hadn't quite.

"Not at all."

He had been invited to take up another post. Headquarters wanted to be fair to him. They had offered him the appointment of director in charge of stationery.

"Well, anyway..." said Elsie.

"Why shouldn't I confide in you, Miss Pilbury? I remember you as a shy young typist with your ginger hair tumbling down your back. Whom should I tell if not you?"

"Thank you, Sir Rodney."

Of course he intended to decline the offer. "So that's it," he said firmly. "I shall be leaving the Pluvius Works." He turned and marched with dignity into his office.

Elsie Pilbury stared after him. So that was his news! Leaving! And how kind he was, telling her, or almost telling her, or doing his best to tell her! The dear old fool! She dabbed her eyes. She was also asking herself who in heaven's name were all these young women with tumbling ginger hair he kept remembering.

*

"Jonty!" said Walter.

"I know," said Jonty. "Come into the cabin."

He did so, shutting out the fettling noises.

"Well, she'll be off the day after tomorrow," said Walter.

"Eh?"

"The jumbo thingie, what else?"

"Oh, aye, the jumbo bloody thingie! And before you say it, it's your twentieth dispatch, not your twenty-first. And you've no need to shake like a raspberry jelly. I've got you through nineteen dispatches. I'll get you through this one."

"I had a dream last night," said Walter.

Jonty groaned, and as Walter went resolutely on through the recital of the familiar nightmare, he said, "I know! I know, I know! I bloody know!"

"I'm sorry you won't be able to sing at the reception," said Walter.

"I'll bet you are. Got yourself another tenor quick enough, didn't you?"

"What?"

"You know what I mean."

"I don't know what you mean. Well... Anyway, Sir Rodney's a very good tenor."

"Maybe you can do without me altogether?"

"If you're going to get humpty about it, maybe I can."

"What!"

"I didn't mean it."

He didn't, but the rag was red enough for the argumentative old bull. "So it's come to this! I'm derundant!"

"You're pretty close."

"I struggled to get here. I forced myself back to work. But I'm not wanted. It's just like I was saying to Charlie Embleton."

"Tommy Wrench."

"Him that's a spronker in the zilted spindle shop."

"He's a zilter in the spindled spronkle shop."

"It's the same thing."

"To a blind horse, it isn't."

"Oh, I told him."

"Told him what?"

"I've forgotten, haven't I?"

There was a knock at the door and Charlie Embleton entered.

"Hello, Tommy!" said Walter.

"What cheer, Charlie!" said Jonty.

"Have you got a minute, Walter?" said Charlie. "A minute! Have you got a minute, like? A bit of news I've got. I've got a bit of news, like."

"Oh, no!" said Walter, naturally fearing the worst. "Don't tell me! It's the Apocalypse!"

"No, it's better than that," said Charlie. "Are you busy, like? I can come back. I thought you might be interested, like. I can come back, though. If you're busy, like."

"News!" said Jonty. "I'm sick of bloody news! After all the palaver, fiddle-faddle and flapdoodle we've had! Stoppages! Mass meetings! Punch-ups! And I lose my voice! All over that bloody bill for the bunting!"

"That's it, though," said Charlie. "That's it, like!"

It occurred to Walter that the excitable and incomprehensible messenger might after all have intelligence of some import. "Nice and easy, Tommy," he said.

"No, but I'm telling you, like! I was talking to old what-d'you-call-him. You know who I mean. Doddery old bloke with Santie Claus whiskers. Works in the office basement. Keeps the historic records. With a quill pen. They let him out in the daylight twice a year. He staggered upstairs yesterday, like. With a roll of parchment. D'you know what he told what-d'you-call-him? You know who I mean, like. Him with the itchy ears. He told him that the cost of the bunting at each and every thingie dispatch, like – well, it's provided for in Sir Rodney's grandfather's will. In his will, like. It's paid for in – in…"

"Perpetuity?" said Walter.

"That's it, like! There's what they call a Bunting Trust. A Bunting Trust, they call it, like. You see, Walter, like? There's never been a bill for the bunting. Ta-ta, well."

*

It wasn't perhaps the worst exit line Charlie Embleton/Tommy Wrench had ever had.

But the time warp crumbles, for him and for all of them. It will reassemble, of course. They will go back to the best times or the worst, whichever they select. The worst times are the best for some of us guilt-ridden inadequates (Tot Needler and the human condition, *passim*).

Still, if you happen to find yourself near the Nostalgia Centre, drop in on us. You'll meet our latest recruit, the former ancient archivist of the Pluvius works, dredged from its basement. He is old Zach Postle, the last quill penpusher in Lastfort. Will he be able to explain why he has a long pole with a hook on the end? Probably not.

*

Elsie Pilbury, tearful but bravely recovering, entered Sir Rodney's office.

"I am fifty-eight, Sir Rodney," she said.

"Are you really?" said Sir Rodney. "Oh! Congratulations! I didn't know it was your birthday."

"No. That was last month."

"Oh, well, as long as you've remembered."

"I mean – I'm due to retire in less than two years. I shan't wait." She had to dab her eyes again. "I'll go when you go."

"Oh, no!"

"Yes! I couldn't stay if you were gone."

Sir Rodney rose. What was this? He was inexpressibly moved. Dear, dear! Well, well! He cleared his throat. "Well, well! Dear, dear!" he said.

"After all," said Miss Pilbury, "the moving Finger writes and having writ moves on."

"Of course! It does, now you mention it."

"I've been reciting that at the club. I don't think they like it."

Sir Rodney said it was the way of the world. That was a truism. What he had noticed about truisms was that they were true. "Perhaps the world no longer has any use for such as we." He went to the window. Well, he was not going to depart this place, he had determined, without a small orgy of defiance.

The naming ceremony of the jumbo thingie – why, he asked himself, should it be performed by the wife of a jackanapes official? "I want you to send off one of those things, Miss Pilbury," he said.

"Which things?"

"In one of those machines."

"A fax?"

"If that's what it is. Send it to the Minister with or without Special Responsibility for Whatsit in the Department of Thingummy."

"I know whom you mean."

"You do?"

"Mr Edgefield."

"That'll be he, yes. Please inform him – with old-fashioned courtesy, of course – that the presence of his wife and himself is, owing to a change of arrangements, no longer requested at my thingie fettling works."

Miss Pilbury was astounded, or fairly close. Wonderful! She would do it! Nevertheless, she felt bound to say, "There are those who will not like it."

Sir Rodney did not doubt that she was right. But the dispatch would be over before the reverberations began to be felt, and by that time he would have rejected outright the derisory stationery supplies appointment and retired to his country house in Coquetdale, there to build model ships for the rest of his days. There would be some place not too far away where he could hold sea trials. Wasn't there water all over Northumberland?

Elsie Pilbury's plans were not dissimilar. "I shall take early retirement," she said. "I shall have my staff pension. And I have my savings in the Post Office. I have a sister in Bishop Auckland."

"Good heavens!" said Sir Rodney.

"She will take me in. She has Rudyard Kipling in her bookcase, you know."

"Good heavens!" Sir Rodney repeated. Savings in the Post Office, a sister in Bishop Auckland and Rudyard Kipling in a bookcase! This was plenitude, if not repletion!

He nodded mistily towards Miss Pilbury. Oh, there was no doubt that he would miss his Pluvius family. But he would make two more departing gestures. He would sing tenor solo at the dispatch reception. And he would invite one of his own people to name the jumbo thingie. He had the very person in mind.

"You'll see that the confounded minister is notified, Miss Pilbury?"

"Yes, Sir Rodney."

"Yes, well..." He looked at the clock. "It seems to be seven-and-a-half minutes to five."

"Twenty-four-and-a-quarter minutes past ten," said Miss Pilbury.

*

On the subject of marriage, Avril said to Elaine, "It seems to me that if a husband works away from home, there's the chance that his wife'll lose him. Or vice versa. If he stays at home, she might wish she *could* lose him."

"Oh, dear!" said Elaine. "I hope you're not being unduly cynical."

"So you think there's no harm in being duly cynical?"

"I've no idea," Elaine said, "but Oswald says you can't know what's enough until you know what's too much. Even though he talks like that, I'm prepared to keep him at home, because I love him, you see."

"Unduly?"

"Yes, for the time being. He thinks a great deal about morality."

"They do, some of them. There's no more virtuous man than my dad, but as he's grown older he's learned to keep it to himself. Well, most of the time."

Not that Elaine was seeking advice. She knew it was entirely reasonable to marry Oswald, in spite of his perfections. The only worry she had was that it was entirely reasonable.

*

"Tonight," Mel Queasy told the listening dozens, "Radio Clarts again presents its incidental series, which it calls *Incidental Series*. And my guest is Mrs Gladys Button, a lady of some topical notoriety. She is going to talk to us about her bad leg. Well, Gladys, this is quite a remarkable leg you've got. Do you think your leg will go down in history?"

Gladys Button said this was quite possible. "After all, why not? We have the precedent of Harry Hotspur's hamshank."

This was beyond the purview, it seemed to Mel Queasy, of even a local radio workhorse. "That's an interesting thought," he said, "but I'm sure our Radio Clarts listeners are rather keen to hear about your left leg."

"My right leg."

"Either leg. Your right leg, we might say, precipitated a certain recent event in the Pluvius Thingie Fettling Works."

159

"We might, and you're very kind. But Harry Hotspur's hamshank did a lot more than that. Shall I tell you in what way?"

"On balance, no. I think it's fair to suggest that if you hadn't had a bad leg, there wouldn't have been a fire in the ladies' at the Pluvius Works."

Gladys said yes, she felt quite proud that her leg had exerted such a powerful influence. "But I hope I can remain modest about that."

"Hard on the heels of the conflagration – a devilish word to put into a man's script, I must say – we had other near-calamities. And now rumour speaks of the imminent departure of an important person."

"Tush!"

"Tush?"

"All this is as nothing compared to the ramifications of Harry Hotspur's hamshank."

"Quite," said Mel Queasy. "But I do feel that our radio audience doesn't want to contemplate Harry Hotspur's hamshank."

"Of course it does! Heed me, young man! I came here in the interests of free speech. I came resolved to dissertate on ginger-haired Harry Hotspur's hamshank. I might have talked about Leonardo's noble velocipede or Sebastian Cabot's brave but doomed North-West Passage venture. But no! I knew I had a duty to plump for Harry Hotspur's hamshank."

Mel Queasy decided that the moment had come when he must say how interesting it had been chatting to her. He said it. "It seems the lines are now open for tonight's 'phone-in," he added. "Thank you, Gladys."

"Ha!"

"The first call is coming in even as I speak. It's from Mrs Pauline Archer of Whickham. Good evening, Mrs Archer. What is your question?"

Mrs Archer said her question was addressed to Mrs Button and she would like to hear more about Harry Hotspur's hamshank.

"And I'll tell you," said Gladys.

But not on Radio Clarts. And not in this story. Perhaps someone will tell it in the sequel, set in Lastfort in 2045 in the Pluvius Chocolate Cream Works. We at the Nostalgia Centre are bullying the publisher even now. Mrs Thirlaway is leaning on him.

*

The rain was pouring. It poured on the drinking trough below Sir Rodney's window. The ghost of his grandfather's horse was there. It gazed up at the leaden sky and shrugged, as who would say, "What did I tell you?" Sir Rodney prodded at his pullover. It was a fairly unworn one, in honour of the ceremony. It would soon have a pretty decent hole in it, given the rub of the green.

The ceremony! Well, the day had arrived. One way and another, he expected to enjoy himself. He was reflecting, after all, that his assembly squad foreman had a daughter, easily the prettiest girl in Lastfort.

Meanwhile, he was also bearing in mind the verse his grandfather had had engraved above the boardroom entrance:

All thingie fettlers, come what may,
Must pack their tools and end their day.

Was it indeed time for the chairman himself to end his day? He believed so. His grandfather's horse looked up at him, nodded approval and vanished forever from his drinking trough.

*

The rain was not pouring on Jonty. He was in the club, entirely alone, having drawn a pint for himself. Everyone was at the thingie dispatch, including the club steward. So it had come to this! He was standing here, talking to himself. Walter had said, "You'd better keep in out of the wet, Jonty. But you'll be at the reception, won't you?" So! It seemed they could do without him. After sixty years, the buggers could do without him! Do without Jonathan Theodore Roosevelt Harwood!

He supped miserably. He would retire, that was what he would do. They would come knocking at his front door when they were in trouble, as they surely would be. But he wouldn't be in. He'd have slipped out of the backyard and gone to Japan to sell his services to the Hakki Mukki Thingie Fettling Company.

He supped some more. Do without him, could they? What? And they thought they'd got a better tenor, did they? Was that it? He cleared his throat and tried to sing a couple of notes. "La-la!" They came out strong and tuneful. Not sing, eh? To hell with the doctor! He tried a whole scale. "La-la-la-la-la-la-la-laaa!" What was wrong with that? Eh?

He would drink another pint. He would go home and have a lie-down. And then? "You'll be at the reception, won't you?" Be at the reception? What? Where else would he go? He had new underpants, hadn't he? He had a new vest. New socks. New shirt and tie. New suspenders. New silk hankie for his breast pocket. What next from that bloody old woman? Top hat and spats?

*

The rain poured on Walter's men, who had so assiduously prepared and fitted the dispatching apparatus and were on hand to undertake any last minute adjustments that might be needed. The hoist, newly tested, loomed overhead. Labourers hovered ready to make fast the jumbo thingie as soon as it was in place on the huge transporter that was to trundle it slowly and agonisingly across country to Gledson's Scupper, Pump and Hatch Emporium. The police motor bikes that were to accompany it scurried and hooted in the lane alongside the Plodge Burn. Cars were standing by, waiting to whisk the guests away to the Julius Caesar Hotel.

The rain poured on Walter, as he supervised and sweated and trembled.

*

"I'm glad I got a powder blue costume," Auntie Dinah said.

"A suit," Beth amended.

"Eh?"

"They call them suits now, Auntie Dinah. Have done since 1945, I believe. The Second World War's got a lot to answer for."

"Powder blue. You get nice things at that shop."

"Oh, yes. Not cheap, mind you, but you've got to be prepared to pay if you deal at Marks and Spencer's."

"It's what Princess Elizabeth would have picked."

"I'm sure. Especially now she's queen."

When the Rolls arrived to take Auntie Dinah to the ceremony, however, the rain

161

was torrential, and not all the promises that her powder blue suit would come to no harm could persuade her to risk its exposure. So she ensured its protection by enveloping herself in her black mackintosh. She called for her wellington boots. The suit would be unveiled later at the reception, for which she would also change into her shoes ("They still call them court shoes," Beth assured her) and some flunkey would no doubt look after her wellies and mackintosh if she tipped him sixpence. Afterwards, the powder blue concoction would be stored away against the day when her errant offspring would flock back home.

Beth kissed her and said, "You're a marvel," and the Rolls departed. Auntie Dinah was telling the chauffeur that on just such a rainy day as this her son Stanley had broken his glasses.

*

In the deserted office, Elaine waited. She must go out soon to present the bouquet to the lady who was about to name the jumbo thingie. What a family occasion this was turning out to be! The duty had been pressed on her by Sir Rodney, for his own indisputable if selfish reasons. By strange chance, Oswald had elected to wait with her.

"It's nice of you to stay in here," Elaine said, "alone with me."

"What else could I do?" said the gallant Oswald. "It's raining out there." The emptiness of the office guaranteed that he could embrace her with what Tot would have recognised as impunity. He adjusted his glasses and added, "Poor old Uncle Jonty…"

"Why?"

"What's to become of him?"

"Now, Oswald," said Elaine, "he'll manage very well without you. Besides, wouldn't it be convenient, providential and desirable if Casablanca the unspeakable uncle got a certain lady as housekeeper?"

"Implausible enough to be possible," Oswald quoted.

"She might even think of marrying him," said Elaine. "In fact, propriety demands it, now that she's seen his bum twice in fifty years. Off we go, then."

*

And yes, Radio Clarts, always boastful that it covered the local scene, was represented at the dispatching ceremony by its omnipresent reporter, Mel Queasy.

"Well, here I am," he told his listeners, "at the Pluvius Works, where all the workers and their families are gathered to watch the latest jumbo dispatch. The rain is pouring on to the jumbo in question, as it stands proudly there, waiting to be named Peacock. The red, white and blue bunting is clinging wetly to the ceremonial platform… I see the bottle of champagne which is to be cracked against the thingie's casing… From the office, I see Sir Rodney Eames emerging, accompanied by the lady who has been invited to perform the naming ceremony…"

The lady's identity was, he informed the unmoved public, something of a mystery. "However, I can describe her ensemble," he said, "for the benefit of our lady listeners. Under the protection of the umbrella held by a security guard, she is dressed in black mackintosh and wellington boots…"

He paused for effect and to find another bit of paper. "At the very hour of the dispatching of this jumbo thingie," he then resumed with rather splendid gravity, "an

162

official announcement has been issued from the industry's headquarters, following consultation at cabinet level. It is to the effect that, owing to lack of orders, on completion of the next three tiddler thingies, the Pluvius Thingie Fettling Works will cease production. A simultaneous announcement was made in the House by the appropriate minister, Mr Michael Edgefield. Opposition spokespersons queried why Mr Edgefield seemed to derive peculiar satisfaction from the situation. The unions have been notified. Closure means that eight hundred men will lose their jobs. We must ask ourselves…"

He paused again. "But at last we come to the all-important moment of dispatch. Sir Rodney, himself in storm coat and sou'wester, having duly kissed the prettiest girl in Lastfort, is now whispering last-minute advice to the lady who is to perform the naming ceremony."

*

"Just say, 'I name this jumbo thingie Peacock,'" Sir Rodney murmured.

"Pardon?" said Auntie Dinah. "Hold my flowers, hinny, will you?"

Sir Rodney clutched the bouquet and repeated his instructions.

"I know, I know!" said Auntie Dinah. She then pronounced grandly, "I name this thumbie mingo Poppycock," adding, in a moment of inspired improvisation, "God bless my soul and all who sail in her!"

Sir Rodney guided Auntie Dinah's hand. The bottle shattered against the casing. There was the old, old heart-stopping pause that comes at precisely this moment at every jumbo dispatch. Then the grips of the hoist tightened and the Peacock ascended gently and unfailingly. Walter smiled. He had achieved his twenty-first (or twentieth) successful jumbo dispatch.

Auntie Dinah watched with wondering eyes. If only Dan could see her now. Or Stanley. Or the one she lost. She wept.

Cheers echoed in the rain.

*

That evening, at the reception, *Bobby Shafto* rang out as always.

In a corner, Mel Queasy thrust a microphone at Tot Needler.

"As I was saying earlier, Tot," he said, "what is to become of them now?"

"We've been here before," Tot said.

"What?"

"In this time warp. You see, Mel, it's my old friend, the human condition."

"In what sense?"

"Well, certain disasters keep recurring. Some of them we can grapple with."

"You mean – slump, recession, political vacillation, failure of hope?"

"Yes. But there are others too big for our comprehension."

"Oh?"

"Like Mrs Button's leg," said Tot.

Bobby Shafto swelled up, sung as a duet by two old men.

By the Same Fellow

Short Stories

Up the Tyne in a Flummox
The Turnip in the Night

Non-Fiction

Bluebottles on my Marmalade
Through My Hat

Verse

Hailstones on Your Father

Stage

Pot Luck
A Little Stiff-Built Chap
Tight at the Back
Cushy Butterfield
The Night of the Snapped Suspender
Come Snow, Come Blow

Radio

I Knew Him, Horatio
The First Night of Tom the Fool
How Shall We Honour Billy Dutton?
Grasp the Nettle Egregiously
Highly Likely
Quintessentially Flummoxed
Eva and Adamson

Television

Cribbins and Livings
Mother Nature's Bloomers
A Pantomime of Sorts
A Funny Old Life